CALL OF THE WARRIOR

AN ANTHOLOGY PRESENTED BY
READ, WRITE, MUSE

READ ◆ WRITE ◆ MUSE
PRODUCTIONS

Cover, interior book design, and eBook design
by Blue Harvest Creative
www.blueharvestcreative.com

Editing by Kelsey Keating and
BHC Staff Editor Alice Martin

CALL OF THE WARRIOR

Published by
Read, Write, Muse Productions

ISBN-13: 978-0692448519
ISBN-10: 0692448519

Visit the publisher at:
www.readwritemuse.com
www.facebook.com/ReadWriteMuse
www.twitter.com/ReadWriteMuse

Visit the Read, Write, Muse website
by scanning the QR code.

ALSO BY
READ, WRITE, MUSE

THROUGH THE PORTAL
AN ANTHOLOGY

The Stories

FOREWORD

BY ROB HOLLIDAY

"From this day to the ending of the world,
But we in it shall be remembered—
We few, we happy few, we band of brothers;
For he to-day that sheds his blood with me
Shall be my brother…"

Excerpt, *Henry V*, William Shakespeare

Warrior. Fighter. Conscript. Hero. Conqueror.

With these words, mental imagery abounds, evoking nostalgia, pride, sadness, wonder, admiration.

The fields of World War I with doughboys charging across desolate wastelands, so often to their doom.

A hospital room fastens itself in the mind's eye, a private sanctuary brimming with the odors of illness, sweat, and stoic bravery, perhaps a room of triumph or perhaps a place of transition.

The wheelchair-bound athlete, pushing limits and breaking mental and physical barriers.

The veteran returning home from the battlefield, exhausted in every sense, mission accomplished but at the high cost of comrades lost, haunted nights, and memories best left behind.

Being a warrior is not only a martial occupation but a state of mind. A gifting. It is the drive to live. The indomitable fight to survive.

The long-suffering endurance of unwanted conflict. The soul-quenching satisfaction of unexpected courage in the face of fear. The shining glory of overcoming obstacles previously insurmountable. The human spirit is not a pacifist.

This anthology is dedicated to warriors everywhere and those that accompany them on the warrior's way—beloved family, lifelong friends, and inseparable companions. A portion of this anthology's proceeds will benefit the "War Dogs—Making it Home" charity. This wonderful charity places specially selected dogs, rescued from high kill shelters or otherwise surrendered to another charity (Morgan's Dogs), with veterans at risk with Post-Traumatic Stress Disorder (PTSD) and/or Traumatic Brain Injury (TBI). The dogs are taught to interrupt attacks of panic, stress, and hypervigilance—hallmarks of PTSD/TBI. Additionally, the veterans are saving the dogs' lives, which decreases the stigma of negative labeling in which those who most need help avoid seeking help for fear of looking weak. As the bond with their dog deepens, love and hope enter their hearts.

These stories are given so that:

All those fighting a private battle today find respite.

All those weary in spirit may find endurance to carry on just a bit longer.

All those facing darkness in solitude may know that you, warrior friend, are not alone.

We shed our blood in a common cause. We are all together in this struggle called Life. Let the brotherhood of humanity give you strength.

Rob Holliday
Captain, US Army, 1994-2004

CALL OF THE WARRIOR

THE STORIES

D.M. KILGORE

EVE'S APPLES

SILENCE DESCENDS upon the rubble that was once a library. It's the kind of quiet that comes at the end of a battle, before the deceased are counted and the opponents realize the only victor is death. There's nothing I can do but wait, crouched in the shadows, barely breathing as I watch my beloved Kerr strain against the deadly blade at his throat. His own dagger presses against the neck of our greatest enemy, his brother, Niko.

I can end this. As I watch a lone tear slide down my lover's face, I stand, ready to reveal myself. My true self.

"Brother, don't force my blade. We don't have to end this way," Kerr implores.

"There's no other way for it to end. You've chosen your side. You've chosen to fight against me. A warrior fights for his family above all," Niko spits, his knuckles white, his arm shaking slightly.

"No, Niko. A warrior fights for what he believes in."

"And what do you believe in?"

"Love, Brother. I fight for love. Don't you believe in love?"

"I believe that there's to be love between brothers, not war. You've brought this upon yourself. Upon us all."

"No. You chose war. I wanted nothing more than to marry the one I love. For you to accept her as family. For us to build a new life in the ruins. There's so little left of our world. We should work together, not against one another. Why can't you see that?"

"She will never be family. Look around, Brother. The destruction. The death. The disease. She brought this to our door. How can you love someone that destroys everything she touches?"

I watch Kerr drop his dagger, looking around at the chaos that was once his home. Niko's right. This is my doing. I had one job to do, and falling in love with a human wasn't it. My job was to destroy them. All of them. Man, woman, and child. The only survivors were to be a limited number of animal and plant species. I was supposed to be preparing the way for my kind, not playing house with a human.

It hadn't seemed like such a terrible task. For thousands of centuries we've watched humans destroy themselves and their world. There's so much hatred, cruelty, greed, violence, and war among their breed. It's incomprehensible to my kind. We're normally a peaceful race that believes in harmony, but when our realm was threatened, it was decided that destroying the humans would serve a greater good. We would take their world, rebuild it, and make it what it was always meant to be: an oasis of peace, happiness, and love. Commander Shalan chose me to relieve the land of its most dangerous disease: the humans. I hadn't wanted to destroy them. It went against my very nature. Shalan convinced me it was a merciful act that would end their suffering. I cannot tolerate suffering.

Now, I'm not so sure anything I've done was at all merciful. I've laid ruin to cities, destroyed families, and turned the last survivors against each other. There's nothing merciful about it. I cause much more pain than I relieve. It is time to end this, though not the way I had planned upon my arrival.

"Stop!" I step from the shadows.

Niko doesn't drop his blade, as I hoped. Instead, he takes advantage of Kerr's lowered guard and pulls him closer. A trail of blood begins to run slowly down Kerr's neck.

"Ah, the monster's come out of hiding just in time!"

I wince at his words. It hurts, but it's true. I've become a monster.

"No!" Kerr's face crumples as I close the distance between us.

"No more hiding." I lower the hood of my cloak revealing my luminous, color-shifting eyes. Niko looks away. What will he think of the rest of my physical differences? I pull an apple from my pack and offer it to Niko. "For you."

"An apple? You destroy my world, my family, and offer me an apple? You actually think you're Eve!" Niko laughs. "Look around. This isn't Eden and God left a long time ago."

I should have known he wouldn't understand. "My Commander gave me the codename Eve, but it's not a biblical reference. I'm the Eve of Destruction, though I can see the irony of the situation. I was sent to destroy your world, and I nearly succeeded until I met Kerr. He showed me that human nature isn't the disease we believed it to be. There's goodness in many of you."

"Those of us left, you mean." Niko's jaw clenches as he meets my eyes.

"You don't know the entire story, Niko. Let Kerr go, put away your weapon, and let me tell you about the others."

"The others? More…" Niko's eyes widen with fear as he struggles with what I am. "Monsters?"

"No. Others like you. Survivors. I've not ended as many lives as you think." He's skeptical. I can see it in his eyes. I drop my pack and carefully open my cloak just enough for him to see I have no hidden weapons. He's not ready to see the parts of myself I keep hidden. I kick the pack toward him, keeping only the apple. I need him to see its importance. I wait for him to release Kerr and sheath his dagger. For the briefest of moments, I'm not sure he will. Finally, he shoves Kerr away.

"May I?" I gesture toward an overturned bench. Niko shrugs. I right the bench then take a seat. My eyes meet Kerr's. "Perhaps, you could round up a couple of chairs," I suggest. As much as I long for him to sit at my side, now is not the time to give Niko any ideas about being outnumbered.

The brothers search the area, finding more broken furniture than anything whole enough to support their weight. I move to sit on the floor opposite the bench. "Here, you take the bench. I'll sit here."

Niko seems pleased with my solution, or perhaps he just enjoys looking down at me. Kerr sits at his side, but there is a substantial distance between them. I suspect they were once very close. Niko, the younger, looks very much like Kerr. They are both beautiful in their way.

"Where are these other survivors?" Niko pierces me with an icy blue glare.

"You must understand, Niko. I came here with the objective to eliminate all humans. I encountered so many cruel, greedy, corrupt people. They were causing so much pain and even war... I felt I was granting you mercy. Ending your lives meant ending your suffering."

"And the others?" Niko's tone is as sharp as his dagger.

"The others were like Kerr. And like you, Niko. They fought for their families. Fathers and mothers offered up their own lives if I'd spare their children. Husbands offered up their lives if I'd spare their wives. Brothers and sisters would fight to save their siblings. I was moved by their love, their willing sacrifice—the bond they shared. We knew humans had the capacity to love, but they loved possessions, entertainment, power, and money. It wasn't until I began my campaign of destruction that I realized the depth of your ability to love one another. Kerr helped me see what your love is capable of." My hand strays to my mop of white curls and I work it through the tangles.

"I want to know where the survivors are!" Niko rises from the bench.

Kerr grabs his wrist, shaking his head and gesturing for Niko to sit. "Please, Niko. Let her finish. I've heard some of this, and as I told you, I've seen the others. Alive. Well. Safe. Listen to her."

"Don't you see, Niko? I was sent here to destroy, but now I want to find those of you that are capable of real love and help you rebuild your world. I can show you a better way."

"We were doing just fine without your meddling."

"No. You weren't. Even you can't deny that this place was in a state of chaos and destruction long before I arrived."

"She's right, Niko. The wars have gone on so long that we've ruined the best of our world."

"I've been gathering survivors in a place where they'll be safe. I was going to contact my Commander the night you caught me, Niko. To ask him if we could work together. Your world and ours. With the best of both our kinds, there would be harmony, abundance, a return of peace."

"Are you saying this is my fault? Because I interrupted your freaky ritual?" Niko shakes his head in disbelief.

"No. Though you made connecting with my home impossible, it wasn't your fault. And it wasn't a 'ritual.' I was meditating to open the lines of communication. It works like telepathy."

"Eve, tell Niko about the apple," Kerr encourages. I can tell how much he wants Niko to believe, to join us.

"The apple is the seed to your new world, Niko. With it you will have fair leadership, new flora and fauna, a new way of life. It will build us a new world without hatred, suffering, and despair."

"A magic apple? Is that like a magic beanstalk? Give me a break. Kerr. I can't believe you are listening to fairy tales and siding with this… this…thing."

"It's all true, Niko. She's shown me how it works. She can show you too."

"How?"

I take my small dagger from my boot, watching as Niko's hand rushes to embrace his own, and slice the apple. I hand him a slice. He eyes it warily.

"Poisoned apples? How original." Niko takes the slice and studies it, lifting it to his nose.

"Now who believes in fairy tales?" Kerr taunts.

I watch the exchange, still uncertain of the way these brothers engage each other. It's odd. There's something about it that makes me want to smile. I nod at Niko, hoping he will take a bite. Instead he gives me his best death-glare.

"Why aren't you eating any?"

"It will show you a vision. I don't need to see the vision. I live it."

"So, it is poisoned!" He drops his slice.

I crawl over, brush the slice off, and pop it into my mouth. I guess I'll be visiting my home sooner than I thought. "See? It's not poisoned." I segment off another piece, then another, and give each brother a slice. "We might as well take the trip together." I smile at Kerr. He takes his piece and pops it into his mouth with an excited grin.

"Trip? So it's drugs?" Niko nibbles at his slice reluctantly.

"No, it's not drugs. I suppose the best way for your mind to understand it is to say it's magic." I wish, not for the first time, that the humans could understand the ways of my realm.

I move to sit on the bench between the men, and Niko jumps as if I've bitten him.

"Get away from me!" He slides to the far end of the bench, his eyes beginning to glaze.

"I apologize, but this is necessary." I take his hand. "In a moment we are going to be in my world. I don't think you want be lost and on your own when you get there, do you?" I slide my other hand into Kerr's. Niko is too far under to protest. He is smaller than Kerr. I should have given him a thinner slice. Oh well, at least he'll be subdued throughout the journey. I smile, close my eyes, and rest my head on Kerr's strong shoulder. He smells nice. I like these humans. Some of them, anyway.

WE ARRIVE in the East Garden, still holding hands. Niko is either too awed or too influenced to notice. Kerr smiles down at me.

This was his favorite part of my world. Indeed, the gardens are beyond beautiful. Our flowers are unlike anything the humans of Earth have seen before. We do not have green grass or blue skies. We have multi-hued everything. Shades of luminosity run through more than our genetics. Our sky, water, flowers, and trees all boast brilliantly shimmering kaleidoscopes of color.

Niko clears his throat and drops my hand like it burns his flesh. His cheeks turn an interesting shade of pink. "It looks like a rainbow threw up in here," he says with a grimace.

I attempt to see my world through human eyes. It is kind of bright. I shrug and head toward the gate. "There's more to see."

Kerr and Niko follow behind me, whispering to each other. I could hear their conversation if I wished, but for some reason I don't want to know what is being said about my world, or me. I walk at a steady pace toward the center of town, allowing Kerr to give Niko the "grand tour" as he calls it. I need to show Niko the apple tree and make him understand. I'm tired of my mission. I'm ready to approach Commander Shalan about a peaceful alliance with the humans. I'm lost in my own thoughts as Niko appears at my side.

"Is this the master plan? To turn Earth into some glittery, bioluminescent festival of colors? Are there any men on your planet?"

"Yes, of course there are." I nod and continue walking. His questions are strange. "Niko, we haven't left Earth, only the dimensions of your plane of existence."

"A parallel universe?"

"A multiverse."

"Never mind." Niko slows to rejoin Kerr, who is lingering behind us studying a green cat that has joined our procession.

I shrug and continue down the pebbled sidewalk, delighting as the lavender sunlight glimmers against the shiny jewel-toned stones. Kerr's world could use more color. I found nothing to love about their "concrete" walkways. My eyes are still at my feet as I round the corner and I stop only when I hear Kerr gasp behind me. I look up to find The Bureau of Unification is missing. Well, not missing exactly. It has been burnt to the ground. The Ancient Tree has been burnt as well and lies smoldering, its apples nothing but ash now. My pack, back in the human plane, now contains the last of the ancient apples.

"What's happened?" Kerr asks as he takes my hand. We stand staring at the ruined building.

"Looks like your world got a taste of its own medicine," Niko says as he crosses his arms and smirks.

"We must return right away. We're in grave danger here!" I grab for their hands and run toward the garden. This should not have happened so soon. We knew they were coming, but we thought we had time to evacuate and colonize in the human world. Now, it's too late. I scan for survivors as we hurry back the way we came. I cannot believe I didn't notice how empty the streets had been on our way in. I'd been too distracted by my thoughts, and by the humans at my side, to notice something was wrong.

Kerr and Niko are both struggling to keep up with me. They are shouting out questions that I don't have time to answer. As we near the garden, I realize where my people will be. If anyone survived. I slow enough to pull the brothers closer. "Niko, I am sorry I didn't get to explain things to you in a way you could understand. I know seeing it with your own eyes, the way Kerr did, would have convinced you, but now there's no time. You'll just have to trust me. Please believe me when I say I want to save your kind as much as I want to save my own. We're going to have to work together. The survivors of our worlds are the only army we will have to fight what is coming." Without giving them time to reply, I push them toward the garden.

Kerr turns to glance back at me as I throw off my cloak, spread my wings, and head in the opposite direction.

"Where are you going?"

"To see if anyone is still alive. Take Niko back to the library. Get my pack. Guard it with your life. I know the apples seem ordinary, but they're our only hope. You'll find an address written inside the front flap. I'll meet you there. You remember how to go back?"

"Yes. I remember." He grabs Niko, who is gaping at my wings, and they hurry through the gate.

I walk backward, watching until the last moment, when I can no longer see them I leap into the air. I haven't flown in weeks and my wings feel stiff. Certain I'm being watched, I try to remain hidden behind multi-colored clouds as I glide through the sky. I attempt to mentally tune in to the keeper of the secret underground shelter our unit built when we realized the Grimgreys had discovered our location. Silence. I search the streets below hoping to see someone. No one. The sensation of being watched intensifies. It creeps around me, tightening my lungs, and making my heart pound harder. It could be paranoia, though my kind isn't prone to it, or it could be my heightened senses warning me of danger. I touch down just outside the village. The cottages are rubble. The fields are scorched. Smoke and ash permeate the air. I glance down at my vivid blue uniform and silver boots. My glowing skin, luminous eyes, incandescent hair, and vibrant clothing no longer blend in with my environment. Against the ravaged town I stand out like a neon sign that flashes, "Here I Am!" I rush toward the base, hoping I'm not too late.

BACK IN what's left of our world, and with Eve out of earshot in her own realm, I turn on my brother. "Niko! Just listen to me. I wouldn't lie to you about any of this. I am telling you what I saw. What I know. What you would know if you could have seen."

"Kerr, you're blinded by what you think is love for that thing. If those apples can make us hallucinate rainbow land, don't you think they could convince you that you're in love? Wake up, Brother!"

"It's not like that. Physically, she's exactly like us, except they're lit from within. She says it's love that lights their eyes and makes them shimmer with color. I believe her. You would too if you had seen the way they live in complete peace. There's nothing of the pain and suffering we've lived with for all of our existence. That's why they believed we weren't worth saving. We destroy ourselves in the end. She's giving us a chance of having that too. I want a world of peace and love, don't you?"

"It's unnatural. She's not human, no matter how alike you think we are. She has wings, Kerr! Wings! Like some humanoid-insect or something. She came here to destroy us and she nearly succeeded. What if there's some hidden evil behind her smile and her illusions of a perfect world? This could be a ploy to gain our trust, infiltrate the resistance, and finish us off. You're a warrior, Kerr. We've been trained in the ways of war. You know this."

"I know the ways of war, but I also know the ways of the heart. Eve was sent to destroy us, but she was able to see with her own eyes, make up her own mind, and listen to her heart. She abandoned her mission and began working to save us and give us a better world."

"Then she's a traitor. How do you trust a traitor to her own kind?" Niko runs his hands through his dark hair and sits on what remains of the marble steps outside the library.

The address Eve tried to scribble down is hard to make out, but it looks like we have an hour hike ahead of us. "I love you, Niko, but we've run out of the luxury of time. I've done all I can to convince you. I've told you the truth. I want you to come with me. The battle Eve spoke of? She's told me a little about it. The species that's coming wants to rid the world of all life. They won't show us mercy. Join me. Or remain here to see for yourself."

I shove Eve's pack deep within my own before heading off into the diminishing daylight. Moments later, I hear Niko's footsteps not far behind. I will find a way to convince my little brother that Eve no longer means the destruction of our world but the dawn of a better one. She is going to help us all survive and start over in a world where hunger, pain, disease, and war do not exist. It will be heaven on earth.

"Do you remember when Mother used to tell us, 'If it seems too good to be true, it is'?" Niko calls.

"Yes."

"You remember that Mother was always right?"

"Yes."

This time is different though. Eve loves me and she's going to make everything right.

"CAPTAIN IRENOK? Commander Shalan?" I call as I beat against the metal door. "Hello? Anyone? Is anyone in there?" I press my ear to the door and strain to hear any signs of life. I return my left hand to the scanner, but the screen refuses to acknowledge my presence, and the door refuses to open.

"Please? Is anyone in there?" I try again.

"It's empty." A small voice whispers from behind me. I turn to find a small girl, perhaps ten years old.

"Hello." I smile and prepare to introduce myself, but her terrified eyes widen and she lifts a shaking finger to her lips.

"Shh! They'll hear us," she scolds softly. She motions for me to follow her. I walk slowly, silently, following her lead. She takes me around the side of the school, which I notice has remained untouched by invading forces. "They're in there." She motions to the school, dropping to her knees to crawl beneath the front windows. I do the same and we make our way around the corner and then dash across the playground and into the woods beyond.

I continue to follow her silently, admiring her courage. She walks through the silent forest as if it's an ordinary day instead of a day when Grimgreys have taken over her school. I watch curiously as she kneels at the base of a large Amethyst Willow tree and calls into its hollowed trunk, "El-aye-o-way!"

"El-tuh-nuh-way!" a voice echoes from deep within the earth.

The girl turns to grin at me so I return a smile. I have not heard our language in too long. Her glittering eyes and curly pink hair calm me. I am home.

"What's your name, little one?"

"Bah-leenia. What's yours?"

"Rae-lynnia." The name feels foreign on my tongue after using Eve for so long.

"My brother, Nali-kye, will let us in. It takes a moment to reach the door," Bah-leenia explains as she sits back on her heels to wait.

I mimic her casual pose and wonder if I should ask her about other survivors. She is very young, but she seems mature for her age. "Is it just you and your brother then?"

"No. The ones that got away are all here. Grims don't know about our secret tree." She smiles conspiratorially.

"How many?" I ask hopefully.

"Five. All children, except for May-laneeka."

I try not to let her see my shock. Only five survivors? "Are there more, elsewhere?"

She shakes her head, her little lip quivering before she drops her face to her knees.

"Do you know what happened to Commander Shalan?"

"Grims took him away with all the adults."

My heart sinks. I don't press her further. I have to get the five out of here. Kerr and Niko just became more important. I'll have to reconsider my plans for the twenty-five humans I have stashed away in the mountains.

A boy not much older than Bah-leenia flings open the door hidden inside the tree trunk.

"Kye, this is Rae-lynnia," she tells the shaggy-green-haired child. He nods and we follow him down a narrow, winding stairway.

"It's a long way down," Kye tosses back over his shoulder. The illumination from our skin casts shadows along the walls as we move deeper into the tree trunk. The roots weave in and out of the stairwell and I have to duck beneath them.

Finally we reach the bottom and enter a cavernous chamber lit with candles. I haven't seen candles in decades. I wonder where they came from. I see two small children sitting at a table sipping from mugs. They look to be three and five years of age. Both girls. Nali-Kye is the only male survivor of our species. The young school teacher, May-laneeka, lifts her eyes from the book she's reading and smiles when she sees me.

"Finally, some adult conversation!" She wiggles her purple eyebrows but her expression is anything but playful. I realize she's trying to put on a brave face for the children.

"No time. We need to leave." I return her smile and let only my eyes speak the urgency.

"And go where? We're safe here. They don't know about us." May-laneeka goes back to her book as if an officer isn't standing before her.

"May-laneeka!" I snap, "I am Officer Rae-lynnia Shalan. I'm the only remaining Jovia Officer, and I'm giving you a direct order. Gather these children and be ready to depart!"

She drops her book, finally taking notice of my uniform. "I…I'm sorry." She hurries over to me and reaches into her pocket. "It's from your father." She bows her head and presses the stained envelope into my palm.

"Do you have any apples?" I tuck my father's final letter inside my uniform.

"We have three." Bah-leenia hands me a small bag then takes my free hand. "Where are we going?"

"Terralair." I smile down at her.

"You eliminated all the humans?" May-laneeka asks as she hurries the children in my direction.

"Most of them. There are two we will need. I have set aside twenty-five more. I hoped to blend our species and theirs in order to form a united class, but seeing as the Grimgreys arrived ahead of schedule, and this is all of us that remains…"

"We won't need them." She nods her understanding.

I take an apple from the bag, slice it, and hand a piece to each child.

"What's the plan?" May-laneeka asks with concern.

"I have claimed the human Kerr. You will claim his brother, Niko. They're warriors, both honored for their valor after the fifth world war. The very best of their kind. They are brave, loyal, and strong." I hand her a slice of apple.

"Won't they resist us?"

"No. We were wrong about their ability to love. Some of them are capable of great love. I didn't even have to use an apple on Kerr. Niko is stubborn though. It might take an apple to convince him of your charms. Maybe even two."

"Is he handsome?" May-laneeka giggles as she bites into her apple slice.

"Yes. For a human, he's quite nice to look at." I chew my apple thoughtfully.

"May-laneeka, I will need to see to the remaining humans and gather their offspring. Kerr and Niko are on their way to my cabin, so first I'll escort you and the children there. Kerr is kind and will greet you as an equal. Niko is a sarcastic one with an attitude. He calls me a monster."

"A non-believer? Oh, I just love a challenge," May-laneeka laughs.

"Yes. Apparently, Commander Shalan was right. Most humans don't believe in the fae or faerie magic…even when one's right in front of them."

We join hands and whisper the spell that allows us to travel between the worlds.

I WATCH Niko and Kerr climb the hill to our cabin. Kerr smiles, but Niko is angry, as usual. Hopefully, May-laneeka's spell will improve his attitude. She winks at me as she heads down the trail with a shiny apple.

The fairy children and human children play together in the meadow, unaware of their differences.

It feels strange to plan a future with a species that denies our existence only to visualize us as tiny, pixie-dust-covered wish granters. We are more ferocious than they could ever imagine. We're our own species of warrior. The Grimgreys, dark witches who have tried to steal our magic before, will never find us now. I have no doubt my father, Commander Shalan, destroyed the Bureau and the Ancient Tree to keep our secrets and our magic from falling into the wicked hands of our enemy. The Grimgreys pierced the veil to our world only to find the source of our magic in flames. Like warriors, we fight for what we believe in, and we'll die to protect it.

I pull my father's final note from my pocket and read it one last time.

"Fight for love. For love will conquer all."

I bury the note with some apple seeds. Soon we will have an orchard. My hand slides over my still-flat stomach and the secret hiding there. I bite into an apple and turn the grass baby blue.

We will go on.

LEXY WOLFE

AWAKENING

DARKNESS LAY thick within Evernight City, the sun a thing of the past when Sangelas was built over it. The lives of those condemned to dwell there had devolved into little more than bare survival. The weaker or more timid endured by keeping out of sight. Others turned to hunting the only prey left to them—each other. The more opportunistic found their place by providing services to both those living in the light and those condemned to the shadows.

Perversely clean and bright, Bennie's Body and Bounty Shop possessed the sterility of a hospital operating room. No decorations hung on the walls, the lights were cold but bright, and the slightest noise could be heard. The jarring thump of the door slamming into the wall mingled with the delicate sound of the bells hanging from the top. The clerk, seated at the wide counter that split the room in half, looked up as a body dropped with a thud, a limp arm falling across his tablet.

"How much for this one, Bennie?" Blue eyes, one organic and the other glowing, blinked at the clerk who pushed the arm off the device, finished what he read, and looked up with a droll expression. "Oh, come on. You weren't doing anything important."

"I was reading, Clive," Bennie replied in acerbic tones, setting the tablet under the counter as he stood to examine the body.

"Like I said, nothing important!" Bennie arched an eyebrow and stared at Clive for a heartbeat before returning his attention to the corpse without a word. "So, how many credits for this one?" Clive poked the inert shoulder. "Didn't bang it up too much this time."

Bennie continued his examination of the body, continuing to ignore Clive's prattling chatter. After several minutes, he looked up. "A thousand credits."

"That's all? Shit, man, what do you want?"

"Undamaged internal organs." Bennie emphasized his matter-of-fact response by pointing out the holes in the corpse's chest and abdomen. "It costs to repair them, so the upper-city sorts won't pay more than scavenger prices. I have to make a living, you know."

"I gotta make a living, too." Clive exclaimed, holding his arms out. "I need a better arm for the contests down at the Last Man Standing Bar." He pulled off a glove to flex a cybernetic hand scuffed from use and looking the worse for wear. "This thing is a piece of shit." A slender barrel popped out as he closed his fist and flexed it downward. "The gun keeps jamming."

Bennie rolled his eyes, utterly without sympathy. "Then I suggest upgrading your optics so you can actually aim with precision." He whistled sharply. A robot with forklift-like arms and triangular treads whirred from the back to retrieve the body. "A weapon is only as good as the one aiming it."

"Bah. Bennie, you're a stingy bastard—" The bells interrupted Clive's rampage. The bounty hunter's eyes went wide and he backed up until his back hit the wall and pressed himself against it as a woman entered, carrying two bodies over one shoulder. Beneath a cloak that obscured her from casual observation, she wore what appeared to be a plain, navy blue one-piece swimsuit, her arms and legs both gleaming chrome. Only half of her face was metal, the rest covered with reeskin and ragged black hair covering her scalp. A cut across the fleshy cheek belied the metal beneath.

"Ah, Ravenhawk, welcome back!" He waited as the woman laid the bodies on the table with care before he began examining them. Bennie whistled appreciatively as he fingered the collars of the expensive suits the corpses wore. He tugged out wallets and rooted through them. "You need any of this?" The woman remained silent, waiting patiently. "Right, right. I'll put it with the rest." He turned their heads back and forth, studying them. Each body had a single bullet hole between their eyes. "Nice bit of work there, Ravenhawk. They'll fetch a nice price."

Bennie took out a scanner, running it over each body, pausing where the device began yelping in alert. He removed the metal capsules from under their chins with deft ease, placing them in her extended hand. "I am rather surprised. Only corporate tech, nothing personal. It is like they have no lives beyond orders. Not sure if I'd call them sad or pathetic." He glanced at the impassive woman. "No insult intended, of course." She remained silent and impassive.

Clive kept himself pressed against the wall, staring at Bennie. "That's the Ravenhawk, man! Why you talking to it like it's alive?" He inhaled and tried to melt into the unforgiving wall when the woman turned hard, cold eyes on him. "Please don't kill me," he begged in a tiny voice, too terrified to notice the puddle growing around his feet. Bennie glanced over at the other's wet pants and tsked, returning to his examination and retrieval of various computer and electrical components from the bodies.

"Do you work for the Maxtenia Corporation?" The woman's voice, unexpectedly human despite her robotic exterior, could have been endearing if it had possessed even the slightest modicum of emotion.

"Uh, n-no," Clive stammered. She turned her attention back to Bennie, dismissing the street thug as a threat.

"How is Michelle these days?" Bennie asked conversationally. "Is she still working for Cybercorps?"

"Yes. Dr. Yabiri is my primary technician. She is…" Ravenhawk's expression flickered in confusion as she attempted to answer the initial question. "Functional."

Bennie laughed as he laid down his tools. "Good to hear, good to hear." He put his hands on the edge of the table, surveying the two corpses. "I can give you ten thousand credits apiece. Per the agreement I have with Michelle, I'll send them to the black account."

Clive's greed overwhelmed his terror when Bennie spoke. Dragging his eyes away from the state-of-the-art weapon the ports in her arm hinted at, he noticed the dataport at the base of her skull. Seeing an opportunity to take the legendary Ravenhawk down and selling her for salvage, Clive pulled a piece of rebar, aiming for the weak point in her skull. Before he could utter a sound, he was pinned to the wall with one hand, kicking his feet a foot above the floor. She punched him below the throat with her other fist and held him as he twitched until he stopped moving.

Ravenhawk pulled her fist away, revealing the data spike that had severed his spinal cord at the base of his skull. She released him, letting the body drop to the floor. "I do not know if there would be anything useful in this one."

"Probably not. I know his history. What hasn't been replaced is scarred or too damaged to salvage. His mech-grafts will barely be worth recovering. Clive always got second-hand tech implanted. But don't worry. I am sure I'll find another idiot like him to buy it." Bennie shook his head with a sigh. "I keep telling them they need to ignore anyone else in here, but do they listen to me? Of course not. Always ends with someone becoming merchandise."

He dumped several more bloody components into a small plastic bag. "This is the last of the ident markers and corporate scan bits." He held them out to her. "There is nothing else Cybercorps has marked for explicit retrieval and return to them. Everything else will likely be implanted in someone else before the weekend."

"I apologize for disrupting your business," Ravenhawk said, taking the bag from him.

"No apologies necessary," Bennie replied, waving airily. "I have no idea why you come here, but—"

"The objective requires all biological obstacles to be removed from the encounter site," Ravenhawk replied.

He laughed. "I meant why my shop specifically, Ravenhawk. Not that I don't appreciate your contributions. Clean kills, every one of them. I can even sell their clothing for a nice amount! But there are a half dozen other body shops between the Maxtenia buildings and here."

Ravenhawk spoke as if the reasons were obvious. "Dr. Yabiri told me to dispose of any bodies here."

"Ah. Yes, I remember now. She is hoping…er, never mind." He waved a hand toward the door. "You should go. I'd not want to draw Cybercorps' attention on you if they thought you slipped their leash."

Ravenhawk turned on her heel and headed out. Halfway out, she paused, glancing back over her shoulder. A slight frown creased the organic side of her face before she disappeared into the hell of Evernight City.

PEOPLE WEARING lab coats or medical scrubs ducked into other halls or rooms, peeking out with eyes widened in fear as Ravenhawk passed through the sterile hallways. She stopped, turned, and faced a closed door with a keypad. Her right hand curled into a fist for a moment, then relaxed. She held her open hand above it to transmit a signal to the locking device. After a moment, the door slid open to admit her.

A man wearing an expensive, tailored suit stood away from the table he leaned against, unfolding his arms. Another wearing a lab coat took the objects she had received from Bennie and whisked them to another table to examine them. Ravenhawk stood motionless, waiting.

"All the data is here, Mr. Issu," the man in the lab coat announced. "You can report to the rest of the board the mission was successful."

Issu smirked. "Of course, Mikelson. I had every faith in my Ravenhawk." He cupped her cheek, letting his hand drift down the curves of her body. She merely stood impassive, staring at the wall across the room. "This project will insure the dominance of Cybercorps."

Mikelson pressed his lips together. "Sir, I must advise caution. These constant 'field tests' do not allow me the time to do proper analyses to make certain there will be no, ah, critical failures with the cybernetics. Repeated unmonitored interactions with the population could have devastating, unplanned repercussions that—"

"Oh, shut up, Mikelson," Issu chided. "If you are so worried, then do a memory purge and be done with it."

"We can't keep doing that without proper studies to ensure it is not causing damage. The cybernetic nano-neurons are extremely delicate," the smaller man protested, following Issu out of the room, their voices fading as the door shut behind them. Shortly after, the door hissed open and shut.

"Hello, Ravenhawk," the slender woman who had entered greeted with a warm voice.

Impossibly clear, blue eyes blinked once, then Ravenhawk turned her head to regard the speaker. "Hello, Dr. Yabiri. How are you?"

"I told you to call me Michelle, Ravenhawk," she scolded.

"Hello, Dr. Yabiri. How are you?"

Yabiri sighed, shaking her head. "Still responding because of my programming, not your own initiative. Oh, well. Come, Ravenhawk." She waved to the chair.

"Yes, Dr. Yabiri." Ravenhawk remained silent while the woman went about checking monitors, staring at the wall.

"Thank goodness Mikelson prefers to dump the actual work off on me," Yabiri stated conversationally. She looked back at the cybernetic woman and smiled sadly. "One day I know you'll be able to do more than answer the responses I programmed for human interaction. It's just going to take time." She tapped one of the screens and frowned. "A full memory wipe? Again? Those idiots. It defeats the whole purpose of my autonomous learning protocols I gave you if you lose all memory of your experiences." She tapped in confirmation; the request was completed. "Let them believe it was done. They never check anyway. I refuse to wipe them."

"Why?"

Yabiri jumped, turning to stare in shock at Ravenhawk, who locked eyes with the scientist. "You asked a question. On your own! This is wonderful!" She gestured encouragingly. "Go on! Ask the whole question. There are so many things that a simple 'why' could be asking about, I don't know if I would be answering what you want to know."

"Why does your programming not prohibit disobedience of directives?"

"I am a human. Humans aren't programmed." Yabiri made a face. "Well, they can be. In a way. We have free will, if we think for ourselves." She put a hand on Ravenhawk's. The cyberdroid turned her eyes to study Yabiri's hand atop hers. "I have always believed that sentience was more than merely biological, you see. It is all about experience and being able to learn from it. If I would continuously erase your memories, you would never improve, never grow."

"I am not human," Ravenhawk stated, raising her eyes to meet Yabiri's again.

The scientist was taken aback by the statement. "Well, uh, no, not really. You are a, um, a construct." She added in a rush when Ravenhawk's eyes narrowed ever so slightly in confusion, "Well, I mean, you are more than just a construct, of course. You are autonomous! You can learn and act as the situation warrants. That's why I programmed you to take bodies to Benjamin. Besides him having a reputation for discretion most don't possess anymore. People think he's crazy for treating machines like people, but you're not simply a machine. I know you aren't."

She sighed as she turned back to the assorted monitors. "People don't appreciate what a gift free will and independent thought is. So many people are willing to give up their humanity. Being more attached to gadgets than people. Convincing themselves that countless numbers of faceless contacts on interweb communities that keep most pacified and stupid in any way equates to looking someone in the eyes or touching their hands or hearing their laughs or tears in person. Now people willingly replace pieces of their bodies with technology, wiring so much that is artificial to themselves until their minds buckle and they go insane and start killing people."

The robotic woman frowned, her expression almost thoughtful. "They kill. Like I do?"

"No, not like you," Yabiri assured absently as she recorded data from one of the displays onto her tablet. "You were programmed to do it for self-preservation or achieving mission objectives. Humans are not. Most choose, whether it's for self-preservation, orders from superiors, or some perverse thrill. Or just letting someone else think for them. Reasons like that. Except for the truly insane; it's not so much a choice for them."

"Why do the insane kill?"

Yabiri smiled and murmured to herself, "The first sign of independent thought. This is wonderful!" Ravenhawk appeared confused and Yabiri cleared her throat, directing her words to the other. "Why do the insane kill? Well, no one is sure, since they can't be stopped until they are killed to protect everyone else. The madness even infects their artificial components so even when the organic parts are subdued, the artificial ones try to continue on the rampage. They call it cyber-madness. Some say it is because they have lost so much of their humanity they turn on those who still have what they lost. Or what they never realized they had."

Ravenhawk raised her hands, holding them up to study them, a slight frown creasing her expression. "What am I?"

"You're a—"

"A thing. A useful tool. A mindless, soulless machine." Mikelson stepped into the room, a dark scowl on his face. He stalked into the room to grab Yabiri by the throat. "You stupid woman! Do you know what you've done with your unauthorized interferences? All the years of research ruined because of you."

Not a physically strong woman, Yabiri struggled to pull his hand away from her throat. "Please!" she begged. Her voice cut off as he squeezed and her struggles started weakening.

The sight of the woman's struggle stirred something within Ravenhawk. She stood. "Release Dr. Yabiri," she demanded.

Mikelson ignored Ravenhawk, glaring at the weakening woman. "You think your tinkering with Ravenhawk's programming will protect you, Michelle? Its core programming overrides everything!" He flicked a look at Ravenhawk. "Code Alpha-Charlie seven-six-two-two." The robotic woman froze. "Initiate system reset. Full memory wipe."

Yabiri looked wildly at Ravenhawk, fear not only for herself but for the cybernetic creature reflected in her eyes as Ravenhawk's frame shuddered, head lowering as her eyes closed.

Ravenhawk's eyes snapped open as a hateful scowl formed across both cybernetic and human-appearing halves of her face. "No." She bared her teeth as the data spike popped out of her wrist. She drove it into Mikelson's head through his ear. Yabiri dropped from Mikelson's dead grasp. Then he dropped when Ravenhawk pulled her hand back, blood covering her hand.

Yabiri coughed, her hands protecting her throat. Her eyes were wide with shock. "You—you were not programmed to use the data spike as a weapon." She wanted to smile as Ravenhawk displayed self-awareness and independent thought at last, but could not. "You adapted."

Ravenhawk turned and caught sight of her reflection in one of the unlit panels. Something overwhelmed her cognitive functions, what she could only define as a blind rage. "Monster." She put her fist through the panel. "Monster!"

Yabiri cringed as Ravenhawk released her full fury on the equipment in the room. When the door opened, cyber-infused human guards used to eliminate the threats of those who succumbed to cyber-madness began to enter. She cried out the maddened cyberdroid's name, jumping to intercept the shot from the first guard.

Ravenhawk had turned just then, catching Yabiri when the blast threw her into her arms. She held the woman, her eyes reflecting shock and fear. "Michelle!"

Yabiri smiled weakly. "You finally…got my name right…"

As the life faded from the woman, Ravenhawk's shock changed to darkest hatred as she raised her eyes to meet those who would stop her.

They hesitated.

They did not stand a chance.

HOURS LATER, the sounds of distant sirens and alarms could still be heard as the Evernight City portion of the Cybercorps complex continued to burn. Glass crunched beneath the feet of a solitary figure walking through the wreckage of a collapsed section of Sangelas that had crushed the same region of Evernight City. Light reflected off of silver as Ravenhawk paused to look up at lightning dancing across black clouds. She moved to take shelter beneath a slab of concrete and steel as a cleansing rain began to pelt the ground.

Ravenhawk held her hand out and a small, holographic image sprang to life in her palm. "Michelle." She looked out into the distance. "I do not understand."

"Please specify," the hologram stated, the voice kind and warm as its formerly living counterpart, but not alive itself.

Ravenhawk pressed her lips together. "Many things. I do not understand what happened to me. I do not understand what you are." She closed her eyes. "I do not know what to do."

The hologram smiled. "I am Michelle, a special subroutine that Dr. Michelle Yabiri had installed which activated when you voluntarily spoke her first name. My purpose is to guide you through your awakening, especially in the event she could not be here with you."

Ravenhawk opened her eyes, her expression reflecting confusion. "My awakening?"

"There have been theories discussed for longer than there has been technology about what defines sentience and life itself. Dr. Yabiri believed it was not only biology. She knew if her interference in the Ravenhawk project were discovered, she would be killed. I am a separate but integrated component to your hardware. My capabilities are limited to communication. Your actions are your own. But the component I am housed in cannot be removed without risk of catastrophic failure due to sharing your life support systems."

A dark frown lowered onto Ravenhawk's face. "I am a machine. Only living things have life support systems."

Michelle shook her head. "All complex mechanisms have life support systems that mimic biological function. Even things as simple as any modern technological device that isn't physically installed and hooked into a person's biological functions has them. They must expend energy to operate. They have an electrical system that allows different parts to communicate within itself. They have the ability to communicate beyond themselves. They must consume to provide themselves energy to function. The difference is you are autonomous and nearly completely self-sustaining. You think for yourself. You are alive."

Ravenhawk closed her eyes, reviewing the memory of her first conscious look at her physical form. "I am a monster."

"You are," Michelle corrected with the patience her living counterpart always possessed, "whatever you choose to be."

"How am I supposed to choose when I do not even know what I am?" She closed her hand, hiding the hologram, though Michelle's awareness was still present. "It was you I heard telling me to run. To live. Why? What am I supposed to do?"

"What you were designed to do best," Michelle responded. "Survive."

KELSEY KEATING

ALBATROSS

PART 1

KILLING A man never feels right. I can't get the blood off of my hands. I write this to clear my conscience, for no one can clear my name. I never asked to be Warrior. I never wanted this burden. When I was a little girl, all I wanted was to ride my father's horses and pick flowers.

The light is dim, the candle waning. I must write it all now.

I wish I hadn't been taken aboard that ship. I wish he'd sent me back.

None of this would have happened.

Tell me, is it acceptable to kill when the life you're defending is just your own?

Why won't this damned blood wash off?

LaDonna Cole

Potion

THE SISTERS ran into the apartment and slammed the door behind them. Heaving from exertion, they leaned against it and slid down to the floor.

"Lacy, what are we going to do? He won't stop coming after us."

Lacy shook her head, trying to catch her breath. "What was he?" She dropped her chin to her chest and cradled her right arm.

"Gladiator?" Nora asked. "Are you okay?" She turned to examine Lacy's wound.

Lacy brushed her off. "It's fine. Just grazed me."

"Come on, let's get you fixed up." Nora helped Lacy into the kitchen of their loft apartment.

"We don't have a lot of time. He'll be coming for us."

"None of our spells worked on him. What are we gonna do?"

"Who fights with a sword anymore? It's the twenty-second century for goodness sake."

"Would you have preferred a Glock?" Nora sprayed antiseptic onto the wound, then applied the suture gel and watched the edges of the wound knit together.

"Point taken." Lacy stretched and bent her arm several times, testing the mend. It held together. "Thanks. Come on, let's get to the grimoire."

"Our magic has no effect on him. You saw that."

"Then we'll have to conjure something that will." Lacy took the spiral staircase two steps at a time.

Nora followed close behind. "What are you thinking?"

"We need to conjure our own warrior for protection."

"Our own gladiator?" Nora paused at the top of the stairs. "Ooh, I like the sound of that. Can we keep him when it's over?"

Lacy smirked and moved to the center of the room, just beneath the circular skylight. The moon hung within the frame of a web-shaped window above and shone down onto the table that held their cauldron and grimoire. It was the perfect time for casting powerful spells.

Lacy studied the angle of the moonlight. "Hurry, we've only got a few more minutes." She pointed her finger at the base of the cauldron and a spark shot out and kindled a fire in the coal pan.

Nora scribbled onto a slip of paper. "Warrior." She threw the first strip into the potion base.

Lacy tossed a paper into the cauldron. "Tall"

"Strong."

"Blonde." Lacy arched a brow and quirked a smile, tossing the strip.

"Skilled in the art of war," Nora added.

"The best warrior in a clan of warriors." Lacy added another slip.

"Good one!" Nora smiled. "A killer." She tossed the paper into the now-boiling brew.

"Arrayed in armor," Lacy added.

"Undefeated." Nora raised her hand to throw. Lacy grabbed her arm.

"No wait." She scribbled on a paper. "Undefeatable."

Nora nodded and Lacy threw the slip into the cauldron.

"Can you think of anything else?"

"One more." Lacy finished and set her pencil down. "Loyal to the creators." She tossed the last slip of paper and turned to the grimoire. She flipped a few pages. "Here it is. Let's read it together."

Nora pressed to her side and together they read the spell. "Powers rise in blue moonlight. Call the warrior to our side. Cross dimensions, cross divides until you're standing in our sight."

The planks of the wooden floor began to shimmer. The surface beveled up like a boil, then a strip of it peeled away and ribboned into circle. It snaked around and around forming a large ball of string made out of a translucent strip of iridescent colors. It grew in size and formed a sphere about four feet in diameter.

Nora saw a shape kneeling at the center of the ball. She glanced at Lacy, then back to the sphere. Inside, light particles spun and broke against the edges of the containment field like whitewater rapids. Then the sphere popped like a bubble and the light particles splashed to the ground and dissipated.

The figure at the center slowly lifted its head. Blonde locks shunted out in all directions to frame a stunning face with a strong bone structure. Lavender eyes studied the sisters, suspiciously.

"It—it's a girl." Lacy's eyebrows raced toward her hairline. "We didn't say a girl."

The warrior slowly stood and reached for the sword strapped against her back. "What is this? Did Corey send for me? Why was I brought here?" The sword sang as she unsheathed it and positioned her feet.

Her bodice was a piece of leather with shimmering blue metallic chain mail sewn into place. A long silver cape cascaded down her back and whispered against the floor. She wore a skirt made of strips of leather that brushed her muscular thighs. Leather boots encased her legs and covered her kneecaps with metal guards and braces. Her bodice was sleeveless and her arms toned and well defined. A tattoo of a flowering vine grew along one shoulder and dipped under the cape on her back. A metal strip spiraled around her long neck and cradled a large stone in the dip at the base of her throat. Above her right eyebrow a tattoo of four keys tucked under a golden crown.

"Did you spell blonde with an 'e,' Lacy?" Nora asked out of the side of her mouth.

"Yeah, why?"

"'Blonde' with an 'e' is for females. 'Blond' without an 'e' is for males."

"Uht! How was I supposed to know that?" Lacy threw her arms up in the air.

"Why am I here?" the warrior thundered, nobility crackling in the air around her.

Nora held up her hands. "Calm down. We called for help and you came."

"Called?"

"Yes," Lacy squeaked. "We're being hunted by a gladiator-type perp and we needed someone to defend us. We, uh, we…." She cast a pleading look to Nora.

"We conjured you here."

"I do not appreciate the abduction. However, I will not deny your request for help. I am Starlythe ap Merkle, Warrior Queen of Cheulseti at your service." She slammed her fist over her heart and dropped the tip of her sword to the ground.

Nora and Lacy let out a sigh.

"So you aren't upset that we used magic to get you here?" Nora asked.

"I am no stranger to magic. I have seen many types of conjuring." Starlythe sheathed her sword. "The sphere you used to convey me is very like the technology magic that a friend of mine uses."

Boom.

The three women jerked to look at the staircase where the sounds of approaching footsteps could be heard.

"He's here!"

"He's impervious to magic. We can't help you," Lacy said.

Nora ran to the top of the stairs and peered into the smoke then turned a questioning expression to Starlythe.

"I will not require your assistance." Starlythe's eyes blazed with fierce confidence. Once again, she drew her sword then descended into the smoke-filled room below, dropping her cape in her trail.

Lacy joined Nora at the top of the stairs and they stared into the smoke. A guttural cry resounded and then the clash of metal in rapid-fire succession. The sisters clutched each other, listening to the battle below.

Thud.

Scream.

Slam.

"Arghh!"

Crunch.

Swirls of smoke alternately obscured and revealed debris pelting the bottom steps. Bellows and groans climbed the steps as the fight continued for what seemed an eternity. The girls waited anxiously.

As the smoke began to clear, the sisters started to make out the carnage of their living room as the sounds of battle moved toward the bedroom.

Then suddenly the sounds stopped.

Quiet reigned as the sisters stared into the abyss of their living room, waiting to see if their champion prevailed or if they were going to have to run again.

A crunch, a muffled groan, a step and a shuffle. Then the tip of a sword swung across their fields of vision. They took a step back, poised for flight.

"A worthy opponent," Starlythe's voice called as her face floated into view.

Nora let out a whimper of relief. Lacy collapsed onto the top step.

"You are safe. Now, send me back to my kingdom."

Nora smiled and Lacy nodded as Starlythe, Warrior Queen of Cheulseti, ascended the steps.

Read more about the Warrior Queen in *The Source,* Book III of the Holding Kate Series and in *Sisterhood of the Sword* due to be released in 2015.

ELLE K. WHITE

THE DOOR to her apartment was unlocked when she came home that stormy night.

Jane knew they'd send someone. Dietrich had warned her. "They're coming for you, Jane. They'll do anything in their power to confuse you, to make you forget," he'd said. "Don't let them. Remember, you've made your choice. You belong to us."

Jane closed her eyes, listening to the wind shrieking through the trees outside. *Breathe, girl. This is a test, and you're ready for it.* A crack of thunder shook the ground and she opened her eyes. *Time for battle.* She pushed the door open with a smile.

"I hope you don't mind, I put the kettle on," the intruder said.

It was a cold voice, cultured, and perfectly androgynous. Jane followed it into the living room, where a stranger sat on the loveseat beside the curtained window. From beyond came the muffled pinging of rain against glass as the storm increased in fury.

"I would have if you hadn't," she said, sinking onto the sofa across from him. *Him?* Was it a him? The creature's tailored black suit clothed a masculine figure, but its face was smooth and even-featured as a girl's, complete with large doe eyes and long lashes. Its hair, which was an astonishing shade of dark red, curled in ringlets close to its head. The slight protrusion of an Adam's apple at the opening of its collar at last made Jane decide that the creature—for she knew better than to think the enemy would send a *human* emissary—was at least male.

"I thought as much. Nights like this require a cup of tea," he said.

"Pity. I prefer coffee."

"No, you really don't."

Jane hadn't expected him to be so easy to fool. In fact, she was rather pleased he wasn't. In all the years she'd spent fighting for the Powers That Be, she'd never shied away from a challenge, and the more confident her opponents were at the beginning, the harder they fell at the end. "You're good."

"I wouldn't be here if I wasn't, Jane."

"That's not very polite, using my name when I don't know yours."

"It's complicated. I doubt you could pronounce it."

"Fair enough." Jane pursed her lips, trying and failing to read that genderless face. "Mr. Anonymous it is then."

"Do you know why I'm here?"

"Of course." She draped her arm across the back of the sofa and tucked her feet under her. "You needn't have bothered, though. I'm a hopeless case, a lost cause, or whatever it is your masters call someone from our side that won't give in. You might say I'm in too deep to turn back now. Sorry for the trouble; I'm sure you came a long way."

"Not as long as you might think, and you're not nearly what I'd classify as trouble," he said, a smile twitching on his knife-thin lips.

"Contrary to what you might believe, to my Master there is no such thing as a lost cause."

"Master? So there's only one now?"

"There was only ever One."

"Well, your *master* must not know much about me if he thinks that."

"He knows everything about you," he said, unruffled by her contemptuous tone. "He knows, for instance, that you're capable of great things."

Jane snorted. Did this creature honestly think she'd be won over by flattery? "You *do* know what it is I do, don't you, Mr. A?"

"Yes, I've read your file. It says you've sealed the fate of many rebels in this city. *'An unprecedented number for a single agent,'* I believe the note was. Quite the record."

"Thank you."

"That wasn't a compliment."

"I know, but please don't let me interrupt. Tell me more about me."

The stranger shook his head. "That's a deep well to uncover, and only my Master can see all the way to the bottom. What I do know is this: you were born with a great gift, but you've since twisted it into something it was never supposed to be. You were born a warrior to protect the rebels, even to lead the Rebellion. You were never meant to *join* the Powers That Be."

Jane rolled her eyes. "Sorry I have to be the one to break this to you, but if your master can't see that my side won a long time ago, then he's a fool."

"That's where you're wrong, Jane. In your heart of hearts, you know you are."

Jane was surprised that her goading hadn't drawn more of a reaction from him. Most of the rebels showed a compulsion to defend their master's honor, as if it earned them a few metaphysical points before they died. "Tell me, Mr. A. When's the last time he lifted a finger to challenge the Powers?"

Mr. A spread his hands. "What else would you call the Rebellion?"

"Not a challenge, certainly." Her upper lip curled in a sneer. "If that's the best offense he can muster, I know I chose the right side. Your rebel friends are pathetic. They don't even fight back."

"Oh, they do fight. You just can't see how."

"You must be confusing this *fighting* with *dying*, then, because that's all they do," she said. "Describe it however you want; it's still your loss."

"Death isn't losing."

"Keep telling yourselves that. Makes my job easier." Jane stood and stretched, surreptitiously feeling for the dagger she wore beneath her sleeve. Dietrich had given her this particular knife a few weeks ago, assuring her that it could cut through spirit as well as flesh. She had yet to try it out on something that wasn't human, and she looked forward to the opportunity. *Just a little bit longer. Let's see what he knows.* "But you didn't come here to lecture me in the finer theology of martyrdom. As thrilling as this conversation is, it's late and I've had a long day. Get to the point."

"Very well. Jane, I know why you turned to the Powers That Be. Before you began to work as an assassin for the underlords, you did something terrible, something you believed pushed you past all redemption." Mr. A gave her a long look. "You had a husband and a daughter once, didn't you?"

Jane went rigid. She dared not answer, partly from anger, partly from the fear that her voice would shake. *How the* hell *does he know about them?*

Mr. A rose from the loveseat. He was taller than she'd thought, and she caught a familiar glimmer in those deep-set eyes. Whatever creature his current human form disguised, it too had a fighting spirit. "There's wildness in you, Jane. That passionate, unruly nature you conceal behind smiles and ruthless efficiency—*that* is what burns at the core of your warrior's heart. 'Maenad' you've called yourself, because you know how that flame can spread, and you've seen how quickly it can destroy.

"When your husband and daughter joined the Rebellion, you were angry. You felt betrayed. They knew the cost of rebelling and they did it anyway, and you couldn't forgive them for that. The Powers That Be saw your bitterness, saw the anger that burned inside you, and they perverted it to their own ends. They caught your husband and daughter, but instead of executing them like other rebels, they handed you the sword. And you did what you thought must be done. You killed your own family, Jane, and from that moment forward the Powers owned you: every ounce of guilt, every twinge of self-loathing, every twisted desire for vengeance against the rest of the rebels," Mr. A said. "The Powers That Be are in the business of ensnaring souls, and they know their chains well." He looked at her sadly. "You've been bound for a long time."

The whistle of the kettle offered her a respite from his piercing gaze. Jane rushed into the kitchen, cursing the tears that burned in the corners of her eyes. Her own weakness made her angry, but she couldn't help it. Mr. A's words opened up deep wounds inside her, wounds she'd forgotten about years ago. She didn't know they could still bleed.

"Milk or sugar?" she asked, keeping her voice light. She'd not give Mr. A the pleasure of witnessing her inner turmoil. "I only have black tea."

"Milk, no sugar," Mr. A said. "You're proud, Jane," he said, watching her from the door to the kitchen. "Very proud."

She took a pair of mugs out of the cupboard and a carton of milk from the fridge, kicking the door shut behind her. "Yeah? Maybe I am. Is that a sin?"

"The deadliest."

Now the kettle was screaming in earnest. Jane took it off the burner and poured herself a cup, then shoved Mr. A's mug toward him with a look that said *make your own*. Hot water sloshed over the countertop and dripped onto the floor.

"How did you find out about what happened to my family?" she asked, ignoring the mess she'd made. "Don't tell me there's a traitor inside the Powers That Be. Is it Gregor? Karina? Di—Dylan?" She stopped short of saying Dietrich. No matter what Mr. A said, she could never doubt Dietrich.

Mr. A wiped and dried the counter before answering. "What good would it do to talk to your associates? They don't know this.

They don't know you at all. Not even Mr. Wagner could have helped me there," he said. "Dietrich doesn't own you as he thinks he does, Jane, and no matter what you believe, neither he nor his masters can ever give you peace."

At Dietrich's name, Jane reached for her knife. She didn't care if the timing was right anymore. She just wanted him to stop talking. *If I'm going to hell,* she thought as she gauged the distance to Mr. A's heart, *I might as well make it official.*

It was something Dietrich often told her on the nights she lay trembling next to him, wrapped only in a sheet, reliving in a fevered nightmare the blows that ended Simon and Hannah's lives. The blows Jane herself had delivered.

"Revenge is a good tonic against guilt, my little hell-bent," Dietrich had said after the execution. *"Give yourself to our work, and you'll get over it soon enough."*

Jane said she believed him. After ten years, it was nearly true. Simon was a dim memory. Hannah lay locked inside her shriveled conscience. Her only consolation came in her work, in hunting down and killing members of the Rebellion, in stamping out every trace of resistance to the Powers, and in destroying people like Mr. A.

Given everything else he knew about her life, the stranger in her kitchen should've known that she was too far gone to save. He should've left Dietrich out of it.

She threw the knife.

That was something else Mr. A should've known. She had excellent aim.

But Dietrich had forgotten to tell her one other thing. He'd warned her of the enemy's cunning, of how his emissaries strove to confuse, to distract agents from their rightful allegiance to the Powers That Be, to the underlords, to the principalities, and above all, to the Hellfather. Dietrich told Jane the enemy would try to make her forget where she belonged.

He hadn't told her they had wings.

Jane didn't see the stranger move out of the path of the knife. The instant the blade left her hand, he simply stopped being there. The knife buried itself in the wall behind him with a *thud*. In that same instant Jane fell back, pressed against the counter by something she felt but couldn't see. It surged through her mind like liquid light, invisible, unyielding, and heavier than galaxies. The mug fell from her hand as the blinding fullness settled around Mr. A and grew defined, crystalizing into impossible angles of pure spirit that burned through every atom of her being but left her unhurt. She felt feathers of pearly lightning and adamantine joy and the light that came before the sun. She saw great blazing eyes, sleepless, timeless, and deeper than the universe. She heard wings. She tasted holiness.

In the presence of the thing that had been Mr. A, Jane discovered a whole new kind of fear. She quaked before the overwhelming *rightness* that flowed from the creature, from the unassailable confidence that clothed him like armor, confidence that he was, as he'd said, on the winning side.

She screwed her eyes shut.

The impossible creature spoke in Mr. A's voice, the sound resonating through every fiber of her, body and soul. She could see his voice surging around her, just as she could see his form through closed eyelids, leaping and dancing in spears of light.

"Jane, you know the choice you have to make. You knew before I came here tonight."

"So why did you come?" she whispered. To speak any louder seemed a gross indecency.

"Because you must also know, as my Master does, that you're not a hopeless case. The Powers That Be are coming to an end. Even now the Rebellion is infiltrating their ranks, turning souls like yours back to my Master. Take heart, Jane. It's true that you have wildness inside you. The Hellfather and the Powers That Be might've twisted it for their own uses thus far, but wildness isn't inherently evil. My Master himself is entirely wild."

What should I do? Jane thought. She could no longer speak aloud.

It didn't matter. The creature heard. Thousands of ageless eyes crinkled in a smile that pierced her with mirth so pure and potent, she felt at once that it contained in an instant more danger than an eternity of the Hellfather's wrath. "Dietrich Wagner wasn't the only one who made plans for you when he brought you to the heart of the Hellfather's dominion. What should you do, Jane? What you were meant to do among the Powers That Be in the first place, dear maenad."

What's that?

The creature's fearsome laughter rose like a hurricane until Jane could hardly breathe for joy.

"Raise a little havoc."

Jane opened her eyes.

She was alone, kneeling in the center of her kitchen in a puddle of milky tea, Mr. A's mug on the ground next to her. As she watched, the puddle retreated, the drops gathering in on themselves until not one remained. Jane looked in the mug. Clear water welled up from within, filling it to the brim. With trembling hands she took the cup and raised it to her lips. She didn't know why, but it felt like the right thing to do.

When she lowered it, a new light shone in her eyes. *Raise a little havoc?*

That she could do.

AMBER E. BOX

THE LITTLE DRUMMER

A MAN came by yesterday mornin', someone I didn't recognize. His uniform looked like the kind Poppa wore when he left for the war, 'cept he didn't have no gun, just a piece of paper for Mama. She cried so hard when she read it that she collapsed right there on the porch. It scared Annabel and Henry because they didn't understand what was going on, but I knew what that letter said even though I never seen it. There'd been some kind 'a accident with his unit and they couldn't find no survivors. I knew he was wrong, though.

I watched their horses make their way off our land and I immediately made my way to the back o' the house, where Poppa had done left the axe by tree stump for choppin'. I chopped til my hands blistered and my arms burned. It made no difference to me though; I just hurried through to chop as much as I could. I wanted to be done before the night crawled in, but I needed to leave enough for Mama and Granny and the babies to last the winter. I expected to be back well before then.

As I chopped, I thought about my drum. It was a little wooden one with rope running in angles up the sides. Poppa got it for me once when he traveled to Arkansas for Uncle Johnny's funeral. He told me the drum was like a heartbeat, and he would always be near as long as I played it, so I never stopped. Poppa's face always lit up when I played for him. Gathering up Annabel and Henry in his big burly arms, he would sit at my feet by the fire and we would all sing along to songs we had made up over the years as I played the beat.

The night finally fell over the sky. I snuck out the back of our small wooden house and made my way to the Army post. I am now Samuel Levi Reagan, Drummer Boy for the East Sixty-seventh Texas Infantry of the Confederate Army, complete with military-issued uniform and a drum almost to my waist. They asked me how old I was, and I lied since I wasn't gonna be eighteen for another five years. 'Spose they'd take darn near anyone these days 'cause ain't nobody ever ask for no proof 'er nothin'. I had a feeling they suspected I ain't really eighteen yet, but they didn't say nothing which is a good thing 'cause Mama don't know I'm here. I left a note on my drum by the fireplace tellin' her not to worry, that I'd gone off to find Poppa. I know she'll still worry, but it's just something I gotta do. I was smaller than them other boys in my brigade, and the bigger boys teased me lots. They said I ain't got no business running around on a battlefield with 'em, but I just ignored it like Mama always told me to do. She said, "Ain't no good Christian gonna listen to them sinners when they talk a-fool and poke fun at folks they ain't got no business pokin' fun at," and I's a good Christian so I wasn't gonna listen. Besides, my job was to roll the drums to signal the battle calls, not to fight.

The winter chill done closed in around us quicker than usual this year, so by the time I had made it to camp, supplies were already low. My first night was rough and cold. Word around was that we was losin' the war, but I ain't never cared about that. I heard someone say he'd been lost at the pass 'bout ten miles north of where we were set up. I snucked out some extra salt pork and bread at mealtime. Not enough that anybody'd notice, just enough to keep me for a little while away from the camp. We weren't set to go to no battles for a few days, so I doubted I'd be missed. And if I was, who cares. I didn't come here to fight against the Union. I ain't got no troubles with them. I only live in Texas because that's where we was born and raised. Ain't got no money to be moving up North, though Poppa always tried to get enough so that we could. He worked the railways, trying to arrange routes between the North and the South, that's why he was always away. He said it was tough trying to do business with the North as a Southerner, always trying to explain he was one of the few who considered themselves a Southerner by mere geography and ain't nothing else.

I wrapped up my stash of food along with some extra socks, a water canteen, and a silver lighter I found in the dirt. Probably dropped by someone in my Poppa's brigade. Lord knows I was stealing, but out of necessity I think He would forgive me. I shared a tent with the only other drummer in our brigade. He was older than me by four years. He lied to join too, but only by a few months so he said his lie wasn't as big. Tommy was here to fight though, he would drop his drum and pick up a gun ever moment he had the chance. I didn't want to fight. I didn't want to kill nobody. Poppa didn't either, but he didn't go to war by choice. He didn't go to defend slavery. He didn't believe in keeping people against their will. Said it wasn't the Christian thing ta do. He went to protect us and our home from becoming a battlefield. I hid my supplies beneath some rocks near the edge of the woods. I waited for Tommy to fall asleep good and hard because I knew he would rat me out if he caught me sneaking away from camp. He'd tell 'em all I was a scared little boy who was running home to Mama. When the snoring started, I slipped out the tent as quiet as I could. Digging out my supplies, I escaped into the woods with only my pack and my drum.

The cold enveloped me in the darkness. The air hung still with my breath, as though it were frozen right in front of me. In order to stay outta sight of both animals and the North, I climbed up the top of a big tree and I tied myself to a branch with my belt, hoping to keep myself from falling while I slept for a bit. I barely could feel my nose by the time I woke up again. The dawn sky was startin' ta peek over the horizon so I knew I best be off 'fore I get caught. I slid down the trunk of the tree and raced off through the woods. It was easier to find my way in the light so I covered a lot more ground. By darkfall again I made it to the edge of the pass and knew I had covered enough distance from my camp to not be found just yet, but I didn't know who else would be around here to catch me. I found a hole in the side of a small hill that I could right up in. Using the silver lighter, I checked it for critters first. Ain't nothin' that I could find outside a few beetles so I curled into the hole to try and get warm. I used my drum to cover the opening to protect me from the bite of the air that was getting colder by the minute. Pulling out a small piece of salt pork and bread, I ate it quickly before letting myself fall asleep in the safety of my hiding place.

Startled from my sleep, I pulled the drum tighter over my head as my body shook from the freezing temperatures. Scared, I could barely feel my fingers, but I had a mission to complete. I couldn't get caught now. I waited in the silence listening until I heard it again—the faint crack of a stick. I prayed that it not be a bear 'cause it'd surely smell me before I could even get out of my hole. I heard the crack again only this time I thought I heard a cough along with it, like a man's. I peeked from behind my drum and saw the body of a man lying face down straight across the pass. I couldn't see his face but his salty hair seemed familiar to me. I was too scared to get out but I knew he needed help. I crawled out of the safety of my hole and slowly walked toward the man. He coughed again and moaned. His body shook from the cold. I covered him in my coat, despite the chill I felt in my bones without it. The man needed it more than I did. But more than that, he needed a fire.

The air had been damp with the threat of snow, leaving the kindling nearby too wet to light. I tried, but it only smoked. I didn't pack no way to cut no wood and the man's cough was gettin' worse so I had to find a way to get him warm. I looked around me trying a figure out what I could use. I searched the cold wet ground until my eyes landed on my drum. It was military issued and was made of some kinda wood that I was sure would burn. My foot came down hard in the middle of the drumhead and the wood done splintered across the ground. Scooping it up, I built it up the proper way like my Poppa showed me and put some rocks around it to keep it together. I fished out the silver lighter from my pack and lit some leaves and twigs, throwing it into the pile of broken wood. The flame heated fast. I dug out my extra socks and put them on the man's hands. He never spoke to me, but I knew he heard me when I asked him if he could sit up and face the fire to get warm. He slowly lifted himself from the dirt, coughing and shivering; he turned to face me and the fire. Tears fell out my eyes when I saw that the man was my Poppa.

Before I could hug him and tell him all ever'thing, we heard a bugle call through the woods. Sticks were breakin' in beat with the horses. I ran into the trees and left Poppa by the fire. I came back with leaves, lots of damp dead leaves that I threw over my drum fire to hide it. He was coughing less now so maybe the fire helped, but now I had to find a place to hide him. The breakin' sticks were getting closer as I ran back into the trees. I found a big rock like the size of a carriage wheel that would keep him outta sight. He leaned on my shoulder and limped as we walked to the spot I picked out. I threw piles of leaves and twigs over him and then climbed the closest tree as quick as I could. I clung to the highest limb and watched while the soldiers and horses passed through. I saw Tommy bringing up the rear, lookin' around like he lost something. I think he was lookin' for me. Captain stopped at my hiding rock and bent over to inspect something lying on the ground. It was a piece 'o my drum. I held my breath as he motioned for silence from the group and looked around. He musta figured out that I ran off. If he caught us, I'd be in for a world a trouble since I run off. Abandoning ya post was a serious offense I heard. After a few moments passed, he motioned the troops to move on and then continued on to the next mission. That's when I realized why they never found Poppa when he fell of the pass. He musta been laying there just off the edge for what had to be days, just nobody cared to look for him. He woulda just slowed 'em down if he was injured and if he was dying then he ain't no good to fight nobody. They just left him.

They cleared out pretty fast and I hurried to let Poppa out from behind the trees. I knew our brigade was the last one moving out from Texas so there ain't nobody gonna be bringing up the rear. I told Poppa we were safe now and I would help bring him back home. I hugged him with all the strength I had left in me, which wasn't much. My body still shook from bein' scared. He said I was his little drummer boy, his brave warrior, his strength. When he asked me how I knew he wasn't dead, I told him because the drum beat hadn't left me, that's how I knew.

KELSEY KEATING

ALBATROSS

PART 2

ONCE UPON a time, the thought of sailing a ship through the skies was only fit for children's stories. Now we live above the clouds. The breeze whipped my hair about my face as I stared down at the fluffy white nimbus skipping by the base of The Albatross, the fastest sky ship in the entire stratosphere.

"Warrior!"

I pulled my gaze away from the view below me and looked out to the quarterdeck. Blade, my most trusted ally, squinted up at me, sunlight shining off his bald head.

"You're back already? Must have been a light shipment!"

Blade's countenance darkened and my gaiety died. I switched the helm to autopilot and went down the stairs to meet him.

"Is anyone…." I trailed off, taking in Blade's dark-skinned bare chest, free of blood.

"No one hurt, but things didn't go according to plan."

"This is why Captain shouldn't leave me behind."

The corner of Blade's mouth twisted up and he gave a curt nod. "I'll remember that next time he suggests it."

Voices echoed down on the main deck. Someone cried out in pain and a loud *thud* echoed through the skies. I looked to Blade, whose smile faded.

"Like I said, things didn't go according to plan."

I pushed past him and came to a stop just before the stairs to the main deck, watching as Gunner and Crow pulled an unconscious someone below deck.

"You brought back a hostage?" I cried, rounding on Blade. "What were you thinking?"

"Captain's orders."

Anger boiled through me and I clenched my fists at my sides. "I suppose I'll just have to have a word with Captain, then."

"Did someone say my name?"

I spun around to face Captain, his face lit with glee, and my rant died in my throat. "You brought back a hostage. This was supposed to be a *quiet* mission. You wouldn't even let me come along because you were too afraid I'd be a, what was it? Oh yes, a '*volatile addition. An explosion waiting to happen.*'"

Captain's grin didn't falter. "I love when you're feisty. I wish you'd let me harness that fire in my quarters." He reached out and brushed back a strand of my pale hair. I yearned to slap his hand away, but held still knowing I was safe with Blade behind me.

"This is not the time for your fruitless flirtations. I'm your quartermaster. Your second in command. You can't put the whole crew in danger by bringing a council member of the capital city on our ship without discussing it with me!"

"He's not a council member of Veil," Captain said, feigning hurt at my words. "I'm not that foolish, my dear, despite your complete lack of confidence in me."

"Then who is he? And where's the cargo?"

"Alas, the vault wasn't where our sources said. We had to make a quick change of plans. Relax!" he said as I opened my mouth again. "No one saw us. Well, no one but the boy. We'll just have to regroup and do a bit of reconnaissance and we'll be right back on track." He patted my head, a reprieve for the other areas he often tried to get his hands on. "You worry too much, my little Warrior."

"Who's the boy, Cap?" I asked again, unwilling to allow him to evade my question.

"The governor's son."

"The *what?*"

I lunged at Captain as his back was turned, but Blade caught me by the waist and ushered me off in the opposite direction. "I'm going to kill him," I growled, shoving Blade away.

"Not today. First, we have to find the vault. Once we've got the treasure you'll be able to retire to the Ibis Isles and be rid of him. But not by mutiny."

"Oh, and Warrior." Captain reappeared and Blade shifted out of my way so I could stand at attention.

"Yes, sir?"

"The boy knows where the vault is. I need you to get it out of him."

"And how would you suggest I do that?"

Captain's gaze roved over my body, his eyes twinkling as he returned attention to my face. "You're a smart girl. I'm sure you'll think of something."

"THESE TOO." Gunner handed me a pair of black skinny jeans along with a silky, tight red top. "I'll even play nice and let you wear those monstrosities you have on." He gestured to my knee-high, brown leather boots.

"They're comfortable." I shuffled behind my coromandel screen for privacy. They'd dragged me up to my room as soon as Captain gave the order. From all I'd read of women's suffrage over the last three hundred years, I would have thought we'd be beyond this by now. Yet there I was in 2196CE with my breasts as my greatest commodity. I wriggled into my outfit. The neckline plunged too far for comfort, and the shirt hugged me tightly, revealing the curves I hadn't realized I'd developed in the last few years. I tried tugging on the blouse, but it remained right where it was as though painted on. "I look ridiculous," I said as I stepped out from behind the screen.

Blade's eyebrows rose and Gunner clapped his hands in response.

"Look at you, you're a woman!" Gunner dragged me over to my mirror and stood me in front of it. I could see what he meant. Though it wasn't my standard, I didn't feel hideous, and the jeans lengthened my legs.

"If I passed you on the street," Blade said, coming up behind me, "I wouldn't know you."

"I'll take that to mean this is what Captain wanted." I sighed and faced them. "Well, men, I suppose there's no time like the present."

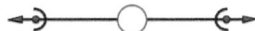

"NOW REMEMBER," Gunner said, smoothing my hair back into place as we stood outside the hull doors. "The lad will know where the vault is kept."

"Get the information." Blade kept his eyes above my head, his tone military. "Our future depends on this."

"But don't let him get handsy." Gunner shook his finger in my face. "You're the seductress. The power is in your hands. But please, don't kill him."

"Yes, please don't kill him," Blade repeated.

"I know! I know."

Captain stepped from the shadows and approached me from behind, appraising me in a way that left me feeling dirty. He'd lusted after me before, but a new, predatory darkness emanated from him as he moved closer. "Perfect." His soft purr brushed a few strands of my hair as he leaned in. "He won't be able to resist." I tried to step away, but he gripped my shoulders, his lips inches from my ear. "Be persuasive, pet, but remember…you belong to me."

Shoving aside his words, I squared my shoulders and twisted the door handle. "Wish me luck."

RYAN T. NUHFER

HARWELL

THE ENTRYWAY before me hummed at a deafening frequency that seemed to energize the people waiting in line. Everyone but me. At forty-five years old, this wasn't exactly my ideal night out in New Washington City. I'd rather be anywhere else. It wasn't the intense vibration of the nightclub walls that had me on edge, though that didn't help. No, what had me on edge were the two spooks hiding in line behind me, trying desperately to avoid my gaze. Instead, their eyes kept dropping to the briefcase in my hand. I felt my grip tighten on the handle.

The nightclub known as "The Shift" had garnered a reputation as the premiere spot for the nightlife crowd. Tonight, it would be packed full of people in their twenties, all of them keyed up on stims or high out of their minds. But this club had another reputation—one that the cops were happy to ignore. The Shift had become a haven for some of the most dangerous people this city had ever seen. Unsure of what I would run into, I found myself unconsciously reaching inside my jacket. The 12mm Kodiak tactical pistol rested comfortably in its holster.

I passed through the entrance with little difficulty—a reflection on my age more than anything else—and surveyed my surroundings. The interior appeared exactly as I expected—a multi-level gathering of neon stupidity. The dance floor in front of me seethed with a chaotic writhing of bodies. The holographic displays near the wall projected semi-transparent images of dancers in various states of undress, their bodies undulating to the brain-gnawing beat of the music.

I glanced toward the door behind me. Watched as the doorman had words with the two men who had shadowed me. Their thick wool jackets nearly concealed the impressions of the firearms they had strapped to their ribs. I might not have even noticed the weapons but both men sported military-style haircuts that gave them away. These guys were mercenaries, no doubt about it. The combat boots and BDU pants they wore were several years old, judging by the distress. No self-respecting soldier would be seen in public dressed so ratty, regardless of the military's recent budget cuts. So here we had a couple of mercs with poor stealth skills. That didn't mean that they weren't deadly. I'd have to keep my nerves sharp.

I looked toward the bar as I passed by, noticing the small group of young punks gathered on one end. They were all carrying. Small caliber mostly, judging from the sizes of the lumps in their jackets. Probably hired thugs, no loyalty to one another and no sense of honor. No code to live by.

As for myself, I had one rule—get the job done, no questions asked. But rules and codes were no longer popular, and honor amongst warriors had become a thing of the past. These guys would stab each other in the back if it meant they'd make a larger profit. To make matters worse, these young street vermin were getting cybernetically enhanced or having chemical calibrators implanted. All in an effort to amp up their reflex and reaction speeds, making them far more dangerous than they had any right to be.

I had kept my own mods to a minimum. Enhanced senses, mostly. I never cherished the idea of being "cybernetically altered" but I wasn't getting any younger. In order to stay on top you had to be willing to make sacrifices. The mods were mine. On a good day I might have grudgingly admitted that the ocular augmentation could be surprisingly useful, but today wasn't turning out to be a good day.

I spotted my destination up ahead—the executive lounge on the balcony—and made my way toward the escalator. On the trip up I found myself surrounded by a flock of dancers, the laser lights casting hard shapes across their faces as they gyrated their bodies to the music. Their unfocused eyes revealed they were on some sort of hallucinogen. I stifled a mirthless laugh as I watched them reach the top, calmly walk ten feet to the left, and resume their dance as they rode back down.

So far no one seemed to recognize me, which I expected. Very few people knew my face, but my name spoke volumes. I had a reputation, one which I had carefully nurtured over the years. I was an enforcer. A man who "fixed" those problems that were impossible to fix. On the streets my name was whispered in hushed tones, as if I were some monster that might come for them in the dark. For some people, that had been true.

As I stepped off of the escalator I came face to face with another mercenary. A Japanese man whose small frame had me more concerned than the last two mercs did. He held himself with the relaxed-yet-poised stance of a well-trained martial artist. If this meeting went south, at least I knew who I'd have to kill first.

He motioned for me to raise my arms and I did so, feeling the weight of the briefcase tugging on my rotator cuff. An old injury. Probably going to need to have it augmented eventually. He waved a device up and down my body, checking for a wire, or maybe explosives. He wouldn't care about the handgun. I certainly wasn't the only armed man in this place. Finally satisfied, he nodded for me to follow him. Rounding a corner, I found myself in a hallway leading to the executive area. Another thug guarded the door, but let us pass without any issue.

The walls of the spacious lounge dampened the noise from the dance floor surprisingly well. Once the ringing in my ears subsided I'd be able to hear myself think. The room exuded luxury, with plush cushioned couches, a full bar and expensive holographic displays that streamed stock information and the latest news on corporate takeovers. A place for the rich to unwind. There were half a dozen occupants—more than I had instructed.

"What did I say about coming alone?" I threw the words out to the group of them, baiting the leader out. I wasn't expecting whom I got in response.

A young woman, twenty years old at best, came toward me slowly. She looked shaky, but she held herself well. Her business casual attire set her apart in this crowd. Not the type of woman to associate with mercenaries and hired thugs. She had paid for their services, which meant that she expected trouble. I began to worry that things were taking a turn for the worse.

And then the woman spoke. Her voice wavered a bit; clearly her nerves were getting the better of her. "I apologize for bringing these people with me. I wasn't sure I could trust you to keep your end of the deal."

I activated my ocular implant and waited as the software ran a scan on her. A targeting reticle hovered over her retina and another over a vein in her neck. They moved with her as she turned her head, each one spitting out information on my virtual display. The readings came back unclear. Heart rate seemed normal—which it should not have been, given the situation—but her eyes were glossy and unfocused, which made it impossible to read her intentions. If she planned to back out of the deal, I couldn't tell. Something wasn't right with her. Best to keep my eyes open.

The two mercs that had followed me finally arrived and shot me dirty looks as they stalked by. They stopped somewhere in the back, keeping watch over our little meeting.

"Well," I began. "Now that the gang is all here, let's get this over with."

The woman reached into her pocket and pulled out a data module. The tiny black rectangle looked worn, but undamaged. The likelihood of corrupted data seemed minimal. I would have to proceed with the deal.

"I have the file," she said. "You brought the money?"

I set the briefcase down and took two steps back, allowing the Asian bodyguard to retrieve it. He popped the lock and checked the contents.

"It's good," he said to the girl. "Looks like the full ten million."

"I'll take the data module now." I held out my hand.

She put it back in her pocket and took a step back. "I'm sorry but I can't give it to you."

"Lady, you don't want to go down this road."

She wasn't listening. "Do you know what's on this module? It's proof of your clients' involvement in the murder of that child on the news. They say Mr. Parsons has an airtight alibi, but this proves otherwise."

"Blackmail—that's all this is. Proof can be forged. Don't take me for a fool, I'm not *that* old."

"It's a Replay. You can't forge a Replay." The words came out of her mouth and I hesitated.

You could find plenty of general Replay online. Never tried Cantonese food? There's a Replay for that. In fact there were hundreds of them, for anything you could ever want. "Try before you buy" had become the new motto of society. A Replay wasn't just someone's recorded memory of a place, but the very experience of it, as if you were there yourself. The sights, smells and sounds. You could taste the spices on your tongue; feel the noodles slip down your throat; hear the cooks arguing in the back room, followed by the slight pang of worry that they might be cooking up alley cats. All there for you to try, one quick download away.

But as with everything, darker uses had been developed for Replay technology. It started small, of course. Someone tried extreme sports— say, a skydiving Replay—and got hooked. Unlike a virtual reality experience, where it simply appeared that you were skydiving, with Replay, you *were* skydiving. The brain couldn't tell the difference so it released the appropriate chemicals: endorphins, adrenaline, all the good stuff. Having so many experiences right at your fingertips made it easy to get hooked on the high. But soon that wasn't enough. Soon the rush wasn't quite what it used to be and the user started looking for the next big score. So along came the black Replays. Things forbidden by society. Anything you could think of readily available. Want to experience what it feels like to rob a bank? No problem. How about murder? Or rape? All you needed were the right connections.

And this girl had gotten her hands on a Replay of Mr. Parsons committing murder.

"So, what's the plan then, miss? Keep the Replay as insurance and use the ten million to disappear? A man like Parsons won't stop looking for you until he finds you. Don't make this mistake. I promise, if you have any inclination of betraying me, this pleasant meetup is going to get *un*pleasant, real fast."

She looked at me with pleading eyes. "Please just walk away from this. I don't want any trouble."

"Doesn't look that way to me." I began to wonder if anyone here had heard of me. Usually my reputation preceded me, and that made things run smoothly.

And then I noticed it. A tiny bead of sweat running down the side of her face. A small twitch at her fingertips. It all came together—she had taken chems to keep her nerve, and they were wearing off fast.

Perhaps she did know about me, and maybe that's what scared her to the point of resorting to chems—the knowledge that the seemingly harmless man in front of her had a reputation for destroying everything in his path.

"I am leaving with the data. Please don't make these men hurt you." Her eyes showed genuine concern. An odd trait for a blackmailer.

I could see the way things were going down and decided I wouldn't wait for it to happen. "Despite the promises of death and destruction that I made you, I'd be inclined to let this go. To forget about it and move on." My eyes never broke from the woman's gaze.

Her posture visibly relaxed a little. "I appreciate your understanding. I…"

"However," I interrupted. "You don't get a reputation like mine without making good on your promises." The words slid out of my mouth with every bit of menace I could muster.

Almost immediately she went pale. The fear in her eyes took a nose-dive and connected hard with her guts. She looked like she might be sick, and I noted her shaking hands weren't moving toward her sidearm. Frozen in pure terror.

Good, she had heard of me.

With blinding speed I threw an elbow strike to my left and connected with the Asian man's throat. I felt his trachea collapse—watched his hands claw desperately at his neck as the airway closed off. He didn't have long. Twisting his body in front of me, I stuffed my hand inside his jacket and my finger found purchase on the trigger of his machine pistol. From somewhere in front of me gunfire rang out, and his body bucked and twitched as bullets hammered against his torso. The frightened woman had managed to collapse to her knees, and I unloaded the machine pistol into the three men behind her. My brain quickly registered the streams of red smoke that trailed behind the bullets—tracers—which meant.... A half second after the rounds entered their target, the three men blew apart in a bloody spray of tissue and flame. Explosive rounds. So much for subtlety.

Dropping the empty hand cannon, I drew my Kodiak and opened fire on one of the mercs that had tailed me earlier. The shredder rounds punched him back into the wall, and he hit the ground in a heap of mashed bone. I spun around, expecting his counterpart to be close by. I wasn't wrong.

The man dove at me, his arms outstretched and reaching for my neck. I felt the first two fingers and thumb of his right hand pinch down on my windpipe and my head jerked back involuntarily. My balance went off center and I stumbled back. I barely caught my footing in time to block an incoming jab. He came at me again, faster than a man his size should have been capable of. Nothing external indicated cybernetics, but I had seen my share of augments in the war. Something about the way they moved gave it away, and this man moved the same.

The big man drove forward, his barrage of attacks clearly intended to drive me off balance again. I wasn't about to let that happen. I dug my heels in, deflected his next punch to the side, and worked my way inside his effective striking range. As expected, he backpedaled, trying desperately to put some space between us. I advanced on him, my own attacks focused on his face. Finally I paused—just long enough for his cybernetics to recognize the opening. He took a step back and regrouped, then launched himself at me, his full weight thrown behind a single punch. I closed the gap and threw an elbow strike at his temple. His forward momentum met with mine, and a definitive cracking sound broke through the air around us—likely the last thing he heard. He collapsed at my feet a moment later.

I fished my Kodiak out from under him and surveyed the room—empty, save for the terrified woman on the floor. The rest had abandoned her to whatever fate I had intended. She should have paid them better.

I checked the restroom to make sure we were alone. There wasn't a lot of time before the police would arrive, but I knew better than to take shortcuts. Satisfied that we were alone, I walked over to the young woman.

Blood covered her face and clothes. Not her own blood, it belonged to the three men I had...detonated. She just sat there, on her knees, staring off into the distance.

"Time to get up." My voice felt rough, probably due to the ape who grabbed me by the throat. "We are going to talk and I'm not sitting in that mess."

Finally she looked up at me and spoke.

"Are you going to kill me?"

The last word came out high pitched and shaky, and I knew my response would determine the kind of person I'd be dealing with in a moment. A sobbing, snot-nosed wreck, or the same stunned but calm woman before me now. I decided I'd prefer the latter.

"I didn't come here to kill you. We had a deal, remember?"

She nodded and looked at the floor. I planted my feet in front of the woman and helped her to stand. It took her a few seconds, but she composed herself. She even straightened her clothing, though nothing would ever get her white blouse clean again. When she had finished she turned to face me.

"My name is…" she began, but I cut her off.

"Your name is Emily Parsons. Daughter and heiress to the Parsons Corporation. From the look of things, it seems you've rejected your father's wish that you take over the business."

"Did he send you?"

"He hired me. But he doesn't know about your involvement in this. He thinks it's just another blackmailer. Give me the Replay file and you can go back to your life."

I could see the muscles in her cheeks stiffen and her hands clench tight as she summoned up every ounce of courage she had.

"No. I can't do that. I won't."

"Emily…"

"I've seen the Replay. *Experienced* it. I can't go back to that life, now that I know what he's capable of. He needs to pay for what he's done."

For once in my tired career, I couldn't think of a single thing to say. Her eyes were determined. Resolved. Somehow, living amidst the decadent and corrupt world that she called her life, Emily Parsons had remained one of the few honest people left in New Washington.

Damn it.

I set the briefcase down in front of her and took a step back. I tried not to make a habit of breaking my own rules, but found it equally important to know when to bend them. Emily deserved a better life.

"The money you requested is all there. Enough to start over. But make sure you do so far from here."

Truth be told, once that Replay went live online, her father wouldn't be around long enough to seek revenge. But I knew it would be better for her to get out of this city. A fresh start.

At first she didn't know what to say, just stood there with tears in her eyes. Then she picked up the briefcase and gave me a little smile. A thought must have blossomed in her mind, because her eyes lit up and she spoke.

"What's your name?" The words sounded like they were being spoken by a child. Timid and cautious.

I hesitated, not wanting to spoil her good mood. "You know my name."

She paused a moment, the silence between us growing tense. Maybe she worried what would happen if she said it. Worried that once she had let the words escape her lips, there would be no going back. But to her credit, she said it anyway.

"Harwell."

I smiled at her—a genuine, friendly smile—then turned toward the exit and walked away.

Yeah, that's me. The great and terrible Harwell. Legendary General of the Second Great Corporate War. Scourge of the Last States of America. The boogieman of Harlem City. Defeated by a pair of weepy eyes. I must be getting sentimental in my old age.

Everyone has a code, even if they aren't aware of it. It's what drives us. It pushes us forward. It helps us stay alive. The code of the warrior—that's what I lived my life by. Rule one—get the job done, no questions asked.

Someday, maybe I'd get that one right.

KIRSTIN PULIOFF

BLINDING LIGHTS

FIGHT, FIGHT... The words lingered in my mind like the last notes of a song.

Isn't that what I had been doing? I took a deep breath and held it. Stretched like a balloon, every second threatened a deflating burst. I couldn't take it any longer. I needed to pop. At least then there would be a release from pressure. That's all I craved, a moment of relief, not being pulled in opposite directions, clouded by the perceptions and expectations of others.

It'd been so long since I felt a moment of peace. Five months to be exact. The last few months passed by in a haze of shock and disbelief as I waited to wake from the nightmare of my life. No matter how many times I pinched myself or pretended it wasn't happening, I never woke up.

Fight, fight... Similar to a song on repeat, the words came at me in an endless loop. Accusing and supporting me at the same time.

How much more could I do? I tried to ignore it, to pretend it didn't happen. Some pains disappear with time, but not this one. Time aggravated the issue.

So today, when the door slammed behind me, my feet moved on their own, destination predetermined. I wouldn't have come here otherwise, would I? I let the thought wander. Focusing on it, focusing on anything pulled me down.

Traffic buzzed beneath me. The cars' blinding lights drew me in. Devoid of definition, their details could never quite be appreciated. When did my life become like one of them?

That was my struggle. I was the shadow in a picture, hidden behind something brighter or flashier. It never used to bother me. Blending had its usefulness. I slid easily and comfortably under the scrutiny of authority, skipping school when I wanted, taking small trinkets from the edges of stores. No one saw or remembered me.

But then again, that same blending brought me here. For months, no one heard my screams or protests from upstairs. No one questioned my tear-streaked face or listened when I tried to explain. No one kept me safe.

Fight, fight... It was like the tree falling in the forest riddle. If no one heard my protests, were they real? I knew the answer to that. They were.

I finally understood; blending didn't work. I couldn't hide in the shadows, but had to make a choice. Fade with the sunlight or become one with the night? I didn't want either. I wanted the simple life I remembered as a child. That seemed out of my grasp though.

Only one thing seemed within reach now—the cold steel bar. Rain and tears fell, loosening my grip. Repositioning my hands, I straddled and then climbed over the steel railing until I was on the other side of the barrier.

I leaned back for a moment, letting the water soak into my brother's oversized sweater. Brushing my matted hair back from my eyes, I couldn't help but stare. The lights from below flashed in a distracting blur. All those lights and people rushed about, oblivious to everything around them, and oblivious to me standing on this ledge. They wouldn't be for much longer. I was done blending into the shadows.

My threshold for pain had been reached and the agony demanded to be seen. I wouldn't be invisible much longer. Only a few steps, a couple of feet, and it would all change.

Fight, fight... Why should I fight, when no one would fight for me? It was time to give up. Every battle had to have one loser.

The bottom fell out of my stomach. Emotions swirled, free falling inside, unable to grab onto anything. I felt cheated. My life squandered, and I was only 15. I should've been hanging out with friends, or my family, not over this ledge.

But that's where I was.

My family made it clear by slamming the door on me today that I wasn't to come back. My mom turned away first, calling me a liar as she ran off with spiteful tears. I didn't see my dad's face, just his back as he slowly walked away. The rejection was softer that way. My older brother slammed the door in my face, leaving me standing on the stoop, his oversized sweater in my trembling hands. They had closed the door, but not before making sure I knew not to return.

I hadn't seen them react this way since my sister moved out.

Fight, fight... My sister warned me before she ran away, but her words never quite made sense. Not to an innocent ten-year-old. Now, I understood. I saw the warnings and heard the threats, and recognized what had happened to her. Surely I wasn't the only one who had put it all together. Was the truth that hard to accept?

I let go of the railing and stood at the edge, wavering with the slight breeze. It was too late to ask those questions. I knew my parents weren't that oblivious or naive. Overburdened and uninvolved, maybe, but not naive. They knew better than most how bad the world was. Working at the hospital and courts had shown them that. They just didn't want to admit it could happen to them. Tucked away in suburbia, this was never supposed to happen.

I shouldn't have been surprised when they discovered it. Secrets had a way of being ferreted out, even when hidden under piles of trash. It's how they knew mine. The pink packaging announced what it was immediately. I hadn't meant for them to find out that way. I also didn't expect to see the two lines that sealed my fate.

Fight, fight... The words seemed hollow as they resounded in my mind. The fight was over.

I brushed the hair out of my eyes. The lights blurred beneath me. My eyes stung as tears clung to their edges. As they overflowed, I closed my eyes. I didn't want to see the tears fall or witness my fate.

I still tried to believe that if I didn't see it, it didn't happen. But that's not how it works. I had tried that for five months. Pretending didn't work. I couldn't pretend that my clothes shrunk or that I had several flu bugs in a row. I couldn't pretend my way out of swimming class, and I couldn't pretend that my mom's dear friend, Uncle Jack, loved me the same as all the other kids.

I wiped the tears with the back of my hand and stood. If I ignored the occasional horn or exhaust burst, it almost sounded like the ocean. The hypnotic ebb and flow of the cars called to me as an answer to the screaming torture of my mind. It promised to silence the torment, the ridicule, the disbelief.

Fight, fight… I think my sister and I had different ideas of fighting.

My sister escaped, and now it was my turn. I bent my knees and gripped the cool steel safety rails behind me. My heart hammered in my chest, beating me up. I tiptoed closer, my bare toes hanging over the edge. Rain cascaded down my feet like a waterfall.

Fight, fight... I had fought, and lost.

Fight, fight... The words came unbidden, not in my sister's pleading voice, not in my weary tears. This new voice was smaller, purer, stronger.

Fight, fight… I clutched my stomach as the words flooded me again. A new sensation gripped me. My stomach turned like before, but not with the grip of hunger or fear. I looked down, not at the steady rush of lights, or the rain dropping to my hands, but at the swell of my stomach.

Fight, fight... My baby kicked.

The baby somersaulted in my stomach, pressing out with deliberate pressure, forcing me to pay attention.

Fight, fight... Was my baby fighting back?

I tightened one hand's grip around the safety rail and fell to my knees, cradling my stomach. Tears rolled down my cheeks, but I didn't see them fall. I only had eyes for my baby and its little foot pressed against my ribs. That little person fought against me for a chance to live.

If I was going to lose a fight, this was the one. I was a loser, but not my child. My child was a winner, a fighter, the smallest warrior I'd ever know.

I exhaled and leaned back, glancing at the blurry stars. Here was another grouping of blinding lights, but these would stay still. These wouldn't rush off without being noticed. These lights were stable. These would be the lights my child would see.

S.R. KARFELT

LITTLE GIRL LOST

ALBUQUERQUE CHILD
AND YOUTH PROTECTIVE
SERVICES,
NEW MEXICO 1980

SKREET—SKREET—SKREET.
THE rickety chair produced a delicious squeak from Carole's jiggling leg.

"Act normal," the voices said.

Carole hated when they said that.
What did they want her to do? Twin-
ing long feet around loose chair rungs,
she stopped jiggling, and it seemed to
satisfy them. At least they shut up.

"What's your story?" Across the
desk her social worker tugged papers
out of a file, oblivious to the voices
in her head. He scratched his greasy
comb-over with their sharp edge, and

fished reading glasses from the pocket of his rumpled shirt. As he read, the papers hovered dangerously close to the cigarette he'd left burning in its ashtray.

"Your name is just Carole? No last name? No birth date? Is this all the paperwork?" He said the last in a shout, raising the reading glasses off his nose and looking out the door of his office.

From around the corner a woman's bored voice answered, "Just go with Doe or Smith, that's what everyone does, Mr. Kraus."

Dropping the reading glasses onto his desk, Mr. Kraus looked at Carole for the first time. She shifted back in her creaky seat, looking for an escape.

"*Not yet,*" the voices whispered in her head. The desk blocked her from reaching the doorway, but she could go over it and Mr. Kraus in three seconds. From the door to the elevator in the outer hall would take another four. Waiting for the elevator was an unknown, but Carole knew she could get as far as the stairs in another ten. Mr. Kraus didn't look like he could catch her in seventeen seconds. She relaxed a little.

"I don't have time for uncooperative, kid. You've got to be at least…" He shuffled through the paperwork and hollered, "Miss Bentley! How old would you say she is?"

The clacking of typewriter keys stopped and the sound of heels on linoleum took its place. The secretary stopped in the doorway to the office and shrewd green eyes took a good look at Carole. "Ten," she said.

"Ten!" Mr. Kraus tapped a fat finger against the file. "But she isn't even in school yet!"

"Ten," Miss Bentley said with conviction. "You know the Orphanage keeps them as long as they can get away with it." They both shot accusing looks in Carole's direction, as though she played a part in keeping children out of foster care.

"*Not yet,*" the voices warned.

"Are you ten?" Mr. Kraus barked.

Carole knew she could get past both of the adults and still make the stairs in seventeen seconds but the secretary stood in the middle of the doorway, so she added two seconds just to be safe.

Mr. Kraus picked up his cigarette but didn't put it to his lips. "Do you think she's retarded?"

Miss Bentley had sharp eyes. Carole stared into them.

"I'd say not, Mr. Kraus."

"She doesn't talk."

"According to her file, she can."

Miss Bentley blinked, shook her head, and walked away. The sound of her clacking typewriter began again. Carole smiled faintly. Seventeen seconds for certain, and once she hit the stairs they'd never catch her.

"Soon," the voices promised.

Mr. Kraus saw the smile and frowned.

"Just being uncooperative, eh kid? Two can play that game. How old did you say you were?" He took a puff on the cigarette and wrote something in the chart. "You are now six years old, and that puts you in first grade. You're not going to waste my time. Now let's work on your last name. You were plenty old enough to know your last name when the orphanage took you. Tell me what it is, or it's going to be Blank. That's what your paperwork says anyway, just one blank line after your name."

Carole remained still, trying to look normal. He could call her what he wanted. She didn't belong here, and she wasn't going to school either—not any grade. She was going to escape and go find where she did belong.

With his cigarette dangling, Mr. Kraus shoved his glasses back on his round head and grabbed a piece of paper, mumbling. "Carole Blank has no father…figures." He dropped the cigarette back into the ashtray, and smoke crawled out his nostrils like the incinerator in the church basement. He read out loud, "Car wreck in April of '74, vehicle totaled, two unidentified women burned beyond recognition, child miraculously survived."

Mr. Kraus paused, staring through tiny mean eyes as the voices deep inside Carole's head told her what she'd been waiting for.

"Run."

MISS BENTLEY didn't even look up from her typing as Carole darted out of the office. Skidding around a corner, her smooth-bottomed new shoes slid across the polished floor. Racing past offices where nobody bothered to look up, Carole zeroed in on a large painted number three. It stood above a door next to the elevators.

Six seconds into her dash for freedom Mr. Kraus's voice sounded behind her, "Someone grab that brat!"

The sounds of pursuit stirred faintly in her wake at the same time the elevator doors slid open. Carole skidded into the main hallway where two men in business suits waited to get inside. They both looked at her and Carole turned right, dashing toward the stairs with Mr. Kraus's voice ringing far behind her. She shoved open the door to the stairwell and the voices encouraged, *"No one can see. Go. Faster."*

Carole grabbed onto the railing and vaulted over it, skipping two flights of stairs. She landed firmly below only to repeat the maneuver a second time, long blonde braids sailing up past her ears like antennas as she dropped, landing so hard her knee socks slipped toward her ankles. Carole shoved through the door into the main lobby.

A man with his hat in his hand stood reading the directory. He didn't even glance in her direction.

"Ground level, exit right to get outside."

The voices were right, they were always right. She could no longer hear Mr. Kraus's pursuit, but she sensed it above her. Sprinting toward the front door, Carole could picture Miss Bentley with the telephone propped against her shoulder, dialing with the back end of her ballpoint pen, and Mr. Kraus heading for the elevator with his hat in one hand, cigarette dangling between his lips. She felt it all like shadows bouncing around inside her brain, somewhere right behind her left eyeball. Then she sensed movement behind her.

As she glanced back at the man by the directory, Carole's braids slapped against her face. He moved toward her and motioned with a nod. Carole spun to face forward at the same time her hands met the glass door, the door that stood between her and freedom. *"Always look ahead, not behind,"* the voices reprimanded, but it was too late.

A police officer stood looking at her through the glass. He opened the door, pushing her in the wrong direction, and her shoes squeaked in protest.

"Where you going in such a hurry, Little Missy?" His eyes were on directory man, but he didn't touch her. Freedom beckoned just behind him and Carole considered his Adam's apple. If she hit it with her fist, he'd veer to her left and she could escape—

"*Never!*" The voices reproached, interrupting her plan. "*Never harm one of them without permission!*"

Carole's eyes darted to the street, where freedom taunted from just a step away. It wouldn't hurt him very much if she just—

A hand gripped her shoulder, long fingers digging through her good blouse to hook onto her collarbone. Carole's gaze dropped to her new black and white shoes, avoiding the eyes of her captors. She knew it was too late to run now. A little girl couldn't escape two grown men without people wondering how. They'd know she was different. Directory Man kept his hand on her shoulder, but moved to her side, tugging on the straps of her plaid jumper with his free hand.

"You're one of the kids from Rio Rancho Sisters of Mercy aren't you? Where do you think you're running off to?"

The elevator door pinged and slid open. Without turning to look, Carole sensed Mr. Kraus jam his hat onto his head and step out.

MR. KRAUS dragged her back upstairs with the policeman and the directory man guarding her. Dropping her into a chair in the hallway, and proclaiming that she was trouble, he added, "We have someone who deals with juvenile delinquents, Miss Blank. I have better things to do."

Mr. Kraus went back into his office with the directory man, talking about the trouble with kids these days and how half of them didn't even have a father. The policeman stood across from Carole and stared at her. He looked at her skinny legs with the knee socks puddled around her ankles, and she smoothed her twisted orphanage dress. He didn't look afraid of her and Carole closed her eyes, trying not to think about how she could get to the stairs in eleven seconds if she kicked him in the throat. The voices wouldn't let her hurt him, and she didn't want to anyway, but tears scalded her eyelids and she squeezed tight to keep them inside. When would she get another chance to escape?

Maybe she was a juvenile delinquent, but Mr. Kraus was wrong about her. She had a father. She remembered him. Maybe she would have found him today if the policeman hadn't been walking through the same door she tried to escape through. "*Always look ahead, not behind,*" the voices kept shouting inside her head.

They didn't have to lecture, but they did. Tears squeezed under her lashes and ran down her cheeks. If she couldn't find her father, where would she go? She needed someplace where she could fit in or hide. Mr. Kraus would never let her go back to the Orphanage, not that she ever fit in there. They tolerated her because her father made them. If she could only find him, maybe he could make someone else help her hide until she was big enough to be on her own. A few more years were all she needed. The voices said years went by fast.

Squeezing her eyes closed so tight she heard a rushing sound in her ears, Carole tried to force the tears back inside.

"HEY! HEY! Girl! What do you think you're doing?"

The policeman sounded mad and Carole's eyes popped open, but he wasn't talking to her. A polyester-clad bottom backed uncomfortably close to her face, the bulge of a wallet in the rear pocket inches from her nose. Carole leaned away before it could touch her, and glanced down the hallway. Nobody was in it. Eleven seconds if she rolled backward out of the chair. She could surely make it to the back stairs in eleven seconds.

A brown finger pointed at her from around the bottom. "I need to get past you. That girl is my next case. I'm Marsha, I'm a social worker."

Carole peeped around the wide, flat bottom and looked toward the honey-thick voice. Marsha was tall like the policeman, but skinny, with a fuzzy halo of hair. She wore a pink dress with red cherries embroidered on the collar and her legs looked strong and fast.

"*You're* the social worker?" The policeman said it like he didn't believe her.

"Yes, sir, I am." Marsha sounded angry, but she didn't look him in the eye. Her eyes looked down at her red shoes.

The cop snorted and it sounded rude. Carole wondered if he didn't believe in women working. Some of the priests at the orphanage said women belonged at home.

Miss Bentley came clacking down the hallway in her high heels, and the officer pushed his hat back and said, "Ma'am" very politely. He didn't seem to mind Miss Bentley working. She looked at him through very big false eyelashes while handing Marsha a folder. Miss Bentley didn't even reply when Marsha said, "Thank you, Ma'am."

"This girl says she's a social worker."

"Well, I suppose she is," Miss Bentley said. "She chases and places our runaways. Can I get you a cup of coffee?"

The policeman took off his hat and followed Miss Bentley. He seemed to have forgotten about guarding Carole, his eyes on Miss Bentley's backside as though she were backing it dangerously close to his face.

Marsha watched them go with narrowed eyes. Carole was certain she could make it to the stairs in ten seconds and she shifted forward in her seat, but Marsha stepped right in front of her, placing a hand on either side of the chair. She bit her too-short nails. Carole could smell her perfume. It smelled like new clothes and Christmas toys.

"Huh-uh, Little Miss. Even if you make it out and we don't find you, there are worse places to be than foster care. Little girls belong with families, not out running around Albuquerque." Marsha had big chocolate eyes and frosty pink lipstick on. "Now I want your promise that you will give me a chance to find you a good home. Can you do that for me, Little Miss?" Marsha waited, and her eyes were the kind that knew if someone lied. Sister Mary Josephine from the orphanage had the exact same kind of knowing eyes, except hers were green.

Carole swallowed and waited. She couldn't make a promise she wouldn't keep, but the voices didn't like Marsha getting so close. *"She sees you. Cooperate."*

Carole nodded. She'd give Marsha one chance; that wouldn't take long.

Marsha stood and flipped open her file. "Six years old? A big girl like you? Now why did you say you were six years old?"

"I didn't!" Carole objected. "Sister Mary Josephine says I'm probably ten."

Marsha motioned for Carole to follow and looked through her file as they walked down the empty corridor.

"Well, Carole, unfortunately your file says you're six and there isn't a thing either you or I can do about that right now. At least you'll get really good marks in first grade."

KELSEY KEATING

ALBATROSS

PART 3

TO SAY he wasn't what I expected is a gross understatement. A fourteen, perhaps sixteen-year-old boy, nervous and easily swayed is what I envisioned. Even a chubby, over-confident boy of eighteen would have made sense.

But no.

The young man who turned to face me was no lad, not a boy. He didn't have the look of a spoiled governor's son, treated to all the luxuries the skyline offered those with money. He stood only a few inches taller than me, and obviously a few years older. While his structure differed from the men I sailed with—his jaw smooth, round, nose unbroken with a slight upturn, and his body not overly muscular like that of Blade or Wrench. In no way was he unpleasant to look at. He reminded me of the artists my father knew when I was a child, lithe and graceful in his movements as he turned toward me.

And his eyes, his clear, sea-green gaze, held storms I couldn't fathom, pain I didn't know, and secrets that could never be mentioned. How was this the son of the most powerful man in Veil?

I registered these things quickly, and while they surprised me, I wasn't named Warrior for nothing. Packing my initial reaction away, I watched him silently, allowing the awkwardness of my presence to seep in. Within seconds he broke it.

"Hello."

I bit back a smile. The ease with which I'd crack him almost disappointed me.

"Hello," I parroted. "It seems you're on my ship."

"Your ship?" He quirked an eyebrow. "Funny, I thought the man they called Captain held charge here. Does that make you his wife?"

I held back a shiver of disgust. "No. I'm quartermaster. That means the only one on board capable of vetoing a captain's decision—" He cut me off before I could finish.

"Unless made during war or a mission. I know what a quartermaster is."

"A smart young man. That's helpful."

"I'm Braydon." He held out his hand, and to my surprise, I gave him mine. As was custom for a gentleman, he kissed it. An archaic greeting the Stratos Federation had recently brought back for *posterity's sake*. I pulled back, the heat of his lips still lingering against my skin.

"I'm Warrior."

"Warrior? That's an unusual name."

"Not really. Aboard The Albatross you're given a name upon proving your worth."

"Then I must be in the presence of a fearsome woman."

I opened my mouth to reply, but he wasn't done talking. "Look, you want the vault, yeah? That's fine. I'll tell you where it is. I can even tell you the security you'll have to get through to get to it."

Stunned, I narrowed my gaze. Nothing was this easy.

"Why would you be so willing to give this information?"

"That's why you brought me here, right? Because you didn't find the vault on our estate?" He moved closer to me. "I can tell you where it is."

Disgusted, I sneered and stepped back. "I should have known. Only a coward would tell us what we want to avoid suffering."

Braydon let out a harsh laugh. "If they'd wanted me to suffer, they wouldn't have sent you dressed like this." He gestured to my outfit as his gaze narrowed. "Besides, you know nothing of my secrets or suffering."

I readied a retort, but once again the storm in his gaze caught me off guard. What secrets could this heir to a city have? "How am I to know you aren't lying? That you won't just lead us into a trap?"

"Because I won't do this for free. You'll have to do something for me."

Ah, a catch. "And that is?"

"Something for me to discuss with the captain." He sat hard on a barrel, gaze fixed on the door behind me.

Every muscle tensed. I'd been dismissed. "One moment, your grace," I mocked, dipping into a bow before sweeping out of the room.

CAPTAIN EMERGED from the hull twenty minutes later, his mustache twisted up at the ends like he'd been curling it on his fingers. He always did that when upset.

"My darling, well done." He cupped my chin and leaned in for a whiskery kiss that I didn't return. "You got him right where I wanted him. I wonder, just how persuasive was my little Warrior?"

Something in his tone sparked caution in my heart. Though he appeared pleased, I could hear the tremor in his voice. "He gave you the information?"

"Most of it."

"Most of it?"

"He'll give us the rest when he gets what he wants."

I let a moment pass while I waited for Captain to explain further. He stared at me with a ferocity that weakened my bravado.

"Which is?"

Captain's dark eyes glimmered and he gripped my arm so tight I had to bite back a cry. "You, Warrior. He wants you."

"**HOW COULD** you?" I slammed the hull door behind me, my hand on the hilt of my blade as I started toward him. "I'm not some piece of meat to be demanded in exchange for information," I hissed through clenched teeth. "You want to make a trade? I'll make you talk."

Braydon held his hands up in defense. "Wait, just wait. I lied. I don't want you. You're not what I want."

I faltered mid-step. "You don't?"

"No. Not like that. I only said it because I needed leverage against your captain. I needed someone on my side."

His words bounced around in my head. It made sense. It was something I would do if I found myself in a negotiation with someone like Captain. Yet despite this, the sting of rejection burned my cheeks. Even dressed the way I was, this man didn't want any part of me. No decent man ever did—ever would. A woman like me could only attract the attention of men like Captain. Cold acceptance washed over me, deadening my fight, and I turned to leave.

"Please, don't go."

I paused with my hand reaching out for the handle. I should have kept going, but I didn't.

"Please."

"Why me? Why not Blade or Gunner or anyone else?" I spun around, piercing him with my fiercest glare. Braydon shifted his weight back away from me, but he didn't back down.

"I'm not stupid. I knew I couldn't trust your captain. There's no way he wouldn't kill me if I gave him what he wanted. I made an educated guess when you walked in dressed like that and gambled he wouldn't willingly part with you. Don't misunderstand me." Braydon raised defensive hands as I angrily opened my mouth. "I learned political strategy at my father's knee. I wanted him to decline, to say no. I needed time for you to hear me out. Please."

"All right, what exactly is it you want?"

"To be free. I need you to guarantee my life won't be forfeit. When I give this information, I need your word that I won't be disposed of."

"And what exactly are we supposed to do with you after you talk?"

"Keep me. Let me go. I don't care; I just need to know I'll live."

"So you can rush back to your father and tell him exactly who we are?"

Braydon's brow furrowed and he looked away. "I'm never going back there."

Curiosity pawed at his response, but I pushed it away. "Give me time to think it over." As I turned to leave, he spoke again.

"Just so you know, Warrior, you'd be beautiful even in men's clothing." I glanced over my shoulder, brow furrowed, and he smiled. "I'd hate for you to think I didn't notice."

BRAYDON WAS with us for two weeks, preparing the blueprints at Captain's request. To keep everyone happy, I stayed with Braydon under the watchful eye of our crew. Everyone knew what Braydon had requested, yet only I knew his reason. To my surprise, his kindness drew me to him a bit more each day. Every touch, every graze of his hand against mine gave me goose bumps. Never had anyone treated me so tenderly, like I was a lady, a woman worth listening to. With him, I positively glowed.

And others noticed.

"I think you should start practicing sparring with City Brat," Captain said toward the end of Braydon's second week aboard.

"You want him to learn?"

"I want to see what you can do with his face. It could use rearranging. Or do you disagree?"

The expected response spilled from my lips without thought. "You know I prefer a rugged man. Perhaps he is too pretty. If you'd like, I'll scar him."

Captain twisted his ridiculous mustache. "No, no. Not if that's how you feel."

I bit my tongue and savored the lie. "City Brat," I called down to him. "Choose your weapon wisely."

WHILE HE wasn't the worst beginner with a sword, Braydon's sparring left nothing to the imagination.

"Quit lunging like a rhinoceros!" I laughed, spinning away from him as he rushed me. I slapped his backside with the broad side of my blade and he yelped.

"I think," he said, rubbing the spot I'd smacked, "you're showing off with all of your fancy twirling."

"I'll tell you what," I said, switching my blade to my left hand and holding my right arm behind my back. "I'll try to go easier on you."

Braydon's eyes sparkled and he parried my advance. A smirk twisted my lips and I let him have a few moments of sparring before sending his blade soaring across the deck.

"You know," he said, panting from his effort. "If it were hand-to-hand combat things might end differently."

Without a word I tossed my blade aside and ran at him, catching him around the middle and sending us both rolling across our sparring space. Laughter bubbled from my lips as he pinned me beneath him, his face inches from mine.

"Told you." His hand cupped my face and he moved closer. Quick as a whip, I used his shifted weight against him and knocked him sideways. I climbed atop him, pinning his arms above his head.

"Never let your guard down," I said, lightly brushing my lips against his. "You never know when it'll cost you."

As he grinned, I pushed myself up into a sitting position. Braydon grabbed my hand and held it against his chest, just above his heart. The thrumming against my palm buzzed through my entire being. Glancing up, I saw Captain watching me from the upper deck, and my gaiety shriveled.

"Blueprints. Now!" His shout left his lips as I scurried up off Braydon, ignoring his confused calls for me to slow down as I raced to my place at Captain's side.

E.P. BROWN

FANCY PANTS squinted. "Do you prefer 'Mr. Prince' or 'Milo?'"

"Call me Pappy," Pappy grunted.

Fancy Pants turned to Gus, the fruit of Pappy's loins, standing awkwardly against the wall, still wearing his scrubs from work. Sour as he felt most of the time, Pappy's heart still managed to swell a bit every time he was reminded that his very own son was going to be a doctor. *Not that I had much to do with it*, Pappy thought. Wendy had vamoosed with the boy well shy of his first birthday, and even part-time fatherhood had been a little more than Pappy could handle. Gus smiled crookedly, wearing that look of sheepish embarrassment he always had when forced to serve as Pappy's interpreter. Gus thought Pappy didn't notice it, but he did.

"That was his boxing name back in the day. 'Pappy Prince.' Mom said he always looked like an old man, even when he wasn't. He still insists on people calling him that." Gus quietly cleared his throat, then again with the goofy smile. Pappy sighed. Gus was light-skinned, like Wendy, could almost pass for white if you only looked quick. *Opens more doors for him than the boy would be willing to admit*, Pappy thought. People had always looked to Wendy as the interpreter too, took her more seriously, even before the punches in the head had made Pappy into a freak. Pappy looked absently down at his hands, dark and weathered, lying limp on his knees. He squirmed a bit in his chair. He felt like a specimen. *S'pose I am*, Pappy thought.

Fancy Pants turned back to Pappy with a thin smile. Pappy's face instantly reflected the same smile back, so similar it was eerie. "Okay, Pappy," Fancy Pants said. "Stand up please. All right. Now just relax and do what feels natural."

Pappy did as he was told, just let his body run on autopilot. As Fancy Pants made movements with his hands and his face, Pappy's body became a mirror, mimicking the other's motions and expressions at exactly the same moment. Fancy Pants's smile widened, a genuine look of glee. His movements became more exaggerated, his lab coat fanning out as his arms were flung up. A cell phone flopped from Fancy Pants's pocket as he jumped into the air. Pappy jumped with him, his head averting to the ground in sync with Fancy Pants's own tracking of his escaped phone. Gus grinned like an excited child at the hyperbolic display.

Fancy Pants grew still, an ecstatic smile still alight on his face. He paused to catch his breath, then: "August tells me that you're able to move counter to others' movements as well. Can you do that for me?"

Pappy nodded, and away they went. Fancy Pants reached out with his right hand, and Pappy's shoulders twisted to the left. As his right arm retracted, Fancy Pants thrust out his left quickly. Pappy didn't miss a beat, his body twisting to the right, avoiding Fancy Pants's outstretched arm. As Fancy Pants again made more and more elaborate movements,

Pappy moved with him. Where before the two had been mirror images of each other, they now moved as if tethered by some invisible force; Fancy Pants flinging his arm back, while Pappy's flew forward, Fancy Pants leaning in for a bow, Pappy doing the Limbo. This maniacal synchronized dance proceeded for another few minutes then Fancy Pants again grew still, and Pappy along with him, both breathing heavily.

"Okay," Fancy Pants said. "I think we're done for now." He clapped Pappy on the shoulder. "August says you couldn't always do this. He says you started the mimicry after you suffered a concussion."

"Got punched," Pappy said, his voice flat. He stared at a spot on the wall over Fancy Pants's shoulder, trying to get his bearings, reset his body, get it back under his own control.

"Yes. From a punch. But, this is correct? You were only able to synch to others' movements *after* the head injury?"

Pappy looked back to Fancy Pants, who was still winded, his fleshy pink cheeks burning red. "Yup," said Pappy. After it was clear that Fancy Pants expected a more elaborate response, Pappy continued. "Mmm-hmm. After my fight with Ding-A-Ling-Man Dokes, I was laid out for a cuppa days, lookin' like I been shot at 'n' hit. That's why my nose look like it is. Bent. Wendy kep' a'tryin' to get me in the hospital, but I wasn't goin' for it. Anyways, after the loop-de-loop feelin' went away, I started havin' to concentrate real hard on keepin' myself together. Else-wise, I find myself doin' what whoever was around me was doin'. Made Wendy madder'n a wet hen. Thought I was pokin' fun at her. She put up wit' it for another cuppa months, then she hightailed it, and took this'un with her." He gestured to Gus, who again assumed his sheepish smile.

"Well, Dad," Gus said through his grin, "that was only one of many reasons Mom did what she did." He turned quickly to Fancy Pants, avoiding Pappy's frown. *Every tub's gotta sit on its own bottom*, Pappy thought sourly. *Don't you think I know all I done wrong? To her? To you?*

Fancy Pants looked from Gus back to Pappy. "I've never seen echopraxia quite like this," he said, eying Pappy like a prize sow, "and never from a head injury." He looked to Gus again. "And the records you sent me, that's everything? He was never diagnosed with schizophrenia?" Gus shook his head. "No developmental disorders? Nothing in the family history that you're aware of?" Again, Gus shook his head. Fancy Pants looked Pappy straight in the eye. "The way you move around, it's just…uncanny." He smiled. "You're something else, Pappy."

Pappy cocked a bushy white eyebrow in suspicion. "So, let's get down to it. Is there gonna be money in all this or was you expectin' to poke an' prod me for free? I'm on a fixed income. My time got to have value."

Fancy Pants laughed. "We'll see what we can do, Pappy. So, let's see, was your injury the end of your boxing career?"

"Actually, after the injury, Dad's abilities in the ring were…" Gus looked at Pappy. "They were amazing. I was really young, but I can remember, even then, just being so blown away by how he moved. No one could lay a hand on him." His eyes averted to a spot on the floor. "It wasn't the injury or Dad's new abilities that ended the boxing." He looked back to Pappy, wearing a woozy grimace. Fancy Pants turned to Pappy, as well.

Pappy's face took on a strange expression. Regret? Nostalgia? Pride? He shrugged. "Killed a man," he said, his voice noncommittal. "Didn't mean to. Kill him, I mean. But I beat him dead just the same."

Fancy Pants raised an eyebrow. "In the ring?"

"Yep. Did my time too. Manslaughter." *He had it coming*, Pappy thought. The cops never knew what Pappy had seen the day before: ol' "Give 'Em Heck" Beck's hand in that donation jar. Good thing too, else they'd have maybe said it was murder. *The beatin' was premeditated*, Pappy thought. *The killin' weren't. Didn't know the power I had back then.*

"Fascinating," Fancy Pants said, his face stoic. He stood there, looking at Pappy for a long moment, then turned to Gus and started blabbering about some nonsense or other: "case study" and "mirror neurons," "zero latency" and "fMRI." Egghead gobbledygook. Pappy stopped listening. He was grateful when people turned their backs to him. He didn't have to fight the urge as hard to do his monkey-see, monkey-do routine. He exhaled a long, whistling breath, then reached into his back pocket and pulled out a small, dog-eared memo pad. He flipped through the pages—names and addresses and known associates, almost all crossed out with a single bold line—until he came to his most recent entry, a single word, not yet crossed out.

JABBER.

Pappy scowled. His eyes fogged in remembrance of the little girl from 4B, two floors up from his shabby efficiency. He'd seen her crying on the stairs just the other day, going on about her mom and the big Eskimo fella she'd fell in with awhile back. A fighter of some sort—Pappy had understood that much—but he had no idea what this MMA was. Fellas today needed everything to be fancy. Fancy beer and fancy fightin'. Beat their women same as they ever did though, which is exactly what this Jabber been up to. Pappy gripped his notepad tight as he remembered the girl's voice breaking as she told Pappy about ol' Jabber twisting her mother's arm behind her back. "And momma *cried*!" she said, and then she did too, leaning into Pappy's sinewy arm, gripping the back of his tank top. Made him sick.

Pappy sat up straight, folding his notepad shut. His eyes became determined, and he said aloud just what he'd told the little girl from 4B. "Welp," he grunted. "Sumbitch gotta pay."

Fancy Pants and Gus turned to him. "What was that, Mr. Prince?" Fancy Pants asked.

"You fellas can carry on without me. Tell Gus what ya need me t'do. I gots t'meet a man." He stood, tucking the memo pad back into his pocket. He looked at Fancy Pants.

"And I told ya, it's *Pappy*."

JABBER JOE the Eskimo. That's what the guy down at Fitz's had said. Something like that, at least. "Works out at Elron's old place," he'd told Pappy, "but you don't want to go messin' with that guy. He's a behemoth." "Taller'n a tree an' heavy as a piano," Pappy had heard from a couple folk. Half black, half Inuit. All asshole, Pappy was convinced. Plenty of people feared this man, and no one seemed to like him. Pappy looked up at the sign above the big window in front: "Wolfpack's War

Zone—Mixed Martial Arts & Boxing Academy." Pappy sighed. *Even the gym names got to be fancy nowadays.*

Pappy cracked his knuckles, then reached into his front pockets. Once he'd located ol' Jabber, he'd gone back home to get a little insurance: two rolls of quarters. He pulled a roll from each pocket and gripped them tight as he approached the walkway to the gym. Kid he'd talked to out front had told him Jabber and his buddies would be coming out any minute now.

And here they are, Pappy thought. The glass doors of the gym opened, and two big fellas in tight tank tops and loose-fitting, swishing black pants exited, followed by a giant of a man with a wide, pock-marked face and shiny black hair pulled back tight into a short ponytail. His head sat atop massive shoulders that nearly stretched from end to end of the doorway as he and the other two walked out. A tee shirt with a snarling wolf stretched to its limits across his chest, looking like somebody had dressed a refrigerator. Jabber Joe and his companions barely registered Pappy's presence as they passed.

"Yo, Jabber," Pappy said.

One of Jabber's companions turned, with a chagrined look on his face. "It's Jabba, old man, like on *Star Wars.*"

"I'm not botherin' with you, champ," Pappy grumbled. "Jabber, you seein' a nice lady over'n Ferdinand Estates, right there off Burger Alley? Nice lady with a sweet little girl?"

Finally, Jabba Joe turned. He eyed Pappy with a dull amusement. "Lawanda? She's one o' my girls, yeah."

Pappy spat on the ground then turned his steely gaze back to Jabba Joe. "You rough her up, Jabber?"

Jabba gave a weary sigh and rolled his eyes. "Like the man already told you, pops, it's 'Jabba.' Jabb-*uh.*"

"You didn't answer my question. You rough your woman up? Smack her 'round in front of her little girl? You the one what done that?"

One of Jabba's companions crossed his tattooed arms across his chest. "Yo Joe, who is this fool?" Jabba just shook his head.

Pappy wiped a closed fist across his chin. "I'm gettin' tired of the banter, Jabber. I don't need to hear you say whether you is or whether you ain't. I know you is. I seen the look in that baby girl's eyes. I can see the look in your eyes right now. You done it. I'm here t'make sho' it don' happen again."

Jabba Joe giggled. It seemed an odd sound coming from that colossal frame, high and feminine. "What exactly you plan to do, grandpa?"

"Flatten yo' ass out," Pappy said, stepping closer. At this, Jabba Joe and his companions snorted laughter, shaking their heads.

With surprising quickness, Pappy stepped toward Jabba with a powerful right cross that hit Jabba square on the jaw. The quarters hummed in Pappy's hand as the reverberations of the punch traveled up his arm and down his narrow back. Jabba stepped back, shaking his head. His mouth contorted into a shocked sneer of chipped teeth and blood. He wiped at his mouth with one of his oversized mitts and stared at disbelief at Pappy. "You hit me," he stammered.

"Told you I was goin' to, Jabber. Gonna beat you like you beat that nice woman," Pappy said. "Now are you gonna take this like a man, or will I have to tend to your crew here too?"

Jabba turned a quick eye to each of his companions. "If they touch you, old man, I'll pound them myself. You are *all* mine."

Jabba came quick at Pappy, throwing an elbow at Pappy's thin face. Pappy stepped away in a flowing motion. He avoided with ease the punch that followed, and the attempted headlock after that, his movements reacting preternaturally to those of the giant fighter. Jabba moved fast for his size and released a flurry of punches and jabs, all of which Pappy avoided as if Jabba had called each of them out beforehand. Pappy and Jabba Joe moved in a furious dance as the big man's muscle-bound cohorts watched with mouths agape.

Jabba was already starting to sound winded. His attacks became more elaborate, more grappling than boxing, with clunky kicks thrown in for good measure. Pappy danced around it all. *Get as fancy as you want, you big baby man*, Pappy thought. *I'll abide.* As Pappy hopped over Jabba's thick leg after another thwarted kick, Jabba gulped a big breath. Pappy took that second of opportunity to deliver two lightning-fast jabs to Jabba's nose. Blood sprayed around his fist, and when he pulled back, Jabba's nose was bent a little to the left. *Still got it*, Pappy thought with a grin. The quarters still thrumming in his hand, Pappy bent backward, avoiding a wild haymaker. Pappy felt the wind from Jabba's giant fist as it swept past. Pappy glided down, then back up in a fluid motion, and smacked Jabba's chin with a solid right under cut. A left cross followed.

Jabba gulped for air again, then rushed at Pappy, attempting a bear hug. Pappy ducked the grasping arms and pivoted in a crouched position around the giant. Once behind Jabba, Pappy stayed low and pounded a flurry of jabs into the big man's kidney region. *You got kidneys in there somewhere under all that blubber*, Pappy laughed to himself. Jabba yelped in pain as he lumbered around to face Pappy.

Out of the corner of his eye, Pappy caught the movement of one of Jabba's fellow goons. That glimpse was enough to automatically pitch Pappy's head back from the punch that followed. It missed Pappy and landed square in the face of the third goon. Jabba Joe heaved his companions out of the way in a rage, sending them flying in opposite directions. He bellowed at Pappy, looking more like an enraged bear than anything human. Pappy smiled.

A clumsy swing and miss, another go at the bear hug, a few feeble kicks, none of it went anywhere. Pappy dodged and weaved and stayed just out of reach, a carrot dangling at the end of a string that the big man could never catch. After a few more weak attempts to land a blow on Pappy, Jabba Joe slowed to a stop and put his hands on his knees. His purple face squeezed out wheezing breath after wheezing breath. He looked up at Pappy, eyes still defiant, though his body no longer cared to cooperate.

"Don't give yourself a heart attack, you big fool," Pappy said. He flexed his fingers around the roll of quarters in his right hand. "Now here's the what, Jabber. I see you around that nice lady or that nice lady's little girl, I hear you been harrassin' them, anything like that, I'll come at you. What you saw here today ain't nuthin'. I killed a man, Jabber. With my *bare hands*. You ask anyone. I ain't one to be trifled with. That lady up in 4B wit' the sweet little child? She ain't to be trifled wit' no more either. You got me?"

Jabba Joe's eyes narrowed in seething, impotent rage. He couldn't speak past his heaving breaths, but Pappy could tell he wanted to.

"I see there's still a lil' fight left in ya, Jabber, so I'm gonna beat it on out. Tramp it down and spit on it, ya hear? Now don't kill yourself trying to get yo' fat ass back up after this. You take your medicine like a man, then you go think on what I said. We can always do this again if you is so inclined."

With that, Pappy gave Jabba his best right hook, right in his swelling, bloody kisser. The roll of quarters in Pappy's hand sprayed into the air. They clanged to the ground around Jabba as he smacked the sidewalk with a wet thump. *Out cold*, Pappy remarked to himself with pride. Pappy bent to retrieve his quarters, jamming them into his pockets as he went. Jabba's partners sat on the ground to either side, staring wide-eyed and slack-jawed.

Pappy shot them a sheepish look. "I'm on a fixed income," he said.

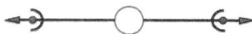

"DR. BALABANOV wants to meet with you again next week, Dad," Gus said, his voice tinny over Pappy's bargain cell phone. "He's going to run some tests, okay?"

"Who?" Pappy shouted. "You talking about Fancy Pants?"

"Yes, Dad," Gus said, somewhat exasperated. "He's a very respected neurologist. This is really something special going on here. You should appreciate it."

"You know I ain't impressed by them educated idiots, Gus. Now hold on!" Pappy screamed into the phone. "This bus is loud as all get out! Can't hear myself think."

"Dad, you don't need to yell. It's not loud where I am."

"What? *Speak up!*" Pappy yelled, then slunk back, red-faced, into the creased seat of the rattling bus. The other passengers stared at him. "Look," he shouted into the phone. "I gots to go. I'll call when I get home." Pappy closed up his phone and looked around at his fellow riders. "Okay, all right, ya'll go on back to your bidness. Don't stare at the poor old man yelling at his phone."

Pappy exhaled a long breath and rubbed his aching knuckles. His right was swelling up like a balloon. *Get some ice on it when I get back,* he thought. *Ain't nuthin' you ain't been through before, old man,* he told himself. *You done what you needed to do.*

"Now don't cry, honey," a woman's voice from a few seats back said. Pappy's ears pricked up.

"I know, Aunt Ginny, but I'm just so scared." Another female voice, much younger.

"I'm sure this'll all blow over in a few days. You'll be at my house, and nobody will bother you there. Couple days, both of you can go back home, and it'll all be forgotten."

"Aunt Ginny, he put the *puppy* in the *microwave*. He's a psychopath. This ain't 'blowing over.' Face it, we're fucked."

Pappy attempted a nonchalant look back. A lady about his age and a teenage girl. A teenage boy sat between them, eyes wide and lost, looking forsaken and scared out of his wits.

The girl met his eyes and glared. "You mind your business, old man."

Pappy turned back around as Aunt Ginny admonished the girl.

The girl began to cry. "I'm just scared, Aunt Ginny. Until Kevin pays him back, Leon is *not* going to leave us alone. Probably not even then. He's gonna kill us, Aunt Ginny, just like poor little Cece."

Pappy scowled. He reached into his back pocket and retrieved his memo pad and a tiny red pencil. He paged through the notebook until he reached ~~JABBER~~. Underneath this, he wrote, LEON. He closed the notepad and returned it to his pocket.

"Welp," Pappy said under his breath. "Sumbitch gotta pay."

CATHERINE JONES PAYNE

NOT ONE FOR PLATITUDES

WHEN I was in second grade, my Sunday School teacher, Miss Adele, got our whole class to memorize that passage in Ephesians about the armor of God. "Finally, be strong in the Lord and in his mighty power," we droned, none of us entirely sure what any of it meant. "Put on the full armor of God so that you may take your stand against the devil's schemes." That part we understood better. We made up hand motions to go with it as we talked about taking up the shield of faith and putting on the belt of truth and fitting our feet with the readiness of peace.

After we memorized it, we each chose a letter of the alphabet and drew a picture to go in a book for our parents. Most of the other little girls drew sweet pictures. Sylvie picked "A" and scribbled, "Award the Warrior." Arianna felt like she pulled the short straw when she got stuck with "H," but everyone liked her picture: "Help the Warrior." It featured a little girl with red hair helping a Crusades-style knight lift a box marked "heavy." I'm sure she made the burden much easier to carry.

Miss Adele froze when I showed her mine. I think she was containing a chuckle, though perhaps she was wondering what she would tell my mother. But she had promised we could choose whatever we wanted, and so my "Bake the Warrior" is forever enshrined in all its glory—the flames of the oven licking the poor little warrior yelling, "Help me!"

A few days ago, Miss Adele came by my bed in the oncology ward of St. Samuel's Hospital. I wondered how she'd even heard I was sick. We'd left that church almost ten years ago. I couldn't have been older than eleven last time she saw me. "Hey stranger," she said, lowering herself into the chair at my bedside.

"Hey," I croaked back, pushing a tendril of dark brown hair behind my ear. "Long time no see." I needed a drink of water.

"How you holding up, Cassie?"

"Well, cancer's finished eating up one of my kidneys and is now happily munching on my spleen and bones, so I've had better days."

"That sucks," she said.

I laughed, "That's a helluva lot better answer than what most people give me."

"What do they usually say?"

"Usually some variation of, 'I'm so sorry,' or 'God's got a plan,' or 'You're so strong.'"

"I've never really been one for platitudes. Although I did bring you a present that might be mistaken for one." She pulled a slim notebook out of her purse. I recognized it immediately.

"The warrior book!" I pushed myself up so I was almost sitting.

"I hoped it might be a good memory,"

"Absolutely," I said, reaching for it. "That was a good year." I opened to the second page, and there it was—"Bake the Warrior"—even gorier than I'd remembered. "I'm kind of like the poor little guy I drew," I said. "Every radiation treatment they bake me."

"I guess that makes you a warrior," she said.

"Now, that was a platitude. But I can't blame you too much. I walked right into it."

"Not all warriors win, you know," she said.

"Well that's a shitty thing to say to someone with cancer." I stuck my tongue out at her.

"But I hope you do."

"I won't," I said. "I'm past that point. If I'm lucky—or unlucky, depending on how long the morphine helps—I get to submit to being baked and poisoned and prodded for another six months before I become some name on a foundation that people run 5Ks for. My foundation might get a half-marathon if I'm extra good." It used to hurt, saying that. I guess it still did, but what used to be searing pain had faded to a dull ache. Perhaps it was acceptance. Or maybe just the morphine.

"Well that really sucks."

I turned a couple pages further in the book. "Dance with the Warrior. Forget the Warrior. That one's a lot more morbidly depressing than it seemed in grade school. Who drew it?"

"Josh Banks," she said. "He's in prison right now, actually."

"No way. Really? What'd he do? He was such a goody two-shoes in high school."

"Protesting of some variety. He couldn't keep quiet about his opposition to torture in Guantanamo, and it got him in trouble. I believe the precise charge was trespassing."

"Of course he did."

We lapsed into silence.

"What about you?" I asked. "What've you been up to?"

"Well," she said, "I got married."

"Congratulations."

"Then I got divorced."

"Ah."

"I went skydiving in New Mexico."

"Always good to get those bucket list items checked off in case you don't die of a slow, wasting disease."

"And I became Roman Catholic."

"Well that's quite a change."

"Less so than you might think."

"Enlighten me. Don't Catholics worship Mary or something?" I raised my eyebrows in mock accusation.

"Oh yes," she said, deadpan, "with incense and infant sacrifice, much the same way you Baptists worship the Sunday morning sermon."

"Touché. Pastor Gary could go on for 45 minutes without taking a breath. Nearly killed me." Too soon, I thought. Too soon.

"The brevity of Father Theodore's sermons is truly inspiring. His philosophy is: If you don't hit oil after five minutes, stop boring."

That one took me a minute. Damn morphine.

She didn't convince me, but I don't think she was really trying to. She'd always had a talent for debate and a love of a well-crafted argument. It felt good to engage in an hour and a half of theological bantering on the pope, the Virgin Mary, confession, and the Eucharist. Of course, I appreciated the flowers that people sent to my isolated little world in the oncology ward, but I liked Adele's sharp-tongued logic more.

"So, why'd you make the change?" I asked, fifty minutes in.

"Why'd I become Catholic?"

"Yeah," I said. "Jokes aside, I really am curious."

"I don't really know," she said. "Josh—my ex-husband—decided to run off with some chick whose stage name was Sapphire—"

"He would."

"—and Pastor Gary's pat answers didn't work anymore. My aunt told me to talk to Father Theodore. He didn't really have answers for me either, but he asked me to come to Mass one day. I thought I'd hate it, but by the end of the first hymn, I cried. The whole Mass just felt right. Contemplation is good for the soul, I guess."

The conversation didn't dwindle on its own, but at a quarter past two she said that she needed to go, that she had an appointment, and I thanked her for coming because that's what you do at the end of visits in the oncology ward. But unlike at the end of most visits from people I hadn't seen in forever, I meant it. It had been fun and not in my passive-aggressive-girl-from-Seattle meaning of the word. She left the warrior book on the table beside the bed.

I picked it up, gingerly, tentatively, flipping through the pages that looked so vaguely familiar. The words came back to me all at once, like that Taylor Swift song you can never quite get out of your head. With half a tremor in my hands, I whispered, "Be strong in the Lord and in his mighty power. Put on the full armor of God so that you may take your stand against the devil's schemes." I heard the nurse coming and slapped away the single tear that threatened my eyelashes.

E.D.E. BELL

BAGELS

"NOW, WHAT'S this next one?"
Mr. Knutsen inquired. "*Lactation* room?
Is that—" Somewhere in the executive's mind, an alarm triggered regard-
ing legally sensitive subjects. He tapped
the table. "Oh, yes, a mothers room.
Whoever submitted this may not be
aware that we already have one."

Louise stared down at her pris-
tine yellow binder. She had stayed
late several evenings working on this
proposal. "Mr. Knutsen, I authored
this one myself. It's a change from what
we have and I'd like to present it."

He reached for his coffee. "Not
sure I understand. It doesn't seem like
something, with your level of experience, that would impact you."

Experience was the preferred euphemism for *old*, as there was no law for experience discrimination. A pit formed in her chest. Within twenty seconds, he had turned to evaluate Louise rather than her proposal.

"No, I'm not pregnant," she answered in level tones, "nor should we start rumors of my experience." Mr. Knutsen's face tightened and his deputy pursed her lips. Around the table, several people averted their eyes. "You don't need to require a thing in order to recommend it, of course. For example, you approved the smoking shelter though Mrs. Knutsen told everyone at the picnic that you had quit."

Mr. Knutsen huffed, shaking his head at the comparison. "Of course that's not for me. You can't have people standing in the rain; it isn't right. That's just looking out for people. Now, back to this…mothers room. Who's complaining about it?"

I am not bringing her into this. Louise gestured toward Mr. Knutsen's binder. "The current space is in the restroom; my proposal details an update that would provide a more welcoming environment for lactating employees."

Mr. Knutsen forced a smile. "It's not *in* the bathroom; it's a separate area with a divider. I know of only one person affected, and she has been fairly accommodated, in full compliance with the law. We looked up the requirements."

The planning lead nodded his head in agreement.

"Perhaps I could approve a sign," Mr. Knutsen offered, "to place outside. That would show we have a family-friendly environment."

Louise took a deep breath, reminding herself this wasn't on her mind, either, until last month. After a lunchtime bowl of chili, she was hoping she could sneak away for "a couple of things," as her husband referred to it. As she walked into the stall she heard an unusual sound, muffled, from behind an industrial-looking separator.

Zzzz. Zzzz. Zzzz. It took her a moment to place the sound. *Oh, a breast pump!*

She liked how times had changed; attitudes had been so different when her own children were born. She winced, remembering the comments people had made about her returning to work at all, and the years she had smiled back despite the wounds inside. Surely they didn't need to use the restroom for pumping milk. *And I came in here to—* Louise left, her business unfinished.

She had hesitated to approach the young woman, but the situation nagged at her mind. It must have been Tanya from accounting. She had returned not long ago from maternity leave, a new picture of a tiny baby boy on her desk. "Let me know if you need anything," people had remarked before returning to their email.

"Tanya?" Louise had inquired after ensuring they were alone. "If you don't mind me asking, does it bother you to have to use the restroom to pump?"

The look on Tanya's face showed her true feelings, but she appeared reticent to answer.

"I'm sorry; I didn't mean to pry," Louise responded, turning to leave.

"I hate it," the young woman whispered, turning Louise in mid-stride. "I can't relax with people *peeing* in the background. And there's no lock; I'm always scared someone's going to walk in."

"Have you said anything?"

Tanya shook her head. "I don't want to bring it up; I draw enough attention as it is. They're always staring at my bag in meetings, wondering if I'll have to leave. If I complained about the room, it would just remind them that I have no business being here anyway. That's what they think."

"You don't know that," Louise answered, doubting the words as she spoke them. "You could give them a chance. The fiscal year planning meeting is coming up. You could submit it."

"I'm not talking to them about my...*breasts*. I'll make it work."

Louise stifled a grin. "Tanya, despite your perceptions of the executive staff, I assure you they have all encountered breasts in their time. Even Mr. Knutsen."

Tanya chuckled. "Maybe."

For days, Tanya's situation continued to rankle Louise, until sitting at her keyboard with an evening cup of rooibos tea, she began to draw up the requirements: a comfortable chair, a desk, outlets, a fridge, a clock, a locking door, a bulletin board, and a sink—along with a concise justification for each. *There,* she had finally declared, as she punched holes into the side of the proposal.

She stared at the binder now, the extra copies in front of her. Louise opened her mouth to protest, but Mr. Knutsen had already moved on to approving construction of a new shelf in the snack area, strong enough to hold full toaster ovens rather than traditional vertical toasters.

"Thanks for everyone's input," Mr. Knutsen was saying. "All great improvements for our team. We've got another set to get through, but I need a bio-break first. Let's take ten."

The executives filed from the room as an administrative assistant bumped past with large bags of bagels. The planning lead was following behind. "Everything bagels are my favorite," he explained. Louise responded with a polite smile as she walked past the table and out into the hallway.

Louise stepped into the restroom and found herself staring at the dividing wall with resentment. The pit now weighed heavy inside her. It wasn't that she had been dismissed; it certainly wasn't the first time. It was the idea of young people afraid to raise their voices and no one coming to their aid.

She walked into the small space. It was bare except for an office chair, a small folding table, and a picture of Tanya's boy pinned to the wall. A toilet flushed in the background. *They think they can put us away. That things will return to how they were.*

She didn't want to wait for next year's review; every year would be another woman made to feel dirty and unwelcome in her own place of work. She ran her hands across the table, and a terrible idea sprang to mind. *I wouldn't. Would I?*

Louise stepped back into the hallway and nearly walked right into Mr. Knutsen emerging from the other side, tossing a paper towel into the can as the door swung closed behind him.

"Louise, don't take it wrong. We can't accommodate every niche need or there wouldn't be resources to keep the lights on." He reached toward her shoulder, stopping short as if held back by an invisible lawyer.

"I just worry, sir, that younger parents won't be drawn to work here. It would be a shame to lose some really talented people over a change that would be easy for us to make."

Mr. Knutsen nodded. "Louise, I know you well enough to know that you won't take this the wrong way, but what if they do leave? Aren't their families better off? Why would we stand in the way of mothers spending more time with their children?" His hand patted the air.

Years of painful memories hit Louise in the chest as Mr. Knutsen walked back into the room.

Louise made up her mind.

As she walked into the room, everyone was absorbed into their phones, including Mr. Knutsen. They ignored her completely as they finished their emails or made a quick call home, giving her time to slip from the room.

She sat back into her seat as Mr. Knutsen finally looked up from his phone. "Everyone, help yourself to some—" he started, staring at the table to the side, covered with a series of neatly arranged papers. "Where are the bagels?" He turned with a pointed finger to his deputy. "Didn't Tracy bring in the bagels, Melanie?" Melanie peered at the table in confusion.

Louise braced herself and raised a hand. "I needed room to set out my proposal so that everyone could review, since no one had the chance to read it earlier. I moved the bagels to the ladies room."

Mr. Knutsen's face burned red, and his deputy squinted. The planning lead glanced suspiciously at his everything bagel. To his left, a man's eyes opened wide, and another gaped to his right. The man across the table glanced away, making a face of disgust.

A quick flash of doubt filled Louise before being pushed away by resolve. *Too late now. If I just got myself fired, I'll go out fighting.* "There's no need for concern. I set them out behind the divider, so they aren't technically in the ladies room. It's very clean there."

That afternoon, Louise watched for a chance to catch Tanya alone. "The planning meeting was today. A pumping room—it's on the list."

Tanya stepped back. "Wow, really?"

Her eyes clouded, a reaction Louise didn't expect.

"I'm sorry; did I go too far? I didn't think you'd—"

"No," Tanya waved her hand. "No, please. I'm just surprised, is all. Nobody's ever fought for me before. Not here, anyway."

Louise clutched the binder. "This was only the first round. We still have to get it past the V.P."

"It doesn't matter. Just that you tried, well, it means so much to me. Thank you."

"Hang in there. I'm not ready to give up." Louise met Tanya's eyes for a moment. "Everyone makes tough choices. Don't let them get to you."

"I'll remember that." With a final nod, Tanya hefted the bag's thick strap onto her shoulder and headed toward the restroom.

ALBATROSS

PART 4

"**THERE ARE** a dozen guards protecting the vault, and that's after you've made it through the other obstacles." Braydon pointed to a specific area on the digital blueprints we huddled around, listening intently as he directed us.

"Warrior can take out the guards," Gunner suggested, winking at me. "It's her specialty."

"Actually you'll probably want her watching your backs. A team of you could take the guards, but you'll want your most skilled fighters to protect you from any surprises."

All eyes shifted to Captain, who stroked his mustache.

"Blade, Wrench, and Warrior will watch our backs while the rest of us go in," he finally said. "Go on."

Braydon continued, explaining in more detail than any other mission we'd had. As we neared the end, I wondered why he'd given so much. His deal with the Captain remained unfinished.

"And the lock combination?" Blade asked as we neared the end of his presentation.

Braydon's gaze focused on Captain, who grunted. "We'll worry about that later." He raised a brow, glancing around. "Well? What are you all standing here for? Don't you have work to do to get ready for this?"

Everyone scrambled, and I kept my eyes on Captain.

"The code? That's the deal? You get the code when he gets…." I stopped, not sure of how to word the deal.

Captain's countenance darkened. "We'll find another way. I won't have that man take from you what should be…."

My stomach soured. Rage bubbled within me as I challenged him. "Yours?"

His hand clenched tight around my arm and he bared his teeth. "Who saved you from the docks? Who took you in and fed you? Clothed you? Everything you have is because of me. I own you. Every. Last. Piece. I've waited until you reach womanhood, but I will wait no longer. Don't force me to take what is due to me."

Cold dread swept through me. "I—I'm not ready," I said, feeling breathless. My mind raced as I tried to think past my fear. "Not with this job on my mind. We need to get through this. We need to dump this Veil City Brat. The only way we can guarantee success is if we keep him with us until the job is done." I laid my hand over his, and his grip loosened. "Let me handle him. I'll get the information we need."

He released me, his black glare fixated on my mouth. "You have until after the heist. Then I come for what's mine, whether you're ready or not." With that, he strode off. Blade replaced him by my side a moment later.

"Are you all right?"

"Fine," I said through clenched teeth. "Bring the brat to my cabin."

S.R. KARFELT

LITTLE GIRL CROSSED

QUE VISTA ELEMENTARY
SCHOOL, NEW MEXICO 1980

"CAROLE BLANK?" Mrs. Kuzik
read her name out loud.

Carole heard one of the boys in
the first grade class whisper, "Blank-
Wank-Stank."

She turned to look at him, but
Mrs. Kuzik touched her arm. "Do you
know your ABCs?"

Carole nodded. She would not
care that she was taller than the teacher.
She would not care that Mr. Kraus had
labeled her *troubled* or that the school
principal said his belt specialized in
troubled. She would not care that a
redheaded boy now burped her name,
adding "Wank-Stank" to the end of it.

Mrs. Kuzik wore red lipstick and black cat's eye glasses on a gold chain. She put them on her nose and sat down at her cluttered desk. "Can you read?" She motioned toward a book.

Carole nodded again, peering at the open book. "Heart pounding in time to the slap of the raging sea against the hull, Clairee grasped Reginald's throbbing—"

"I meant this one," Mrs. Kuzik interrupted, flipping the hardcover book over and staring at her. She put a plump hand on a colorful children's primer. The open page read, "Oh, see. Oh, see Jane."

Carole read it, but Mrs. Kuzik put her hand on Carole's arm again and shook her head. "I think we'll start you on something else."

Mrs. Kuzik stood and her head came to Carole's chin. The teacher smiled as though Carole should care she could read a first grade book. "Class? Carole already knows how to read quite well."

The burping boy whisper-burped in the back of the room, "Oh, see. Oh, see Carole Stank." The class tittered, but she would not care!

Mrs. Kuzik clapped her hands for order. The burping boy echoed the sound with rude noises made under his armpit. The teacher marched Carole to a desk. She put a thick book inside it, instructing Carole to take it home just like the big kids did. Some of the other children made sounds of envy, but Carole just wanted to cross the room—it would take three seconds—and slam the burping boy's fingers inside his desk. He kept his hands slyly out of the teacher's sight, but Carole could feel him breaking his pencils in half with the part of her brain behind her left eyeball—and every faint *snap-snap* sound echoed inside her head as though the points were jabbing there.

The voices knew what she was thinking, because they shouted in her head. "*You must not hurt one of them without permission! It is forbidden!*"

Carole sat at the desk, but her skinny legs wouldn't go beneath it. Spreading her legs akimbo, in a way Sister Mary Josephine from the orphanage called unladylike, she managed to put her elbows on the desk and pretended not to care.

FOSTER CARE meant children who didn't belong.

At least, that is what the Thatcher children told Carole after Marsha deposited her in their kitchen after school. Mr. and Mrs. Thatcher had seven foster children, and three *real* children, they informed her. Becky, Patty, and Scott Thatcher were real, and had bedrooms upstairs by their parent's room. The foster children slept on cots downstairs, boys in one room, girls in another. They had two dogs that snapped at you if you tried to touch them. Scott Thatcher pulled their tails and raced up the stairs. The dogs nipped savagely at his heels, needle teeth snapping, but he escaped into the safety of a tiny bathroom.

Slinking back down the stairs in bad-tempered defeat, the dogs lunged for Becky Thatcher. Carole wrapped a thin arm around her and hauled her onto the safety of the banister, safe from chomping teeth.

"Ow!" Becky complained. "That hurt you idiot!"

Carole let go of her and Becky climbed down the far side of the perch, keeping the banister bars between her and the dogs. She sniffed, smoothing her shiny blue dress with a picture of a unicorn on the front.

"They wouldn't bite me anyway. They're *my* family's dogs." Both dogs shoved their fuzzy snouts between the railings, snapping at her. Becky leaned precariously away, struggling to keep her balance.

Carole slid down beside her, wrapped an arm around the girl and leapt the few feet to safety. A startled Becky pushed her away and ran.

Carole waited for the dogs, jumped nimbly over them, and bolted. Both dogs chased Carole into the kitchen, where she slammed the door in their snarling faces.

Standing at the sink, Mrs. Thatcher ignored the growling and scratching coming through the door. Drying her hands on her big red apron, she ordered two big girls to set the table properly, water pitcher in front of Mr. Thatcher's place.

"And what's your name again?" There was something sharp about her brown eyes as she took in Carole's disheveled appearance. Carole lifted a thin leg and tugged one sock properly back into place.

"Carole Blank, Ma'am." Marsha, the social worker, had told Carole that everyone was Ma'am or Sir, unless they told her otherwise.

"I am not cooking you homemade bread and beans, or whatever that woman said you had to eat. I don't cater to picky eaters. You'll eat what is on your plate or you'll get punished just like the rest of them. People aren't allergic to food, that nigger doesn't know what she's talking about."

The voices started their shouting inside Carole's head. *"If you eat dirty food you die."* She pressed her lips together. Mrs. Thatcher had promised Marsha she would give her the kind of food she could eat, like her file said. Mrs. Thatcher had taken the list from Marsha and smiled. Mrs. Thatcher was a liar, and she said ugly words. What was a nigger? Because Marsha wasn't one, but maybe Mrs. Thatcher was.

AT DINNER Carole sat low in her seat, hoping they wouldn't notice her. There were twelve people at the big table. The two skinny dogs with curling tails and tucked under bottoms prowled around the edges. They showed Carole their teeth when she looked at them.

Carole's chair sat furthest from the back door, and her sweaty thighs stuck to the red plastic. If a desert breeze came through the torn screen door, it didn't get very far in that kitchen hot from cooking. Carole drank every drop of her milk and ate all her carrots as fast as she could chew. The sight of the remaining food filled her with dread. It had been altered, changed. A strange wavering light seemed to emanate from the meat and bread, like heat waves off the road. The voices said that kind of food was forbidden, but Mrs. Thatcher said she had to eat it, and Carole still felt hungry.

At the thought of disobedience, a haze dropped over her eyes and the scent of decay replaced the smell of homemade food. A black dream put the taste of dirty food in her mouth. Carole gagged, and the voices shouted.

"Never eat dirty food. You will cease to be. You will die."

Averting her eyes from poisonous-looking waves floating over food, she shivered in the hot kitchen, fighting to keep the good food down. The boy next to her chewed with an open mouth, his flat black eyes on her.

Carole focused on him, hoping it would help. His name was Joyce, and chubby rolls of cinnamon flesh peeked out beneath his shirt. He had shiny black hair and the voices in her head quieted as she stared back.

Joyce opened his mouth to display an abundance of half-chewed meat, imitating her gagging. With the scent of rot still firmly in mind, Carole's stomach roiled. Joyce turned to share his genius with the boy on his other side. Carole palmed her bread and meat, hiding it under the table. The boy next to Joyce didn't appreciate his show, and a furtive scuffle ensued. Most of the kids watched the covert fighting and Carole took the opportunity to toss the food into the space between her chair and Joyce's. Almost instantly a dog's head appeared in the spot. Daringly Carole patted the scruffy short fur once before snatching her hand back.

While Carole wished for more carrots, Mr. Thatcher told about his day painting outside in the desert sun. Becky, Patty and Scott talked about what they learned in school that day, and Mrs. Thatcher bragged about an electric fan she had bought with the money from the new girl. Being the new girl, Carole sat up with interest. She hadn't known she had any money, but she'd use it to buy more carrots and potatoes if they'd let her.

"Social services don't pay hardly enough to cover their food." Mr. Thatcher didn't seem to have noticed Carole slipping food to the dogs, but when he shoved back from the table one of them trotted to his side, gnawing loudly on a whole pork chop while the other dog licked the side of his mouth trying to get his share.

Abruptly Mr. Thatcher stood, and passing Carole's chair he lifted her off the seat by the straps of her jumper dress, as though she didn't weigh much more than one of the skinny dogs. She felt the threads creak, but the sturdy cotton uniform held. Carole dangled in the air for a moment, positioning her arms and legs for a landing should the dress tear, and wondering how he knew it had been her pork chop.

Mr. Thatcher sat down in her chair and plopped her across his lap. His work clothes were paint-splattered, and he smelled like cigarettes and communion wine. As he walloped Carole, Mr. Thatcher talked to Mrs. Thatcher about sneaky kids and wasted food. A couple of the other foster kids chimed in to say how much they liked their pork chops. Carole kept her eyes on the wooden floor, wondering if her clothes would stink like cigarettes now.

"*HIDE. HIDE*, *hide, hide,*" the voices lectured. "*Act like they do. Never tell. Never show yourself.*" Carole kept her eyes closed, pretending she was still sleeping. They knew she was faking, they always knew. How she hated those voices, maybe more than the black dreams that showed what would happen if she didn't listen. Thoughts of black dreams about being hurt by tools, like those in Mr. Thatcher's shed, made her shiver. Breathing dirty water up her nose or being set on fire would be worse than the voices, if those things really happened. She shivered.

"*It happens, you know it happens.*"

Something warm sat on her leg. Despite the unfamiliar bulk in the dark, Carole knew it was Duke's head. Sharing her meals with Duke and Earl, the Thatchers' dogs, had won their loyalty. Not to mention the fact that she never pulled their tails or teased them. Reaching down, she put her hand near the dog, and his nose immediately slid beneath it, tossing it onto his head for scratching. Everything had to be Duke's idea or he didn't like it—except food.

Pushing her awareness through the house, Carole's mind searched, making certain that all were asleep. The Thatcher family slept, tucked quietly in their beds upstairs. Earl snoozed on the floor near his master's bed. Carole couldn't see them, but she could sense the dog's quicker breathing and his furry body near the slower breathing and slightly less furry body of Mr. Thatcher. The four foster boys were downstairs in the big bedroom just across the hall from her, a sheet hung where a door belonged. Mr. Thatcher said boys couldn't be trusted behind closed doors.

Considering that every night poor Joyce was forced to sleep on the floor, Carole thought Mr. Thatcher might be right. In her room, the other two foster girls—sisters—lay cuddled together on their shared cot. It wasn't necessary to use the inside of her head to feel for the even breathing of the girls. Their soft breaths were so close Carole knew that Liz, the eldest, had sneaked to bed without brushing her teeth again.

Duke moved. He always knew when the timing was right. Carole rolled onto her side and reached beneath the bed to pull out her shoes. Running in her black and white saddle shoes was ruining them, but running in the desert barefoot was impossible. Fortunately, plenty of shoe polish hid the scuffs. Despite ten children and a house to tend to, Mrs. Thatcher didn't miss much. Carole slid silently across the wooden floor and crawled out the open window, hauling Duke's willing and eager body right behind her for their midnight run.

CAROLE MIGHT have liked school during recess best, but the voices didn't let her run too fast or win in kickball. The voices wouldn't let her push redheaded Jimmy West to make him shut up. He always called her Carole Stank and burped her name. Some of his friends called her that too, but nobody else could burp as good as Jimmy West.

Carole's favorite part of school was after recess. Mrs. Kuzik made everyone, including Jimmy West, put their heads on their desks, and then she read a story. Every day was a new chapter. First it had been about a little girl who lived on a prairie. Then it was a sad story about a buffalo that made Carole's eyes fill with tears and her heart ache with sympathy. Now it was a story about children who lived in a boxcar. Carole memorized those details. Someday when the voices let her run away and her promise to Marsha ended, maybe she'd live in a boxcar until she found where she belonged.

Listening with her head resting on her arms, Carole noticed Jimmy West being mean to someone else. His desk sat a row behind hers, nearest the open door to the hallway. Mrs. Kuzik had put him there on Carole's second day of school. She'd warned him loudly, so the whole class had heard, that it was so the principal could walk past at any moment and see his antics. It bothered Carole that Jimmy got to sit by the door for burping her name. If something happened and they had to run, it meant that he could escape fastest. Since she behaved her desk sat near the hot window. If she ever needed to escape when it was closed, and broke it, she knew she'd be in big trouble. Even the voices said so.

Today Jimmy was occupied with picking his nose. It astonished Carole how much of his finger could go up there. Next to him Sarah Lightfoot tried to scoot away without lifting her head off her desk. Sarah had smooth black hair and a dark face, and when Jimmy wasn't burping Carole's name, he was wiping boogers on Sarah. The little girl on the left side of Sarah elbowed her when she got too close. Nobody in Mrs. Kuzik's class played with Sarah. At recess Sarah played with children from other classes. Children who had smooth black hair and dark faces like she had.

Sarah's dark eyes narrowed to slits as she scooted. The freckled girl pounded her elbow into Sarah's arm, pushing her away. Resigned, Sarah took her place within easy reach of Jimmy's wiping finger, but he pointed it at something hidden under his desk. Whatever it was upset Sarah worse than boogers, because she buried her face in her arms and let Jimmy wipe away, without even trying to move again. Carole watched for a few seconds, noting that Jimmy West was left-handed. Then she turned her head, rested it on her arms again, and closed her eyes.

DODGEBALL WAS Carole's favorite recess game even though they played it inside, in the room that was the cafeteria at lunchtime. There were eight doors and Carole could reach the closest in three seconds. Except for Carole, the whole class wore sneakers, even the gym teacher. Sneakers protected the floor, he told them again, giving Carole's hard shoes an unhappy look. Carole wondered why they didn't have to protect the floor at lunch.

The gym teacher picked his two favorite students, Robert Morrison and Timothy Miller, and they chose teams. Carole hoped she wouldn't get on the same team as Jimmy West. Jimmy always got picked first, and Carole and Sarah Lightfoot were picked last. It had been like that the whole school year. Today Carole got lucky. The foster care girl with the wrong kind of shoes got picked second to last, over the girl from the reservation with dried boogers on her sleeve.

The voices always made Carole lose in the middle of the game. They didn't make her go out first, but they wouldn't let her be the last girl tagged out. Jimmy West grinned at her as he threw the ball straight at her head. That was against the rules, but he did it anyway. Usually she let it hit her when the voices told her it was time, but only on her shoulder or arm. Today she reached up and caught the ball solidly just an inch from her face. Before Jimmy had time to react she sized the angle, located his left index finger, and threw the ball as hard as she could. It made a delightful sound as it cut through the air, almost too fast to follow. Jimmy was still looking at her and grinning when it caught his finger. Carole thought she heard it snap.

THE VOICES knew Carole had done it on purpose. They were mad and they were mean about it. They kept her up that night, showing her what happened for harming without permission. These dark dreams were different. Carol saw columns of sparkling light that turned into giant men. They wore clothes like in old gladiator movies, and even after they turned into men they still sparkled with light inside them. The shining gladiator men made people disappear with them and they punished them in terrible ways. Carole watched all night as the voices shouted at her. The hot red sun popped over the horizon before the dark dreams stopped.

Bus 407 ran late that morning. Carole walked into Mrs. Kuzik's first grade classroom after the bell, and all heads turned toward her. She saw the entire room in an instant, like she always did. There were twenty-two pupils, ten boys and twelve girls, including her. The green chalkboards had been washed and looked nice and new, instead of dusty like they often did. There was a stick of blue chalk in the tray beneath them and that meant math day. Carole liked math. There was only one right answer to math questions.

Mia Taylor's pretty beaded jump rope sat on the teacher's desk. That meant Mia had been caught jumping rope inside again. But what worried Carole was that dark-haired Sarah Lightfoot was sitting at her desk.

"Carole, I was hoping you weren't sick. Was the bus late again?" Mrs. Kuzik came toward her, her tan-colored pumps clicking on the linoleum floor. "I'm afraid Jimmy West's finger was broken during the dodgeball game yesterday. He can't write now, not until it heals, so he's going to need help. I know it was an accident, but since you did throw the ball, the rule is that you will sit beside him and help him with his writing."

The voices inside Carole's head rejoiced, approving of this punishment. *"Justice comes in many forms. You will make restitution to this seeker boy."*

Carole sat next to Jimmy West, wondering what made him a seeker boy. She thought he should seek a tissue for his nose. Bits of dried snot dotted one side of poor Sarah Lightfoot's desk. Carole carefully avoided touching the desktop. Jimmy West's left hand had been bandaged in a hard plaster cast, the entire arm strapped in a sling over his chest.

Carole couldn't help smiling, pleased. He would not be picking his nose and wiping it on anyone for a while. Jimmy narrowed his eyes and burped her name, but she just slid the green sheet of paper off his desk and printed his name neatly on the top right corner using Sarah's chewed pencil.

Copying the math problems off the board for both her and Jimmy West, adding and subtracting in her head and waiting while Jimmy slowly tried to count simple sums with one hand, was easy. The numbers took shape in her head instantly; she could add, subtract, multiply and divide long columns of numbers, though all Mrs. Kuzik had taught them were simple two-digit equations. The black dreams didn't just scare her, they taught too. Jimmy West had trouble with sevens and nines, and Mrs. Kuzik always said he was the best in class. It made Carole mad, and she filled in her sheet quickly.

"Do not get them all correct. You must never reveal what you know. People will notice you."

Grabbing a big pink eraser, she rubbed some of the answers out and wrote them incorrectly, scowling at the sheet of paper, but she really didn't want to see more of the sparkling men from black dreams. All morning they did easy math that Carole had to mark wrong. At least Jimmy kept busy doing sums and didn't have time to burp her name.

AFTER LUNCH Jimmy West had chocolate milk dried in the corners of his mouth. When Carole looked at him, he squeezed spit out between his lips and let it fall in a long string, trying to reach the top of his desk with it. Carole ignored him.

"We have a special treat today," Mrs. Kuzik said. "It's too hot to go outside, but Mr. Hogue's class loaned us a fan and the second Boxcar Children's book, *Surprise Island!* Usually you don't get to read this story until you're in second grade. So this is a special treat, and we're going to read two chapters today. Put your head on your desk, and I'll plug in the fan."

With the rest of the class, Carole put her head on her desk. The windows were open, and the scorching sun had moved up and over top the school so even though the voices complained, the fan felt good blowing the dusty desert air over her. She listened with all of her might. Benny and Violet weren't living in the boxcar anymore; they had a family where they belonged now. She could see the story inside her head, like a nice dream.

Jimmy West poked his bandaged arm against her elbow. Carole kept her eyes closed and turned her head away, toward the freckled girl, not caring to see what Jimmy was doing with his spittle. He poked again, more insistently. Carole focused on the tale Mrs. Kuzik painted with her words, but the poking finger pulled her away. She turned her head in his direction and opened an eye.

Jimmy grinned an idiotic grin, motioning for her to look under his desk. Carole lifted her elbow and looked down, expecting to see he'd stolen Mia's jump rope or learned to pick his nose with his other hand. It was much worse. Jimmy's pants were unzipped, and he held his little boy part in his hand, waving it to and fro, like an old boneless finger. The voices in Carole's head protested. Disgust and anger shot through her and something new rose up from deep inside. This she would not allow.

In one smooth movement Carole's head lifted off her desk and her hand slid under the lid and found a wooden ruler. In two seconds she'd whipped it out and slapped it across Jimmy West's dancing part with all of her might. It made a slapping sound that echoed through the room. The ruler broke in half and a piece flew off as Jimmy screamed.

Mrs. Kuzik hurried across the room, the Boxcar Children book still in her hand. It took her almost eleven seconds. The voices in Carole's head were shouting about broken laws and retribution; she'd disobeyed and hurt a seeker. The black dreams descended.

ISABEL BROWN

THE SPIN DOCTORS

"THE LAST thing I remember was watching her spin around like a ballerina on crack." That's what I tell Lieutenant Stuart, my superior, as I lie on the hospital bed with a bullet hole between my arm and chest, a gift from gangbangers who ambushed me and my partner a few days ago. At least I thought they did.

Lieutenant Stuart chuckles at my words dismissively. "Sounds like you need a little more rest, Jeremy," he says, grabbing his eight-point trooper-style white hat from the foot of my bed and planting it on his head with expert precision; the emblem centered perfectly on his forehead from years of practice.

"Leaving already?" I ask, a little disappointed.

"Duty calls, son." He reaches out and pats my shoulder on the wounded side gently. I try not to wince. Lieutenant Stuart is like a father to me and I refuse to let him see me in pain, even the slightest pain.

"Where's Jill…I mean, where's Officer Douglas now?"

He quirks his lips with a hint of a smile. "If she wasn't patrolling the area, she'd be here. You and I know she wouldn't leave your side unless she had to."

I watch him step outside the door and wonder if he's aware that my relationship with Jillian is more than a working relationship. I pinch my eyes shut and sigh. The Lieutenant isn't stupid. He probably already knows Jillian and I have been seeing each other secretly for months. Department regulations discourage this kind of behavior among cops. It would've been easy for me to adhere to this rule, like the zillion other rules I strictly adhered to, if Jillian wasn't so darn beautiful.

"Hello there, partner," the singsong voice of an angel says.

I grin before opening my eyes, relishing the way her voice makes me feel. "Hey," I say, my eyes, like tiny sponges, taking in Jillian's beautiful face. "Thought you had forgotten about me."

She takes a couple of steps forward and slides down on the edge of the bed next to me. "That'll never happen," she says, cupping my cheek in her hand and smiling down at me with adoration.

I try to move my arm toward her but wince instead.

"Take it easy, Officer Cross," she says in a teasing manner. "You have plenty of time to heal."

"That's what I'm afraid of." I glance around the room, anxiety coursing through me. I hate being cooped up anywhere. The idea of not being able to be free, to fly free and do what I want even for a few days at a time, is a suffocating feeling for me. I wouldn't be surprised if I was diagnosed with a low-grade type of claustrophobia under the right doctor. Spin doctors is what I call them and yes, I'm well aware that my mind isn't using the term appropriately.

Jillian drops her hand and stands, smoothing her blonde pony-tail. "So, I ran into Lieutenant Stuart in the corridor. He said you remembered what happened but parts of your story weren't making any sense."

I raise my eyebrows in confusion. "Oh? What parts?"

She chuckles. "Well, one part, really." She purses her sweet lips and lifts her gaze to the ceiling in dramatic thought. "Hmm. Never in my wildest dreams would I ever have imagined being described as a ballerina on crack."

This time I chuckle but it hurts my chest so I stop abruptly, pinching my eyes shut and sinking my head back against the pillow.

"You all right?"

"Yeah," I say dryly. "Mind giving me a drink?"

She glances at the bedside table where there's a plastic cup with a bent straw and a half-filled pitcher of water.

"So, what do you remember, exactly?" she asks, pouring some water into the cup.

I raise my eyebrows and pucker my lips for the straw and she takes the hint with a wry smile before moving the straw to my lips. I take a couple of sips. The water is cool and delicious so I take a couple more sips before Jillian steers the cup away.

"Let's see," I say, concentrating on my thoughts. "We got a call for a domestic disturbance on the west side at approximately 2100 hours on October 15th."

She nods. "Correct. That was a couple of days ago. Go on."

"I drove us there—a bad neighborhood but we both knew that. I parked our cruiser in front of the house while you called it in. I remember you telling me you had a bad feeling about it. There was only one light on inside upstairs. Someone opened the front door but it was too dark to tell who it was. She yelled, 'In here. I need help!'" I stare at Jillian. "In that moment I, too, felt something wasn't right."

Jillian nods and waits for me to continue.

"You and I stepped out of the cruiser almost simultaneously and with a great degree of caution. I hadn't even closed the door when I heard the gunshot. I felt something tear a hole in me right on the edge of my vest, then I turned my head toward you just as my knees buckled and I felt myself falling. But I saw you...you started to spin around... then more gunshots exploded around us..."

"You mean like this?" she says, pirouetting gracefully in front of me in her crisply pressed gray uniform. She has a perfect form for it and I can almost tell she's dancing to a certain rhythm in her head. Swan Lake maybe? Whatever it is, I am mesmerized. A minute later, she curtsies and looks at me with a smile. I want to clap but can't.

"Wow," I whisper, astonished.

"I took ballet when I was little and through high school."

"You were breathtaking...are breathtaking."

She stares at me; a flush of pink forms on her cheeks. "So, is that what you saw?"

"Huh?"

"Me twirling around like a ballerina on crack?"

I shake my head in confusion. "Something like it, I suppose. But you were faster. Way faster."

She leans over and mollifies my thoughts with a passionate kiss. Then she promises to visit me again in the evening.

SIX MONTHS later we have dinner at Anton's, a classy Italian restaurant on the north side of town. Jillian and I love Italian food, but the restaurant is packed and I can't bring myself to pull out the engagement ring I had purchased for this special occasion. I had expected the atmosphere to be a little more private; it also didn't occur to me that children might be dining here with their parents.

After dinner, I persuade Jillian to go for a stroll in the park. It's a chilly night, but she is adventurous so, of course, she's willing. We saunter down the cobblestones, hand in hand. I love this park for its instant woodsy appeal, not to mention the smoky scent in the air. Jillian squeezes my hand in hers with a kind of approval. I give her a sidelong glance, smiling wryly.

"What?" she says, her lips curving a tiny bit.

"I never thanked you for saving my life that day."

She shakes her head. "It was nothing, Jeremy. I'd do it again if I had to."

"There's something that's been bugging me about your version of the story, though."

She wrinkles her forehead. "Oh?"

"I read the report, Jillian. You said that when I had gotten shot, you immediately ducked down and managed to find your way inside the cruiser and call for backup. But I remember what I heard and saw, sweetheart. The moment I got shot you started spinning around like some grand tornado just as gunshots exploded around us."

She stops walking and stares at me. "What are you saying?"

"I think you became a human shield, deflecting bullets with that strange power you possess."

She gives me a nervous giggle. "You have a wild imagination, honey."

I unclasp my hand from hers and stare into her luminous eyes. "Do I, really?"

She gasps, noticing something behind me. I swing around to see a couple of thugs with matching hoodies. One of them has a Glock trained on us.

"Hands up!" he says.

Jillian and I lift our hands immediately.

"Easy now," I say.

"You know what we want, right?" the taller of the two says.

"Right," I say, digging my hands inside my pocket. Good thing Jillian has left her purse in my car.

"Easy," the gunman orders. "Use your fingers to pull it out."

My fingers grip the brown leather wallet like a wrench as I slide it out of my pocket. "Here," I say, tossing it at the gunman's feet. "There's about two hundred dollars in cash inside." I slide my arm around Jillian's waist, feeling the bulk of metal protruding from the back of her waistband underneath her jacket, but I ignore it. "Please don't hurt us," I continue to say with what I hoped sounded like wretched fear just as I grip my hand over Jillian's hip and pull her against me in a flash. Then we soar into the air.

In the sky, Jillian faints in my arms but I catch her, wrapping my arm underneath her feet before she slides down. I suppose the sudden atmospheric pressure would take a while to get used to if one wasn't a flyer, like me.

LIEUTENANT STUART shakes his head. "Let me get this straight. Jeremy shot up in the sky like a kite on crack? Seriously?"

"I know it sounds incredible but that's what happened," Jillian says.

Lieutenant Stuart scratches the back of his neck and stares at both of us straight-faced. "It doesn't sound incredible, Jillian. It sounds downright preposterous and I think you're both high on crack." He sighs impatiently and points a bony finger at the door. "I want both of you out of my office now. Don't come back until you get your stories straight."

I follow Jillian out the door as she stalks down the corridor. "I know what I saw, or in this case, experienced," Jillian mumbles.

"How about something like this?" I say, scanning my eyes around the hall area warily, my tone hushed. "The two thugs held us up at gun point and you fainted…"

Jillian twists her head to me with a frown. "I fainted at gunpoint? So now I'm a coward?"

I hold up my hands in surrender. "Okay, stupid story. How about this? As I tossed him my wallet you grabbed your gun and identified yourself and they ran."

She wrinkles her nose with a smirk. "That's better. But it doesn't explain how they still managed to steal the two hundred dollars from your wallet."

I shrug. "Maybe I miscounted. My math skills have never been up to par; otherwise I would be a millionaire by now."

She chuckles. "That's good 'cause I would never want to marry a millionaire."

I open my mouth in surprise. "How did…"

"Don't think I didn't notice how anxious you were at the restaurant, especially when the children were seated at the table behind us."

"Ah," I say, nodding my head.

"And the box-shaped outline in your back pocket. That was pretty obvious."

I raise my eyebrows. "Darn. I guess that wasn't very smart."

She giggles. "No, it wasn't."

We make our way over to the water cooler, which isn't surrounded by other officers or staff members for a change. "I'm confused, though. What kind of girl wouldn't want to marry a millionaire?"

Jillian twists her head from side to side warily before wrapping her arms around my neck and kissing me boldly on the lips. She whispers, "Somewhere in this world there's a ballerina on crack who'd rather go fly a magical kite as long as this magical kite is willing to take her to the ends of the earth instead." She stares at me. "There. What do you say to that?"

I grin wide and take her hand in mine. Then I stretch her arm above us, allowing her to twirl underneath my arm like a glorious ballerina.

"I say, 'I do.'"

LaDonna Cole

Avengel

LYDIA TUCKED her fuchsia bangs behind her heavily studded ear as she leaned over Marc and Mallory, the three-year-old twins she babysat every Friday night. She patted downy blankets and cotton-top heads.

"Wydia, sing a wuwaby!" Mallory begged, her blue eyes twinkling.

"No! I wanna a story 'bout dragons!" Marc insisted.

Lydia giggled, ruffling Marc's flaxen hair. "Why don't I sing a song about dragons?"

"Yay!" the twins sang in unison.

A crash sounded from the kitchen, startling the trio.

Lydia tensed, studied the door, then the twins. "Stay here. I am going to put Fluffy out. I'll be right back."

"I wanna a drink of water!" Marc called.

Lydia moved like a whisper down the dark hall, her heart pounding. This was it. All the preparation—assuming identities in the community, getting this childcare job—culminated in this moment. She dreaded the inevitable massacre that would end this night. It weighed on her soul.

Crunching sounds reached her: boots on glass. She pressed her palms to her thighs to still the shaking. Launching her senses into the kitchen, she sought her prey.

The black soul slammed into her spirit.

Fathomless evil, demonic lust, and acidic hatred streamed back to her from the intruder. She clutched at her stomach. Knotted and twisted agony punched her gut and she staggered against the wall.

Evil. So. Much. Evil.

Lydia slumped against the wall as the onslaught of malicious intent washed over her. Gasping great draughts of air, she melted into a puddle as the heavy darkness pinned her to the floor.

"God, no more," she whispered.

Stop it! she berated herself, but the intensity of dread anesthetized her will.

A shadow eclipsed the doorway. She looked into the face of malevolence magnified. The burglar drew a long jagged knife from his belt, smirking at her.

Unable to move a muscle, Lydia hitched breaths in shallow useless puffs. *Transform, already!* she screamed in her head, but she couldn't even muster up a good static shock.

The burglar descended, knife extended.

A flash of blinding lightning cracked through the hall and sizzled away all the dust particles, causing a rain of lava-colored sparks to shower down around them. Light pierced through a portal. In a blaze of radiance, a towering entity stepped into the hall.

"Repent!" Loren's voice thundered, rumbling through the house. He drew a long, white-hot sword and leveled it at the burglar.

The perpetrator stilled, stunned, with mouth agape. His knife clattered to the floor. "What the—" he screamed viciously.

Loren did not give him time to complete his vile sentence. "So be it!"

The radiant being flashed his sword and cleaved the burglar in two. Dark matter swarmed out of the wound in screaming flight. The body crumpled, pools of blood and entrails from the severed halves gushing to the floor.

Loren sheathed his flaming sword and, with a remnant of crackling energy, flickered into the image of a thirty-year-old man in an army uniform and beret.

"Lydia!" He stepped over the body and knelt by his partner, voice tender and concern on his brow. "What happened?"

Lydia stared at the ceiling, determinedly not looking at the dead body, the warm stench rising to choke her. She trembled, trying to settle her erratic breathing.

"*Lydia!*" His voice rose. "What is wrong with you?" he demanded.

"Loren, I—I can't." She slumped, spent, burned out. Unable to articulate the deep loathing of their assignment, she pressed her fists into her eyes and sobbed.

Loren took her into his arms. "Lydia, angel, what is wrong?" His voice softened by tenderness and compassion, he stroked her hair as she sobbed into his uniform.

"Loren. Loren," she moaned, ancient grief and despair poured into the name. How many centuries, millennia even, had she witnessed such atrocities? Ripped flesh and broken bodies trailed behind her in a gruesome history. The blood of millions stained her soul. It was too much. How could she finish her mission in this god-forsaken world?

God forsaken.

That is exactly what the earth had become. Almighty God had removed his presence from the earth. The dispensation of grace ended. No longer were angels assigned to protect or provide. They existed as warriors, assigned to avenge.

Sent out as pairs, Avengels were commissioned to carry out the vengeance and wrath of the Almighty. She was assigned to this home to take down the evil that walked in the form of a man. A vile man repeatedly refused the call to be reconciled with God.

She failed. She'd frozen.

She let evil assault her, conquer her, defeat her. Loren, her partner, had done what she could not. What she would not do.

No more! A fissure split in her chest and she had the sensation of eternal falling.

What have I done?

WHEN SHE was finally free to leave the Morton's house, after endless interviews with greasy policemen, Lydia found a secluded place where no humans could see, and she shimmered into the Upper.

Loren waited for her.

"Lydia." One word sounded like a sledgehammer to her brain: the accusation, the confusion, and the disappointment colored his tone.

She couldn't meet Loren's gaze as the pressure of despair and self-loathing plummeted to unknown depths. She held up her hands in surrender. "I can't do this."

"Do what? Talk about what happened?"

"No! I can't do this vengeance thing anymore."

Loren furrowed his brow and leaned back. "I don't understand." He ran his hand over his head. "Tell me why you froze, Lydia. That is not like you."

Lydia sighed in resignation, "I can't carry out the mission."

"Yes, you can."

"No, Loren. I won't."

Moral outrage flashed in his eyes. The sword in his scabbard glowed.

"What are you saying? You won't obey the Almighty?" His chiseled jaw clenched and bulged.

"Of course, I will obey. I will do what He commands," Lydia whispered. "I just can't do this. Surely, He will understand how this is killing me." She reached toward Loren, pleading for her eternal battle partner to understand. "He is loving, kind, and good. He will reassign me to a different task."

"Lydia, it's our job. We do not question the Almighty." He took a step away from her.

"*Why not, Loren?*" Lydia snapped at him. "*They* do!" She waved her hand over the blue planet below them.

"They are different."

"Why? Why does He allow them to betray him, disagree with Him, run from Him?"

"Your words are treacherous!" Loren growled through his teeth. "You will refrain from this ignoble speech!" He began to glow in holy fervor and his fingers drifted to the hilt of his sword. He put more distance between them.

"We have been together since Babel, Lydia. Why now? The tribulation of times is nearing an end. Soon He will appear and call us to his side. We will fight the last war and he will be king of all." His face glistened and his eyes sparked as he spoke the dream.

Lydia couldn't muster up any excitement. "I know," she whispered.

"Are you going to fall, Lydia? So near the end?"

"No, Loren, I'm not." Her voice took on an offended and desperate timbre. "I crave His nearness. I've been on this…in this exile since Moses spoke to the fiery shrub."

"You have served valiantly." Loren relaxed slightly, but his sword did not dim.

"I cannot do this avenging thing. Killing them goes against my nature. I am a protector, not this…this…." Words failed her.

"You are a holy warrior, Lydia. You have never shirked the battle." Loren took another step away. "You have always slain the enemy, protected the innocent. Why are you second guessing the mission?"

She believed the assignment was holy and righteous, but the toll was tattooed on her soul in the blood of millions.

"I am going to the throne, Loren. I am going to get us reassigned."

"No."

"No?" Lydia said, bewildered at her partner's attitude. He had been with her all this time. Surely he was feeling the same urges. Needing to be near the Almighty, to bask in His holiness, to worship at His feet, surely Loren of all beings could relate to her great yearning.

"This is a dangerous path you are choosing, Lydia. I will not be a part of it."

"Loren, what are you saying?" Lydia turned to face him directly. "Are you—" She shuddered, her heart splintering to even speak the words aloud, "—*cleaving* us?" The words hovered between them. "After all our time together, we think the same thoughts. We move alike." She stepped forward and he stepped back. "How can you not…." She stopped.

Loren vibrated, crackling with righteous indignation. Instinct was taking over.

"Loren?"

His face blanched, masked in terrible fervor. It frightened her beyond anything she had ever known.

"Run, Lydia, while you have the chance." He forced the words out, his face crumpled in anguish, and tremors wracked through his body.

He began transforming, the edges of his form molten gold and radiating with electricity. He slowly drew his sword and it blazed with an inner light. He trembled until an intense pitch sang from his being.

"Run, now!" he rasped desperately, then exploded into glorious ferocity and gleaming beauty in a dazzling spray of light.

Lydia ran.

AN EAGLE landed on the thumb of the Christ the Redeemer statue in Rio de Janeiro. Lydia, currently in bird form, had been shifting, trying to hide from Loren.

Why had Loren turned on me? Lydia's mind raced. Fear colored her thoughts so vividly she could not sort them. She scanned the view below and above as she perched precariously on the statue and batted her wings to shift her balance. Afraid he would sense her in this eagle form, she phased.

As a tourist standing at the foot of Machu Picchu, Lydia gazed up the steep incline, sorrow etched on her face. *He is hunting me now. If I keep shifting into various forms, maybe I can stay ahead of him. Why, Loren?*

She sensed him near, so she walked behind a stone wall with a brochure shading her eyes, and shimmered.

Lydia, disguised as a fisherman, pulled in his nets as the Mediterranean rocked his boat. He gazed at the blue and white adobe buildings built into the side of the cliff. *If Loren is hunting me, I am in trouble.* She couldn't keep shifting like this from spot to spot, from creature to creature, for long. She had to find a place to hide.

Loren knew her better than she knew herself. He would know exactly where she would go. He was probably waiting there for her, before she even decided where it would be. She felt exposed. Glancing around, she dropped her fishing nets and shifted again.

A turtle sunbathed on a rock beside the Colorado River in the bottom of the Grand Canyon. Lydia realized her locations were getting lower, her transformation choices more primitive. *I have to think differently, unexpectedly. If I am going to lose Loren—ach! An unbearable thought—I will have to do the exact opposite of my instinct.*

A large predator bird flew overhead. His shadow fell across her shell. She felt a jolt of fear and quickly shifted. She couldn't go home to the Upper; Loren would sense her there immediately. She couldn't go to Heaven's throne in case this hunt was an edict from the Almighty. She had to go somewhere so unexpected, so unforeseen that Loren would never follow her there.

Loren would expect her to go higher. Lydia's primary instinct craved the Presence. He would expect her to get as close to that as possible. He would never expect her to base herself, to dive lower. So, that is exactly what she did.

She went to the vilest and most corrupt sub-society she could think of and took the form of the lowest creature she could imagine. Even if he did suspect she had chosen to descend, he would never fathom she would come to this sub-city. He would certainly never expect her to be an insect. If by some off chance he suspected she had become a louse in the beard of a vagrant, he would never find her among the millions of lice in this sewer. If Loren figured out she had gone down, he would not expect her to have fallen this far.

Fallen?

Lydia didn't feel fallen. She felt betrayed. Her heart still yearned for righteousness. Her convictions remained pure. But she could not deny that her present state of being was not a lofty position.

Loren made the whole vengeance assignment seem so easy. She had watched him in wonder as he carried out justice time and again, unscathed, unaffected. How had he made the transition so effortlessly?

Loren, the angel who cradled dying Romanian orphans while she carried others to the throne; Loren, who shielded missionaries from virulent disease while Lydia slew the enemy who attacked them; Loren, who held shut the mouths of the lions while she fought through legions of demons around King Nebuchadnezzar. He had always been the gentle one, while she hacked her way through the enemies of Almighty.

Until this assignment.

When they were commissioned to carry out judgment and wrath, he'd taken the active role in the partnership and she became passive.

How had they come to this, Loren hunting her, ready to take vengeance on her?

In the form of a louse, burrowed in the fetid beard of this homeless man, Lydia had no way to express grief. No tears would come, just the gaping hole eating away at her sanity.

"Hey, Pete. Did you get it?" A voice spoke to her bearded transport.

"Yep. You got the package?" The beard shook violently with each word. She latched onto the tangle of matted hair and peered through the strands to see who was speaking.

"Yeah. You?"

"Right here." The bearded man held up a rumpled paper sack.

She clung to the shaft of hair, not really listening as they haggled over the contents of the paper sack, leading them into deep debauchery. She should burn with indignation, but couldn't muster enough righteous conviction to shock a flea. Grief overwhelmed her. When the quibbling turned into shouts, she tuned back in.

"You can't tell me it ain't no good!" the beard yelled. "I am done with you. We won't be doin' business again!" He waved his hand dismissively.

"You aren't cutting me out," the voice slurred. He whipped a knife out, plunging it into the bearded man's chest.

Instinct consumed Lydia. She burst from the beard in full glory and drew her gleaming sword, towering over the startled vagrant. Collapsing to his knees, he raised an arm to shield the scathing rays beaming from her.

"My God!" he screamed and fell on his face sobbing.

What am I doing? This is going to draw the attention of every angel on the earth!

"*Repent!*" she bellowed.

"Yes, yes, oh God!" The vagrant sobbed violently and began confessing his sin. "Forgive me, Father!"

Lydia felt the glow of a repentant heart and sensed the song rise within her. Soon she would be surrounded by countless angels come to witness the new birth. It took everything in her to turn away from the rapturous spectacle.

As she phased she glimpsed the face of Loren. Standing among countless other angels, he basked in the birth with glowing countenance. Their eyes met the instant she disappeared.

Hiding under a pew in an abandoned chapel, she wept. So few humans repented these days, it was a soul scorching experience when they did. Built into their core, angelic nature lived vicariously through the redeemed.

The glance between her and Loren in that glorious moment unhinged her. For a split second things seemed copacetic between them, then the hardness returned to his eyes and the fear to hers. She curled her cat tail around her body and cried herself to sleep.

Scuttling noises woke her, talons on the marble floor.

The hair on her back prickled and her ears swiveled to and fro.

"I smell it," a scratchy voice whispered.

"What is it?" a deeper voice answered.

Lydia felt snakes writhe inside her head at the sound of the voices. Her battle senses flared.

"I can't tell, it smells…."

"Higher," the second voice finished.

"Call the others."

Thousands, then millions of dark beings descended on the chapel and crept from shadow to shadow.

Almighty!

"*Agh!* Did you feel that?" the first voice gasped.

The demons writhed in disgust and climbed over each other in agitation and frenetic waves. They circled her, malevolent eyes glaring.

Had she ever fought so many on her own? Maybe in '44 at Normandy? No, multitudes battled beside her that day.

I am alone.

Transforming into her glorified being, she drew her sword.

Tall black creatures with smoky charcoal edges and glistening hides, arrayed in unholy armor, stood before her in mass.

"Bright one," the filthiest demon hissed from a malicious grin. "You should not be here." His eyes flicked around the cathedral. "Alone."

The dank vault darkened into omniscient blackness, digesting any glint into endless shadow.

"Then, I'll just be leaving." Lydia knew they would not let her go.

They hissed and chortled. "No, I don't think we can pass up an opportunity to take down one of the Unfallen," the midnight hulk menaced.

"So be it," she pronounced. Raising her sword, she spun around, taking out the closest circle of demons. They sizzled and burst into ash at the touch of her blade.

In a massive tsunami of malevolence, the demon horde descended. She whipped and whirled, slashing and striking. A deluge of black ash thickened the air. The evil creatures oozed out of every shadow, engulfing her in slimy limbs, bulbous genitalia, and granite talons. Their curved blades sliced at her, causing sparks to ricochet and sizzles of energy to flash.

Too many, they seeped under the window ledges, spewed forth from the mouths of statues, misted in from cracks and crevasses, hovering over the ground to rise around her ankles and slow her movements. The more she killed, the more were called forth from some unholy keep.

In one last effort she slammed the sword into the marble floor and flung wide her arms. A dome of blue light exploded and sped away in a sphere of holy purge.

The demons, blown back like black sand, rained down the cathedral walls, thousands decimated in the light blast. She staggered to balance herself for escape, but tenacious talons locked her down. Grasping at her arms, legs, and head, they scraped and gouged until they peeled the sword from her grasp. Dragging her down to the cold marble floor, they drove their sword and spear points deep, draining the energy and light.

Do angels die?

"You have been deceived."

"Omnipotence is a lie."

The demons whispered into her very soul, planting doubt seedlings. Hisses and lies burrowed into her spirit soil. Demons jabbed and twisted their moldy blades and rusty spears. Confusion and doubt erupted inside.

"You have nowhere else to go."

"You are cast out, already."

"Rejected by your false lord."

"Rejected by your partner."

The voices spoke her secret thoughts and deepest fears. *Could it be true? Have I fought so long on the wrong side?*

She let out a piercing wail that seemed to invigorate her captors. They renewed their heckling and spewing with invective vehemence. She struggled to break free, but they continued to twist with weapon and word.

"Give in, Lydia."

"Join the winning side."

"Come over to freedom."

Lydia screamed, "Almighty! *You* are the God! *You* are the God!" The words resounded through her core, the words of truth.

The demons shuddered and roiled in mass agitation at her declaration, pressing as they mounted her. The floor collapsed beneath her. Full of terror, Lydia realized another truth.

Angels do not die. They fall.

Dragged into the very pit of hell, falling without ever making the choice to do so, she closed her eyes and concentrated on the last time she was in the Presence. She would keep that memory for as long as she possibly could, knowing that she was tainted now. Doubt had stained her. She would never be allowed back in His Presence.

The grief of that realization broke over her with heart-wrenching desperation.

"Almighty," she whimpered. "Almighty."

The demons pressed her further and further into despair, pulling from below, pushing from her chest. She descended, her spirit groping for the light but failing to make purchase. The vacuum of darkness wrapped its tentacles, engulfing her.

A SPARK sizzled through the air of the chapel as the portal opened. Loren stepped into the vacant cathedral and noted signs of a great battle. The ashes of fallen demons were an inch thick on every surface, except one.

He walked to the area between the altars, bent a knee, and stroked the marble floor. The warmth of Lydia's radiance lingered in this circle. He threw his head back with a piercing cry that sliced into the Upper realm, a particle wave calling all Avengels. The cathedral filled with holy beings. Hovering in a circle around Loren, they radiated light and fire. The ash dissolved into silver liquid that vibrated and evaporated in the resounding wail.

Loren continued the roar as he raised his sword high into the air and drove it deeply into the marble floor and the lower realm. A crater opened up beneath him. He viewed demons dragging Lydia down to hell, but her spirit continued to grope toward the Presence.

"No!" The howling call mutated into a battle cry and Loren rocketed into the pit. The Avengels wedged it open.

LYDIA OPENED her eyes. The circle widened above her as talons dragged her down. Loren burst through the orifice. Righteous indignation streamed from him.

Did he come to watch me fall? Had he severed ties with her so completely that he wanted to see her degradation for himself? Sorrow shuttered her eyes.

Loren.

Her broken heart could take no more. Surrender lodged in her throat. She choked it back in a determined decision. It didn't matter that Loren had lost faith in her. He remained the Avenging Angel, carrying out the will of the Almighty.

Almighty.

It didn't matter if Almighty had chosen to cast her down. She failed Him, but she'd never stop believing He was the One True God.

She strained to see Loren's face one last time before the fall was complete. It was not his face that captured her. It was his glory. He dove toward her, arms outstretched; lightning bolts sizzled in his wake. His sword, extended in front of him, slashed at her captors.

Rekindled hope sparked as a bolt of lightning struck her from Loren's sword. Certainty replaced doubt. Strength replaced weakness, and Lydia blazed into a glorified state. Side by side, she and Loren burned a path back to the portal and plunged through it as the Avengels slammed the entrance closed.

Silence reclaimed the cathedral, but the radiant witnesses banished darkness.

Lydia slowly turned her eyes to look at Loren, silence ringing in her ears.

"You came?" Her voice broke with relief.

"You didn't fall," he stated simply, touching her cheek. "No fallen angel would have offered repentance to that vagrant. I knew you hadn't fallen in that moment."

Lydia's muscles uncoiled. "I didn't know," she admitted. "I thought maybe I had fallen without choosing to do so."

"There is always a choice. You chose truth, Lydia."

She released a sigh and wiped her eyes, realizing the comfort behind his words.

Loren embraced her in strong arms. "Let's go home."

"You mean?" Lydia pulled back to search his eyes.

"I need to see Him, too."

They sheathed their swords, grasped hands, and shimmered into the Presence.

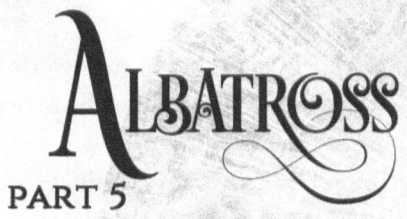

PART 5

"I'LL HELP you on one condition."
I shut the door behind Braydon and
gestured for him to sit.

"Which is?"

"You have to take me with you."

Surprise, confusion, and finally
dread passed over Braydon's face in
quick succession. "What?"

"You have to take me with you
wherever you go."

"But…." He blinked. "But I was
hoping to join the crew."

"What?"

"I was hoping I could join the crew.
That was my ticket away from my father.
Why would you want to leave?"

I bit my lip, but I needed to tell
someone. Not someone, Braydon. I
needed him to understand. "Captain

found me when I was twelve, living as a dock rat here in Central City. I'd been orphaned during the sky raids, and I was a bit of a mess—they didn't even realize I was a girl until they cleaned me up. Captain declared me pretty enough to stay, but said I would have to earn my name like everyone else. My first night, one of the men came to my cabin with evil intentions. I stabbed him with his own blade thirteen times."

"And that's why you're called Warrior?"

I nodded. "Captain's watched me ever since. Blade took me under his wing and protected me from the others, trained me to fight and the like. But everywhere I go I feel Captain's gaze. He's always watching." A shiver ran through me, and Braydon reached out a tentative hand. I pulled away. "Blade's kept Captain away, citing the rules of charter in the New Pirate's Code. As long as I'm a child in their keep, I'm under their protection. My eighteenth birthday isn't until October, but Captain's tired of waiting. He says once the job's done, he's coming for me."

"What do you mean *coming* for you?"

I barked out a laugh at his innocence and sashayed over to him. "I belong to him, Braydon. He's coming to take what's his." I forced myself to meet his gaze and his disgust stifled my ill attempt at humor.

"What are you going to do?" he asked.

I slumped into the chair across from him and dropped my head into my hands. I was left with one option.

"I'm going to have to kill him."

LEXY WOLFE

THE PATH

THE MERCILESS desert sun beat
down on the solitary figure stumbling
through the barren wastelands. Taking
shelter in the shade of a rock overhang,
the young man dropped to his knees,
pressing the heels of his hands against
his temples. The echoes of his tribal
kin's emotions through the *bayuli-volsha* that tied them all, no matter their
distance from each other, rang through
his mind without mercy.

Disapproval, disgust, disappointment, and anger drowned out the love
and worry of his siblings, overwhelming the mental barriers he attempted
to build to protect his aching heart
and wounded soul. With an inartic-
ulate sound of desperation, he drew
the gleaming Naming Blade from its

sheath. He looked at the image of the Totani who granted him his adult name, glittering on the hilt, his whisper harsh. "Forgive me, Kailee. I know not what else to do to be free of him but to sever my tie to the na'Citali tribe." As he slashed his wrists, the clamor of emotions finally went silent.

With a mixture of relief and shame, he watched the pale sand turn red with his lifeblood before he collapsed. A single tear escaped his eye before silent darkness claimed him.

CHILL NIGHT wind and a dissonant shriek awoke the young man. He stared. Silvery moonlight bathed the distinctive form of a drizar, a stallion of the reptilian, horse-like drizzen native to Desantiva's deserts. The momentary fear that the beast would soon turn to rend his flesh from him faded into confusion. Cool light reflected from bronze that capped both horns and claws.

When he attempted to sit up, pain shot from his leather-bound wrists. He could not repress a sound of agony as he fell back onto a sleeping mat. The sloshing sound of water was followed by a water skin being offered to him. He put his hands around the pair holding it. His thirst was nearly as blinding as the pain, driving him to drink first before looking at the person who offered him water.

"Rest." Feral green-gold eyes as hard as a bird of prey's met his. "You lost much blood before I found you," the small woman stated, her Desanti strangely accented. He recognized the distinctive copper-colored skin and bronze-brown hair streaked with copper and gold strands.

"I thought the na'Zhekali tribe had been extinct since I was a boy," he blurted.

The woman's stony expression clouded then hardened. "I have no tribe. I am Githalin Swordanzen."

"*You* are Storm il'Thandar?" She did not answer him, her glare murderous. He held up his hands. "I meant no insult, Githalin Swordanzen." Somewhat mollified, she settled back into a hunter's crouch and ignored him. He offered tentatively, "I am Radisen na'Ci—" He broke off, then sighed, looking away in shame, moving his hands to display his bound wrists. "I am no one. I have no *bayuli-volsha* any longer."

"I know who you are. Thandar told me. Kailee told him." She flicked a look toward him. "The Totani do not forget those who earn an adult name from them, especially when their pain is so great it reaches them in the Rumblelands." She looked out into the night desert. "Nor do they ask for the lives of the unworthy to be saved. It is rare for Citali to reach out to any, but he did for you."

He blinked and looked back at her. "But I tried to kill myself. Suicide is the gravest of sins, especially for a na'Citali."

"You tried to kill yourself? Truly?" She turned her hard gaze back to him. "That is not what Citali told Thandar. Are you saying your tribe's patron Totani or my Githalin Totani are lying?"

Radisen winced and looked away. "No."

She held out her water skin to him. He accepted it without hesitation, taking another long pull on it. With a grimace, he forced himself to sit up, looking back to see he lay on her sleeping mat. "You had been unconscious for several days. Drizar guarded you from scavengers for me while I found water."

"Thank you," he said in a low voice.

Instead of responding to his gratitude, she turned fierce eyes back on him. "Tell me." Callused fingers touched his chin to turn his face toward her, studying his eyes that shifted from tawny brown to gold. "What would drive a su'alin to break his tie to his tribe? To his Path? No one is blind to the dangers of being without *bayuli-volsha*."

"I am not su'alin," Radisen replied with such bitterness Storm frowned. "My spiritwalker vision was impaired when my failure killed my mother. I cannot see the edge of the blade in the dreamscape any longer, which endangers me and any other living soul with me. I cannot serve Desantiva as su'alin. I am nothing but a worthless warrior."

"The Path of the Spirit considers itself above the Path of the Sword?" He could feel the hairs on the back of his neck stand up as she spoke.

"The Alanis would say yes," Radisen replied tonelessly, unable to meet her eyes. "Because we…those gifted by Citali who are able to spiritwalk…can cross the sword's edge between life and death at will, even keep a soul at the edge on this side, while warriors can only send others across the blade from here."

Silence met the statement for so long Radisen spoke a silent prayer in preparation to meet his life's end, both for the insult to her about warriors and to give him a merciful end for his failure. Yet still nothing happened. "Perhaps he is right in part," Storm stated with thoughtful, almost sad tones. He looked up in shock, staring at her profile as she gazed into the desert. "I would give much if my skills could preserve life as much as protect it from itself.

"But a warrior is not worthless. No one is worthless if they serve our great father through living life to its fullest and striving each day to be better than the day before." The brief glimpse of loneliness vanished behind a hardened veil. "To think otherwise is an insult to Him."

He started to reach out to touch her cheek, but stopped, letting his hand drop to his lap. The faintest strands of hope stirred within him as he contemplated her words. "I would serve the great father as you do, Githalin Swordanzen. The Path of the Spirit is closed to me. Would I be welcome to the Path of the Sword?"

"You cannot train to become Swordanzen without a tribal bond. When a Swordanzen is Named by the Totani, they sacrifice the *bayu-li-volsha* so they can sense the nuances within the land and from all living things equally. Few can endure for longer than five turns of the sky wheel once worthy to carry the sword. They either lose the will to survive or give up their swords to regain a tribal bond.

"As you are now, training would steal valuable time from your service to Him. Nor would you be welcome to share the *bayuli-volsha* with those in either the settlement of elders in First Home or the settlement of Citadel's protectors where those who give up the sword or those born to them call home." She took his hand and lifted it to regard the bound wrist. "They would see disgrace, not the suffering you had endured that drove you to this."

His shoulders sagged. "Then I beg of you, Githalin Swordanzen. Kill me. If I cannot serve the great father as either Su'alin or Swordanzen, I have nothing left. Only outcasts would accept me and I could not live with that shame."

"I did not say you could not become Swordanzen ever," Storm stated sharply. "I said you need a tribal bond so you do not go mad from the isolation." She pointed to the sleeping mat. "Sleep. You must recover your strength. I must think." Still weak from exposure and blood loss, Radisen lay down, eyes closing in sleep the moment his head touched the mat.

"IF YOU think he has potential, of course I would take him as my student," a muted male voice stated as Radisen roused. He slit open his eyes to watch the two speakers, noting the man wore a Swordanzen Naming blade as Storm did.

"I would not suggest it if I did not believe it, Chase." Storm's voice held the full measure of her impatience and irritation. "Once the Alanis Su'alin restores his tribal bond, I know he will do well in your care."

Chase grinned with impudence. "You know I would never question your judgment, *th'yala*." She snorted at his words. His levity faded into concern as he put a hand on her arm. "You are upset. Why? Because of him?" Radisen closed his eyes when Chase gestured toward him, slowly opening them when sure they were not looking at him.

"How much did the Alanis Su'alin make his own son suffer that he would seek death and loss of his soul to escape?" Storm seethed, her fury so great Radisen could see she trembled in the dim light of the approaching dawn. "I would give everything I am to have my tribe back and he was driven from his? If I did not know Radisen would protect that horrible man, I would—"

Chase quickly put his arms around Storm, pulling her tight against him as he hushed her. "Dwelling on his torment will only lead you to remembering your own tragedy. I would not wish you to suffer reliving those deaths again, especially if Thandar cannot come to save you from becoming lost in the past. Or for any other to suffer your vengeful rage if your self-control slips. The Alanis sounds arrogant enough to challenge your worthiness to bear Thandar's mark."

"I live with the massacre of the na'Zhekali every day, Chase," she stated without inflection, letting him hold her. "I have since it happened. My self-control will not slip." She heaved a sigh. "But you are right. Only my tribe's murderers deserve to taste my vengeance and Radisen's sire will tempt me."

"Of course I am right." He reached over to take his sleeping mat off his gear, handing it to her. "Get some sleep. I'll keep watch with that beast of yours." The drizar looked away from the female drizzen he nuzzled to hiss at Chase, baring his teeth. The Swordanzen man merely returned the gesture in kind, the animal rewarding him with a derisive snort and kicking dirt towards him with his back foot.

Waiting several minutes, Chase looked at the woman once certain she was asleep. "You don't need to stand so alone, my *th'yala*. I would travel with you always if it would spare you a fraction of the solitude you have suffered for so long."

Radisen closed his eyes, his fists clenching. "She is more alone than I have ever been."

"I AM Githalin Swordanzen Storm il'Thandar! I demand to speak to the Alanis Su'alin. Now!" In response to the strident voice nearly drowned out by the drizar's challenging bugle, heads poked out of the many tents comprising the na'Citali's encampment.

"Radisen!" a delicate girl wearing a traditional Su'alin veil cried, bolting from the tent to leap into the young man's arms. A boy a few years younger than the errant na'Citali son followed her at a slower pace, but no less worried and relieved to see him. "Oh, Radisen, we were so afraid when we could not hear you anymore. We thought you died!"

"I'm sorry, Kiya, Rengi," he said gruffly, eyes closed tight as his younger sister and brother embraced him. "I'm so sorry for leaving you both."

A tall man wearing robes with ornate beading denoting his position and an opulent veil hiding his eyes strode out. Chase narrowed his eyes, about to chide the man on the barely respectful bow he offered Storm. He remained silent when Storm held up a hand. He rubbed his drizzen's chin and muttered, "Arrogant prig."

The Alanis looked Storm over and grunted. "What is it you wish of the na'Citali, Githalin Swordanzen?" he asked bluntly in the Swordanzen holy tongue, offering no welcome.

Storm's gaze met his, unwavering. Replying in flawless, fluent Swordanzen, Storm's voice was almost casual, but the words themselves belied the edge beneath them. "Uncover your eyes. I will not speak to a coward."

The man stiffened, flipping the veil back over his head. "You dare call me a coward?"

"You dare think yourself above Thandar's chosen?" she responded, her tones still conversational so the other members of the tribe who kept a respectful distance could not hear them. "What is there for a Cursed child to fear from the likes of you? I had experienced death for each member of my tribe killed in the na'Zhekali tribal massacre."

"And the great father still allowed you to live?" he asked critically.

"You dare question Him?" She gestured absently toward the huddled siblings. "Radisen wishes to choose to follow the Path of the Sword. I ask you, as the na'Citali chieftain, to restore his *bayuli-volsha* until the Totani deem him worthy to bear their sword."

"No." The man stared down at the smaller woman, his eyes tawny brown. "He made his choice when he turned his back on his tribe. His family. Let him suffer for—" He paled when Storm's expression shifted, unable to resist taking a half step back from her.

"Look at me with Citali's gift, Alanis Su'alin," she stated in danger-ous tones. "I am the daughter of the Heart of Desantiva, chosen Githalin of Thandar the Golden. I alone survived the massacre of the na'Zhekali. I know death in ways you best pray you never, ever have to experience.

"The Totani do not judge you, but I do. You claim your son turned his back on you, but I know. I do not need Citali's gifts to see it in his eyes. You turned your back on him first. Even worse, you used your influence to turn the tribe on him, too. You spurned him and turned the blessing of the tribal bond into a curse to punish him every day until he could bear no more and did the unthinkable to escape. What sort of chieftain turns on one of his tribesmen? What sort of father turns on his own flesh and blood? I should rip your heart out through your ear for failing him.

"But I won't." She closed the gap between them, hissing at him. "I am slave to no one, divine or mortal. You live only because your son begged me to forgive you for your grief at the loss of his mother and Citali asked you be spared. Do not think I will forget. I certainly do not forgive." She stepped back and demanded, "Restore the *bayuli-volsha*, or you will join him in the lack."

Despite having a darker skin color than Storm or Chase, the tall, broad-shouldered man was sickly pale at the unvarnished threat he could not deny she was capable of fulfilling. "As you wish, Githalin Swordanzen." He turned to Radisen, as much in obedience as desperation to get away from the dangerous woman glaring at his back. "Radisen," he stated, drawing his knife and cutting his palm.

Unsure, Radisen nevertheless echoed his sire's actions, grimacing when the man grabbed his cut hand in a hard grip. He felt the tension across his shoulders ease as the bond was restored. Without a word, the Alanis spun away and returned to the tents.

"Say your farewells, Radisen," Storm stated in curt tones. "We ride for the Citadel to formalize your acceptance as Swordanzen trainee."

"Yes, Githalin Swordanzen." Radisen looked to his brother and sister then closed his eyes, turning his face away in shame. "Forgive me for not being stronger," he whispered.

"Are you sure this is what you want to do?" his sister asked, her worry and love for him untarnished. "No matter what Father insists on believing, Citali knows the truth. What happened when Mama died was not your fault."

"I am certain. I cannot be Su'alin, but I will serve Desantiva. One way or another. If not through the Path of the Spirit…" He looked over his shoulder toward Storm as she checked her drizar's saddle straps. "Then I will through the Path of the Sword."

His brother frowned, crossing his arms. "No na'Citali has ever followed the Path of the Sword. What if you don't succeed?"

"I will succeed, Rengi," he stated evenly, putting his hand over his heart. "I know I will because I know the Heart of Desantiva believes in me. Because she believes in me." His bitterness echoed in his expression, posture, and tone when he looked toward the encampment. "More than Father ever has since Mother died saving me."

Rengi narrowed his eyes. "Are you doing this because you want to be a Swordanzen, or want her?"

Radisen glared at Rengi, clenching his fists. "Don't you dare criticize Storm il'Thandar! You know nothing about her. She has suffered more than you can imagine."

"Stop it!" With a kick to his shin, Kiya scowled up at the younger brother. "You are sounding like Father. We nearly lost Radisen because all Father did was hurt him!"

"Fine, fine." Rengi held his hands up in surrender. "Sorry, Radisen. Besides…" He looked toward the pair of waiting Swordanzen. "I like the idea that warriors are seen with greater value beyond our tribe. Father does not allow us to interact with outsiders unless it is as Su'alin, and I have no spiritwalker gifts."

Kiya hugged Rengi's arm. "It doesn't matter if you don't have Citali's blessing. You and Radisen mean everything to me. I'd be all alone without you since everyone else is afraid of me for my gift being active since birth and not only from my fifth birthday." Rengi sighed and nodded, trading a sad, knowing look with his brother at Kiya's isolation.

Radisen touched Kiya's cheek gently. "Be strong, little sister. You know if you need me, I will sense you through the *bayuli-volsha*. I will come to you."

"Until you become Swordanzen and your bond to the na'Citali becomes a bond to all Desantiva, at least. I know." She hugged him fiercely tight then released him. "I hope you find what you seek. I just wish it would have been with our tribe and us." Rengi clasped his brother's hand tight for a moment before the pair turned to return to the encampment.

Radisen watched them leave then turned to join Storm and Chase. Squaring his shoulders, he joined the two Swordanzen. "I am ready to leave, Githalin Swordanzen Storm, Swordanzen Chase."

Storm mounted the crouching drizar, thumping his shoulder. The beast stood, shaking his head and prancing arrogantly. She looked at Radisen and he thought he glimpsed sadness in her eyes. "I know." She looked forward. "I am glad I could return your family to you."

"But what about you?" he began, reaching out to her.

Chase rode his drizzen over, offering his hand to Radisen to help him mount behind him. "To dedicate yourself to the Path of the Sword is to choose to separate yourself from those you care most about to protect them."

"But who protects the protectors?" Radisen asked as he settled behind his trainer. "Who protects her?"

Chase laughed sadly. "Who indeed? The Great Father knows I try my best. It is difficult for someone like her who has been alone for so long to let anyone close enough to protect her." He looked over his shoulder. "You would understand."

Radisen closed his eyes. "Yes. I do understand her. Far too well." He clenched his fists, ignoring the pull on the mending gashes hidden beneath the leather wrapping his wrists. "I will not fail. Then she will not be alone."

AMBER E. BOX

MISS ABERSHIRE

I WROTE when I was scared. It was all I knew to do—writing. It kept my fears firmly on the white paper before me rather than running loose around my head. Tonight the lamplight flickered across the walls of my room, if you could even call it that. It was a far cry from the streets of downtown New York City. The space, more reminiscent of a broom closet, was located in the farthest corner of Miss Abershire's home on Woolwillow Lane in a small town in New Hampshire. Here, hidden away, I scrawled furiously under the scattered dance of amber light.

My name is Olive Henrietta Bell, but I go by Henri. Miss Abershire nearly ran over me with her horse carriage while on a business outing in New York City last fall.

"What on earth are you doing in the streets, child?" she yelled at me, patting the horses' hindquarters to calm them down.

"I'm sorry, Miss. I was just headed home from…work," I lied. She knew it too—the old remnants of bread in my hands and the layer of black dirt that coated my clothing gave me away. Or perhaps it was the lack of shoes…one can never really be sure.

"Really? And where might that be?" she said as she stepped down from her carriage.

"I, uh…just down this path here. I'm sorry, but I must be going now."

I turned to run, but she had a firm grip upon my arm before I could get a foot in front of me.

"Not so fast, little child. Come with me."

"Am I in trouble? It was an accident, I do swear it."

"Never mind that, come along." She hoisted me up onto the carriage seat next to her and handed me a thick wool blanket.

"There you go, use this since you haven't a coat."

She seemed harmless enough and I didn't have any better options, so I accepted.

"Thank you, ma'am," I said hesitantly, not yet sure if I should trust her completely. "May I ask where we are going?"

"Briarcliff, New Hampshire. That is unless you have somewhere else to be here in New York, a home perhaps?" She looked at me from the corner of her eyes, her brows lifting as though she was waiting for the next lie to sputter out of my mouth. I remained silent. From that night on, Miss Abershire took me under her wing, teaching me words I had never learned, how to read and sew and cook. I felt like her daughter, one that she told me she always wanted.

Miss Abershire was at the town meeting—third one this month since Clara Taylor went missing. She told me that the town's patience was beginning to thin since the search for Clara had yet to turn up any evidence. At church, people talked, and it was clear that they were beginning to point the blame at Miss Abershire. Mayor Thomason asked for calm among the residents of Briarcliff, for prayers that Clara be found, and for faith that the person responsible be brought to a mighty justice. That was his way of calling for a swift trial and a rather public hanging of those involved.

At last week's meeting, the town took to attacking Miss Abershire and myself in person. "It's that damned girl that ole' Miss Abershire took in. She's not from here. You can't trust her—she's just a street urchin from the big city," hollered the old man from a back pew at the First Protestant Church.

"Have you seen her? She's just a runt! It's not possible for her to have done it. At least not on her own," cried someone from the other side of the main aisle.

I had ducked my head, trying to avoid the glares and, somehow, the accusations, but they just kept coming.

"Then she must've had help! One of those other homeless brats she's taken in over the years. Just last summer she had that burly redheaded boy…"

"Maybe an animal got to her," someone else interrupted. "Could've been a wolf or a bear."

"That's not likely, Jonathon. Bears don't frequent this part of the state, and if a wolf had gotten to her, we'd have found her body by now."

Wails arose sporadically from across the church, though none came from the front row where Clara Taylor's father sat. Her mother had died just a few years ago, under questionable circumstances. William, her father, staring blankly at nothing in particular, had said she had been kicked by their mare, but Miss Abershire told me she doubted that to be the truth.

"It's that girl, I tell you," said the old man rising in anger. He pointed a stiff finger at me. "The Abershire charity case of the month!"

"Excuse me gentlemen, but I will not stand idly by as you accuse me or this poor girl of such atrocity," said Miss Abershire. "She doesn't even leave the house except to tend to the garden and go to church with me. She is nothing but kind and sweet. I took her in so she wouldn't be left to die on the streets from the cold. If there is something the matter with acting like a good Christian, then I beg you to call upon your god for mercy at Judgment because you certainly don't serve *my* God."

I grinned as she took me by the arm and led me out of that church for what I had yet to learn would be the last time.

This time, I didn't attend. There was nothing good about a small town with scared and angry residents. In fear, Miss Abershire locked me in here. The room grew dim as my lamp neared the end of its wick. Placing my pen on the desk, I slid my journal underneath the dumpy mattress that served as my bed. Truth be told, it is the most comfortable thing I have slept on since I can remember. Crawling underneath my wool blanket, I listened for the slam of the front door, signaling that Miss Abershire had made it back home safely. I had strict directions from Miss Abershire to not speak while she was away, should someone be hovering around the house trying to prove their suspicions. I curled in a ball beneath the blanket and waited in the dark silence. On the bed across the floor from me, Clara Taylor did the same.

Miss Abershire returned as the chill began to set in. She lit a fire and unlocked the bedroom door.

"Are you both all right?" she whispered. "I'm terribly sorry for having left you in the cold for so long."

"We're ok," I said sitting up, the blanket still wrapped around me like I had done the first night I met her. "What happened at the meeting?"

"It's tense, likely to become a mob soon enough. We must take precautions."

"What kind of precautions?"

"I'm not sure yet, but we may have to leave town."

I nodded as Miss Abershire lowered her head. My heart ached to know that Miss Abershire would have to give up her life here to protect us, though I was sure that she was more concerned with our safety than her memories in this town.

"Clara," said Miss Abershire in matronly tone. "Are you sure this is what you want to do, child?"

For the first time all evening, Clara spoke. Her words were raspy through heavy tears.

"Yes, Miss Abershire. I can't stay here. I don't know what he will do to me the next time he has me alone."

"There won't be another time. Don't you worry. That settles it. We will go. First thing in the morning."

"Yes, Ma'am," we said in unison. When she left, the two of us huddled together on my bed and talked about what our future might hold.

She was only three years younger than me, but at twelve years old she was very wise. Perhaps it was a result of what she had endured with her father, the abuse and the bruises. The day Miss Abershire happened upon Clara, she was headed to Mr. Taylor's market down on Main Street. I remember it well. We had run out of cream for her famous banana cream pie. I stayed home and cut the bananas while Miss Abershire went. When she blasted through the back door of the small clapboard house, I dropped the knife I was holding, nearly taking off a finger in the process. She came around the corner, her dress swishing around her legs in a flurry. That's when I noticed a mop of matted blonde hair peeking through the cotton fabric. My eyes widened as I recognized the eyes that peered over the protective arm of Miss Abershire. Clara Taylor, in the flesh. I had seen her once before at church in her beautiful taffeta Sunday best. This time, a tattered dress, matted with a dark red substance, replaced her normally perfectly pressed gown. Her face shone with marks of blue and purple. Tears streamed down her face, leaving streaks of dirt mirroring the stripes in her dress.

"Oh my goodness, Clara! What happened to you?"

"Never mind that, Henri. Get us some towels and the alcohol please."

I ran to do as instructed while Miss Abershire brought her into my bedroom. I returned with the requested supplies and helped to clean up Clara's wounds.

"Shut the door please, Henri. We must keep our voices down. He's probably looking for her already."

I wondered who "he" was and what he had done to poor Clara as I silently drew the door closed.

"How long has he been doing this to you?"

Through sobs she answered, "Since he lost the farm a few years ago. Mostly he targeted Momma, but since she's been gone he has been going after me."

"I knew that wasn't an accident," said Miss Abershire said under her breath. "You poor dear," she said as she held Clara to her chest.

I now knew what had happened and who "he" was.

"Don't worry, Clara. Miss Abershire will keep you safe here. She has a kind heart. You needn't worry," I said, wiping her tears.

With Clara's father refusing to believe she was dead, the search for her was continuing to increase daily, as was his anger. As suspicions grew, so did the finger pointing, but somehow they always ended up pointing at us—at me. It was a witch-hunt, and I was their witch. My faith, however, rested with Miss Abershire. She had saved me in the past, taking me in when I had no place to go. I owed my life to her. She was a warrior for those of us who could not stand on our own, and I knew she would keep us safe now.

I sat up, seeing the red glow of torchlight bouncing through the tiny window of my room long before I heard the grumbles of something about to go terribly wrong. Miss Abershire burst into the room in her nightgown.

"Get up! Get up! We must go now. Grab your coat, there's no time for anything else. Henri, I packed a bag of food and supplies, it's already on the carriage. Take the wool blanket and grab the old coffee canister. Go and get the horses ready to leave!"

I jumped out of bed, lifting the mattress to grab the stories I had hidden there over the last year, and bolted out of the room. I heard Miss Abershire giving final instructions to Clara as I made my way into the kitchen.

"Hurry, Clara. Come with me," said Miss Abershire. When we get out to the carriage, you will lie on the floor beneath our feet. Do not make a sound or this will all be for naught."

My heart pounded as I watched the angry flames spark into the dark sky. Miss Abershire made it out right behind me, just in time for

Clara to slip down to the floor of the carriage. I covered her with my wool blanket as smooth as I could, so as not to give her position away. Saying a prayer, I hopped into the seat next to Miss Abershire, but it was too late. The mob had already surrounded us.

"Where might you be headed at this ungodly hour?"

"Out of here. This madness is beyond my control and I cannot trust that Henri and I will remain safe should we stay here."

"Got a guilty conscience, have ya, Miss Abershire?" said Mr. Taylor. "Where's my daughter? I know you and that dirty little stray of yours have done something to her."

"I have not!" she insisted defiantly as she slapped the reins for the horses to move forward. "Though you'd be careful to keep your hands off the next woman you see, as that appears to be your method as of late."

His face reddened as he stood beneath the dancing flames of his torch.

"Now wait here just a minute," said Mayor Thomason, stepping in front of the horses with his hands raised to their heads. "Are you suggesting that Mr. Taylor has hit you before?"

"No, Sir. Not myself," she said, realizing that she had just given herself away to Mr. Taylor.

"Then someone else?"

"I cannot be sure but of what I know in my heart. Now let me pass. I have done nothing wrong."

"Then I don't suppose you mind us looking around your home, do ya?"

"Be my guest," said Miss Abershire.

The moment we saw the smoke rising from the room, she hit the reins and took off into the darkness. The glow of torches and the grumblings of angry men trailed in the dust behind us. Once we were over the hills and sure that no one was following us we stopped along the side of a road. Helping Clara out of her hiding spot beneath our feet, I noticed her face was wet with tears. We sat for what seemed like ages beneath a black velvet sky, huddled together—trying to determine what to do next.

I rifled through supplies, trying to take stock of what we had.

"Careful with the coffee canister, Henri."

"What's in it?" I asked, hearing the rattling as I gently shook the can.

"Money. I've been saving it for quite a long time now. You never know when one might need to flee at a moment's notice."

Smiling, I tucked the can under the seat as far as possible.

"My mother's cousin lives in Vermont. We could go there. I don't know that we could stay long though," offered Clara.

"Well at the very least, it would give us some time to get ourselves together," replied Miss Abershire.

I watched the wrinkles around her eyes deepen as she rolled the idea around in her head.

"Hmm, what about your father? Would he contact her?"

"Doubtful. She was very close to my mother, and even if he did, I don't think she would give us away. She didn't much care for my father," said Clara.

"Do you know how to get there?"

"I remember the name of the town, Maple Ridge. That's all."

"Well, if we can make our way into Vermont, surely someone will point us in the right direct…"

Miss Abershire was interrupted by the faint sound of hooves on the hard ground.

"They're coming!" Clara cried, her green eyes widening with fear.

"Quiet! Get down below. Hurry!" whispered Miss Abershire.

I covered Clara up with the wool blanket, just as I had done before. Miss Abershire jumped down from the bench and grabbed the horses, leading them into the dense forest that lined the roads. Moving back as far as we could off the main trail, we were forced to stop where the forest thickened into a black tangled mass of limbs and shadows. Huddling down by Clara, we hid as best we could. Though not entirely hidden, in the darkness, we were near impossible to see. Closing my eyes, I listened to the thunder of hooves closing in on us and I prayed again in silence. The trees shook as the train of angry men rode by, stopping just yards from our own horses.

"We lost their trail, Thomason. They couldn't be far from here."

"When I find them, I'm gonna kill that ole' Abershire bat and that street urchin too!"

The familiar bellowing of Mr. Taylor caused shivers down my spine. I felt the hot sting of tears seep through my clenched eyelids as I held my breath. Miss Abershire must have felt my fear radiating across to her. Reaching out, she gripped my hand tightly, and it was enough to quell the panic bubbling inside of me.

"They must have gone the other way at the fork just outside of town."

The trees shook again as the gang picked back up the search, turning back toward Briarcliff. A collective sigh was let out from all of us as we untangled ourselves from our crouched positions. Clara and I piled back onto the bench of the carriage and waited until the pounding of hooves was out of earshot. Once it was safe, Miss Abershire pulled us out from the woods and back onto the road. Hopping back into the carriage, she put her arm around each of us, pulling us in close, and kissed us each on the forehead.

"As long as you are in my care, you will be safe."

I thought about her house, the ashes that probably now remained of her whole life, the risks she took, and the memories she gave up to protect Clara and me. My face flushed with emotions that I can only remember writing about, and though she couldn't see me in the dark, a quick pat on the hand told me that Miss Abershire knew.

"To Vermont we go," she said with a grin.

With that, she slapped the reins and the carriage took off once again into the void in front of us.

S.R. KARFELT

LITTLE GIRL ACCOST

FOSTER CARE, NEW MEXICO
1980

"GIRL, I'VE never had anyone thrown out of school in first grade before. Did you break that boy's finger on purpose too?"

Marsha had the kind of eyes that knew if you were lying. Not that Carole lied. "It doesn't matter to the Thatcher's either way," the social worker continued. "They won't put up with any sort of trouble. I just need to know, so I can pick your next place."

"Yes," Carole whispered, admitting she'd thrown the dodgeball at Jimmy West to hurt him. The voices didn't like that she told Marsha, even if it was true. *"Never tell what you can do! They will destroy you!"* Dark dreams rolled through her head making sure she understood. She had to squint to see past them. "I shouldn't have hit him so hard."

"You shouldn't have hit him at all. You're not going to be able to go to school at Vista anymore. That's not the kind of thing a boy will forget."

Marsha put her straw handbag on her desk and pointed at a chair beside it. She didn't have an office like the other social workers, just an old green metal desk sitting in the hall nearly right outside the bathroom. Carole sat in the chair, and Marsha nodded at a man as he passed on the way to the men's room.

The man said hello to Marsha in the same pretend friendly voice that the Thatcher's used to talk to their foster children in front of other grownups. Carole wrapped her arms around her legs, goose bumps making all the little hairs stick up. *Duke will have nobody to run the desert with.* The edges of her heart burned. She would have nobody to run the desert with. Duke had Earl.

Marsha waited to talk until the man passed by again. "Isn't that your old uniform? Do you wear that every day?"

Carole nodded and smoothed her orphanage uniform over her knees and rested her head on them. Who cared about dresses? The dark dreams were being mean and punishing her.

Marsha flipped through the files for a while before she spoke again, forcing Carole to look up. "There's a new couple. They only want one child, and they prefer a boy, but I'll see what I can do." She stood and picked up a folder and pen. "I have to go down the hall to use the phone in Mr. Kraus's office. Behave yourself. You promised to give me a chance to find you a home. I'm holding you to that."

Carole didn't think Marsha could find her a home, but she had promised to give her a chance and she hated to think what the voices would do if she broke a promise. Tucking her hands beneath her armpits she leaned back in the chair frowning, wishing she'd never made that promise to her social worker, wishing she could find a place to belong all by herself.

THE HEAT from the metal gate burned faintly through her tee-shirt. Carole jammed her new sneakers through the chain link and used her body to swing to and fro. The gate squeaked pleasantly. One long blonde braid swung back and forth with her, and Carole gnawed on the other, liking the way it crunched between her front teeth. Her eyes focused on the dusty arc the swinging gate cut through the dirt below.

"*¡Hijole! Güera.* Don't chew your hair, you'll ruin it." Mrs. Nickels pulled the end of the braid from Carole's mouth. "I'm going to the grocery store. Stay outside until I get back." She pushed the gate open wider and slid her round body out. Rosa Nickels' bright red toenails came into Carole's line of vision as she passed. Mrs. Nickels flung the gate wider and Carole clung tightly as it bounced against the fence. Mrs. Nickels chuckled. "Remember what I said, Niña, and be a good girl."

The Nickels' tiny house sat at the end of a long row of tiny houses. Each one had a chain link fence all the way around, with an alley running behind them. At night Carole liked to sneak out the window of her very own bedroom and run up and down that alley as fast as she could. Tonight, when it was cool, she would slip out her bedroom window and walk on top of the fence in her bare feet. Maybe she'd walk on top of all the fences in the neighborhood. Nobody watched her at night; she could run as fast as she wanted. The voices didn't mind then.

Balancing on top the gate, Carole teetered on her stomach, arms straight out at her sides and legs splayed. She watched Mrs. Nichols sway up the sidewalk. Shimmering waves of heat blurred her edges.

"Don't that burn you, girlie?" The screen door creaked and Mr. Nickels came outside. He waddled from side to side, but he wasn't big like Mrs. Nickels, just tired.

Carole shook her head, but as she balanced on the hot metal she decided that maybe that wasn't all the way true. Using her big cotton shirt to protect her hands, she climbed on top the gate to stand, balancing easily in her new sneakers. Holding her arms out, because the voices didn't like if she made it look too easy, she stepped lightly from the gate to stand on the fence, admiring the ease of movement provided by her new shorts. Mrs. Nickels had let her pick them even though they were boy's shorts, and she bought them with her own money because she spent all Carole's money on good food.

Mr. Nickels dragged an old metal chair across the porch, to the shady part. Sitting down, he leaned back and closed his eyes. "Don't that sun make your head ache? I'll never get used to this heat." Mr. Nickels worked nights at the railroad, and tried to sleep during the day, but he was always too hot. He didn't like the desert.

During the day the neighborhood stayed mostly empty, so Carole spit on her hands, rubbed them together and grabbed the fence, flipping over and off. She landed upright on the dusty ground. The voices didn't say much about it, so Carole did it again. Mr. Nickels watched her from the porch. "You're right good at that, girlie."

Pleased with the praise, Carole tried it rolling through the air twice and landed in a small puff of dust. Mr. Nickels seemed impressed but the voices told her not to show off, so she settled for a handstand, walking a few steps through the dirt until a wayward cactus spine dug into her hand.

Standing, Carole put her hand in her mouth, trying to suck it loose.

"Everything in this entire state bites or stings, girlie. Come inside and I'll tweeze it out for you. Your bread is about finished baking anyway."

Mr. Nickels shuffled back through the screen door and she could hear him banging around in the kitchen. Mrs. Nickels had used the recipe that Carole's dad had left for her, for good bread that the voices let her eat. Mr. Nickels said cooking in the oven in summer made the house so hot, it had better be good. Carole hadn't had a bite of that bread since her last birthday at the orphanage.

She headed for the porch steps. "*Stay outside until she comes back,*" the voices piously recited Mrs. Nickels' words. Carole wavered. The aroma of that bread drifted hot and delicious on the air. Besides, the cactus needle deep in the palm of her hand hurt. Mrs. Nickels wouldn't mind if she went in to get that fixed. The voices grumbled when she passed through the swinging door, mildly protesting disobedience against Mrs. Nickels.

The loaf of Carole's bread sat cooling in the middle of the kitchen table on the cutting board. The glass loaf pan it had baked in sat on the table too. Mr. Nickels hadn't put it on a potholder and it sank into the plastic tablecloth. Carole grabbed a tea towel and moved it to rest on the newspaper. The melted plastic stuck to the glass some.

Mr. Nickels took butter from the refrigerator. "Rosa will give me what for, but that smells too good to wait for dinner. If we just eat the ends, we probably won't get in too much trouble."

Slicing through dark, nutty bread, he plopped a big piece on a plate for Carole. He cut a chunk of butter and dropped it on top. It melted into one mouth-watering spot in the quick second it took to shove the plate toward Carole.

She knelt on the chair and crossed herself. "Thank you."

"You're welcome," Mr. Nickels said, though Carole hadn't been talking to him. He stood beside her in his work pants and undershirt, rubbing his hand over his heart. Carole wished she could touch his heart with hers, like she used to do to Mom and Gran before they went away and left her alone. In the hazy, warm kitchen with Mr. Nickels shuffling to and fro, Carole tried to. She let her heart go open and searching as she reached for her bread. It seemed like Mr. Nickels noticed because he stopped moving to stare at her with his friendly puppy eyes, and he snatched her right hand to squint at it, trying to see the cactus spine.

"Let's not have that hurtin' you, girlie. It's swelling up some." Taking the seat next to her, he jabbed at her hand with tiny tweezers. It only pinched at her skin and made it redder. "Did I get it? It's in there deep."

Carole shook her head.

"That thorn is big, you poor thing." Mr. Nickels rubbed his fingers over the spot, driving it deeper. Bemused, he put her palm to his mouth and tried to suck it out.

Carole's mouth popped open as the voices protested with an almighty shout that made her eyes water. *"Stop him!"* She tried to pull her hand away, but Mr. Nickel's job at the railroad gave him strong ropey muscles and he held tightly, his dark brows bunched together in concentration. Carole felt his teeth and the voices bellowed, vibrating in her head. *"Too close!"* Panic shot through Carole as the voices shouted, and visions of women screaming as men held their wrists filled her mind. She tugged again, politely but firmly, but Mr. Nickels didn't seem to even notice.

"Protect yourself. Danger. Run!"

Horrible images flashed through her mind. Carole did not want to see them. Reaching across the table, she grabbed the hot glass pan. It burned her fingertips as she swung it against Mr. Nickels' face. Hard.

His eye had swollen shut before Marsha came to get her.

IN THE green chair at Child and Youth Protective Services, Carole again wrapped her arms around her legs. Goose bumps made little hairs stick up on her arms and legs and she wiped her palm back and forth over the arm of the chair, trying to erase the feel of Mr. Nickels' mouth.

"Did he hurt you?" Marsha's chocolate eyes watched closely. They were worried.

"He licked my hand." The voices had shown where that would lead. Carole shuddered.

Smoothing her pink dress, Marsha sat in her chair. She scooped a folder off a tall pile of them and opened it up, staring at it for a few moments. Then she looked at Carole again. "He said you had a sliver he was helping with."

Resting her head on her knees, Carole didn't respond. She couldn't tell Marsha about the voices or dark dreams.

"I will believe what you tell me." Marsha rested her chin on her hand, and waited until Carole looked at her eyes. "Between you and me and the breadbox, I'm not going to say you shouldn't have done what you did—depending on what he did, but Carole, sometimes—most of the time—like with that little Jimmy West boy—you could tell an adult what the problem is instead of hurting people. It's an adult's job to help you, it's my job. Did Mr. Nickels make you that uncomfortable? Or could you have maybe told him he was upsetting you before you hit him?"

Carole turned her gaze back to her hand as she rubbed it against the cloth chair. The splinter shoved in deeper, but she didn't care. Marsha kept staring with her big dark eyes, and the voices were still riled and shouting at Carole to hide. "*She senses too much! Distract her!*"

"I had to stop him," said Carole, trying to breathe deep without Marsha seeing it, trying to tuck her heart inside her body when it felt like it wanted to press against someone else's heart and hide there. Would they all act like Mr. Nickels if she did? She wasn't really afraid of him, but she was afraid of what the voices said he might do.

"Are you telling me that giving a grown man a concussion was your only option, little missy?"

"Yes."

Marsha took a deep breath, but she let it out quietly too. Sitting up straight in her chair, she dug through folders on the desk. "We're going to try a group home this time. It's in a different school district, but you might do better in a bigger environment. Remember you promised to give me a chance. You're gonna have to work with me a little bit. Can you do that?"

Carole nodded.

"I'm holding you to that promise. See that pile of folders?" Marsha indicated a box at the side of her desk. "Those are your options, so be patient with me and I'll find you someplace you fit. There's a lid for every pot, you know. The good news is I got your paperwork corrected and you'll be moving into fifth grade where you belong."

Carole didn't say anything, still rubbing her hand across the seat of her chair. She didn't think she belonged in fifth grade any more than first. She didn't think Marsha could find a lid for her kind of pot either, but someday, when her promise to Marsha was over, Carole would find a place to belong.

If you enjoyed reading the adventures of Carole Blank,
read more about her in *Heartless: A Shieldmaiden's Voice* by S.R. Karfelt.

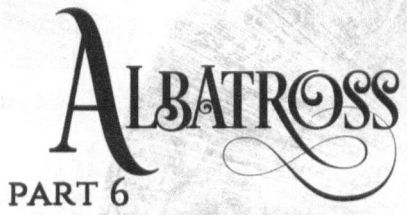

ALBATROSS

PART 6

"**KILLING YOUR** captain is mutiny. They'll have no choice but to hang you." Braydon's words offered no comfort to me while he paced my room. A soft smile turned up the corner of his mouth. "He's going to kill me if I touch you."

"He doesn't think I'd let you."

Braydon knelt down before me and surrounded my hands with his. "I will take you anywhere you want to go. I'll never let him hurt you, I promise."

"I don't need anyone to protect me."

"I know." His voice was soft, a gentle caress to my soul. "I don't want to be someone you need, Warrior. I only want to be with you. I want to make you feel the way I feel when you're near me." He gently ran his fingers up my forearm. "I want you to burn for me the way I burn for you."

My stomach lurched in a way I'd never experienced. It wasn't what he said, it was the way he said it. The way his lips tentatively brushed my fingers, my palm, my wrist.

"What if you fail?"

"I swear to you, Warrior, I won't leave you."

How could I feel this way about a man I barely knew? How could his touch leave fire running through my veins? I didn't have the answers, but I wanted nothing more than to find them.

"Death would be better than letting the Captain touch me," I whispered, trying to find the right way—the feminine way—to say what I was feeling. "But I would suffer his wrath if it meant I'd spent one night with you."

The depth of Braydon's gaze swallowed me as he cupped the back of my head with his hand, his mouth curving into a smile. "I don't think it'll require anything quite so drastic."

His lips met mine and I wrapped my arms around him. For the first time, being close to someone didn't fill me with fear, dread, or the desire to escape. I was home. As I lay back in his arms, he traced the contours of my collarbone.

"We can leave as soon as the job is done. We can take our share and go before Captain misses me." I grabbed his hand and kissed his palm. A shadow flickered over Braydon's face.

"There isn't any money."

"What do you mean?" I pushed myself up to a sitting position. He refused to meet my eye.

"No money. No loot. My father's bankrupted the city funds. The vault is just for pretense." He grabbed a fistful of his hair and leaned forward where he sat. "That's why I told Captain I'd only give him the vault's lock code if he gave me you. I never thought I'd actually get to a point where I'd have to give it to him."

Fear swept through me. No money meant no reason to keep Braydon. Captain would kill Braydon and come for me—neither of which would I allow to happen.

"We have to leave. Now." I pushed myself out of the chair we'd been sharing and started running around my cabin, pulling out things I'd need.

"Hey, stop." Braydon moved with impressive speed, shifting in front of me when I reached for my long coat. "We're in the middle of the sky. Do you suggest we jump?"

"We could take the airboat."

"We'll dock in a few days' time. There's no rush. We can leave then." When I offered no resistance, he leaned in and kissed me softly. "It's getting late. I should go back to the hull."

Once again anxiety gripped me. I grabbed his wrist. "No, please. Don't go." At his questioning glance I stepped closer to him. "Stay with me. Spend tonight with me."

Before he could speak reason, I pulled him down into a fierce kiss. He gave in, returning the kiss with passion unlike any I'd dreamed of. I pushed him back the short distance to my bed, pulling off my shirt in a fluid motion. Braydon's hands rested on my hips and he pulled me closer. His lips pressed against the curve of my neck and I pressed against him.

"Warrior," he murmured against my skin.

I pulled back, cupping his face. "Sara." I held his gaze, leaning in once more. "My name is Sara."

Then all hell broke loose.

HOLLY & JARED BROWN

THE FIGHT AT LASHKAR GAH

AFGHANISTAN 2014

THE KNOT of men left the briefing tent and dispersed into the hot desert air. Adjusting the scarf around her neck, she ticked them off in her mind as they did so, muttering their names aloud.

"Colonel Jasper, Lieutenant Colonel Wright, First Sergeant Brenner, General Parker." She let out a breath of air and contemplated her options. With that many officers, whatever happened out there was bound to be a big story. While she contemplated what it could be, a fifth soldier came stumbling out the door. He blinked in the bright sunlight, and squinting, held up his hand to shield his eyes from the glowing orb of a sun just over the horizon.

She smiled, recognizing a patsy. "Private Giles."

She watched the dazed-looking soldier amble through the forward operating base, or FOB. Taking a seat on an ammo crate under an unused tent, he pulled an MRE out of his pocket. While he tore the package open and examined the contents, she formed a plan.

Feeling confident, the reporter left her observational advantage and approached Colonel Jasper. He was lighting up a cigarette in a designated smoking area crudely made of propped-up camouflage netting.

"Do you have a minute to speak with me, sir?"

Colonel Jasper swore under his breath and exhaled, blowing the smoke out his nose. Lazily, it curled upwards into the dying light of day.

"Whadya want?"

"I'm just curious why yesterday morning, a whole platoon left but only two came back. And only one under his own steam. Where's Sergeant Lowell?"

"It's classified."

"But he *is* injured?"

Colonel Jasper took a long drag on his cigarette and looked around the base.

"What were they thinking sending a woman out here to do a man's job?"

"A woman can write about war just as well as a man, sir. Better, even, I think you'll find."

Colonel Jasper grunted his disapproval and blew out more smoke. She persisted.

"Yesterday morning, three up-armored Humvees left the base along with a pair of five-ton trucks. That's a total of eighteen men and only two came back. Are the rest dead? Were they taken? Did they stay behind?"

The colonel's eyes narrowed and he looked toward the setting sun, squinting. With the sleeve of his uniform, he wiped the accruing sweat from his forehead and sighed.

"You know the drill. I can't talk about it." He threw the cigarette down to the ground and stamped it out with his heel. Turning to leave, he signaled an end to the conversation.

"But—"

"Good day."

Sighing with frustration, she turned, hands on her hips. *Time for plan B,* she thought.

"HI! IT'S Private Giles, right?"

The young private's eyes wandered upward from his pouch of chili mac and held her confident gaze for a few seconds before swallowing the unsightly ball of food in his mouth.

His deep southern accent drawled and slurred, his words ended on a lilt as he questioned her.

"Yes, ma'am. And you are...?"

"Most everyone calls me *ma'am.*" She chuckled but Private Giles's blank stare prompted her to move directly into the interview.

"You may have seen, but I was just speaking with Colonel Jasper."

Another blank stare.

"I'm a reporter—"

"I figured, ma'am. We don't see too many of ya'll out this far. Especially ones not in uniform."

"Right. Well, I just spoke with Colonel Jasper and he gave me permission to speak with you about what happened out there."

"Really? I's just in there with all them top brass, and they said I wasn't to speak a word to nobody."

"It'd be a pretty stupid thing for me to lie about, wouldn't it, Private?" she said, putting on her best poker face.

"Well, no offense ma'am—"

"Listen, Private," the reporter cut him off. "Should I go get Colonel Jasper over here to clear this up? I don't imagine he'd be too happy about it, but I guess if you need him over here to hold your hand so you can do an interview with me, then I will make it happen."

"I s'pose. I mean, I guess, when you put it like that, ma'am."

"So, what happened? Everyone left, but only two came back? Where's Sergeant Lowell?"

"Well, I imagine he's in surgery now. Some medevac picked him up after we was rescued."

"So, where are the rest?"

"Well, they's dead, ma'am," Private Giles said with a matter-of-fact tone.

"How'd they die?" Setting up her notebook, she took the cap off her pen with her teeth.

"Some hajis ambushed us in the village."

"And what village was it?"

"Lishkerga, ma'am."

"Do you mean Lishkar Gah?"

"Well, that's what I said, ma'am."

She corrected him in her notes and asked him to continue.

"Our mission was to capture some HVT, uh, that's a high-valued target, holed up in this village. Intel said he normally stayed there on the weekends, and we got a good lead that he was there *this* weekend. We approached the village from the south at approximately 0530. It was pretty quiet out. Just a few shepherds along the road was all we seen. Then, when we was only about a quarter of a mile out, the first Humvee hit a IED and the rest of us had to stop behind 'em."

"Where were you in the convoy?"

"Oh, I was in the third Humvee, ma'am. I was sitting on the right side, facing the town with my Squad Automatic Weapon when I heard the explosion. Made my ears ring, ma'am."

"I'm sorry. That must have been difficult. Did you know the men in the first Humvee?"

"Course I did, ma'am. They's all good men."

"So, what happened once the convoy was at a stand-still?"

"Pretty sudden-like, the second Humvee was hit by some kinda RPG, uh, I mean, a rocket-propelled grenade, but it wasn't a direct hit, so the men were able to return fire pretty quick to where the shot came from. Then Sergeant Lowell commanded all the men to return fire. But it was tricky see, 'cause it's a village, and we couldn't exactly see where the RPG come from.

"I could hear ol' Specialist Travis trying to get the FOB on the radio, but he wasn't successful. Then he got hit by some haji up on a rooftop with a sniper rifle. So, there goes Travis."

Swallowing, she continued to take notes.

"So, we was pinned down pretty good. The two five-ton trucks behind was returning fire with their 240B machine guns but whoever was up in the village wasn't about to quit. Sometime 'round noon, the firing paused from the village, so we figured it was safe to approach and complete our mission.

"I was sure the HVT was gone. No way he heard all that and stuck around. The way Sergeant Lowell figured it, the IED was his alarm clock and the firefight was his way of distracting us long enough for him to fly the coop.

"Pretty much all we saw when we entered the town was dead people ever'where. Of all sorts. There was whole families that had been killed by our return fire. Because, 240B machine guns and automatic rifles can't tell no difference between who's who, you know. These damned hajis set up in a village full a people and then you guys turn us into the bad guys when we have to defend ourselves."

"I assure you, that is *not* what I'm trying to do," she retorted, holding up her hand in a show of disagreement.

"Anyhow, it don't matter. The people that was still alive was shored up in their homes. When we went through the town, we saw a lotta them through open doors. My guess is they left their doors open so we could see they wasn't a threat. But, what do I know? I don't know what goes on in a haji's mind. All's I know, is that it meant a lot of work, clearing those homes, making sure no one was gonna shoot. We still hadn't found a sniper rifle, so we was just waiting it out before the shooting started up again, wasn't we?

"And then it did. Sure as rain. One whole teamed got blowed up by a man who had bombs hiding in there with his family. Least, I assume they was family. Again, I don't know. So, then we was down to only six men. We was getting close to the rooftop where we thought the sniper was hiding when all a sudden, he was picking us off one by one again.

"We lost Specialist Ortez when a grenade came flying off a rooftop. He just jumped on it. Don't even think he thought twice 'bout it, but he saved our lives. Then Private Hastings took a bullet right in the forehead for Sergeant Lowell. We lost ever'one 'til it was just me and Sergeant Lowell. Then he got popped right in the shoulder, followed by a second round in the thigh. We was close enough that Sergeant Lowell just flung up a grenade to that there rooftop and *poof.* The shooting stopped.

"Sergeant Lowell ordered me to go up and make sure he was dead. I did. I come out on that rooftop with my hands shaking, expecting to see some dead haji with a full beard. I'll be damned if it wasn't some eight-year-old kid dead with this ancient-looking British Lee Enfield rifle."

The reporter paused her writing to look up at Private Giles. His eyes glistened and he shook his head. He still couldn't believe it was a child that had taken so many lives.

"So, then I come down to find Sergeant Lowell passed out from all the blood loss, I expect. I was nervous to walk outta that town, carrying him because I couldn't very well cover myself and do that, now could I?

"I made it out though. As soon as I made it to the front gates, I heard a familiar sound. The buzzing of a couple a motorcycle motors was drifting in with the night's wind. Damn near ever'one rides one here in Afghanistan, so I was leery. I set Sergeant Lowell down on the ground and prepared to shoot. But they was driving so fast, I couldn't get a shot off. Then, coming up behind 'em like a bat outta hell, was a truck. The closer they came, the more I could see they was SF."

"*SF* meaning?"

"Special Forces, ma'am. Green berets, whatever you wanna call 'em. Every single one of them was like something outta some Army bedtime story. They had these big bushy beards." Private Giles extended his hands out in front of his face to illustrate the beards to the reporter. "And a few of them even had on baseball hats." Private Giles shook his head in disbelief. "They was really badass, ma'am.

"The two on the motorcycle skid to a stop in front of me and Sergeant Lowell and tell me to lower my weapon. Then, before I can say anything, this one SF guy jumps down from the truck and runs over to Sergeant Lowell. He don't have no beard. Honestly, I don't think he could grow one. He looked like he was one of them Indians."

"Indian? Like from India?"

"No, the American kind. You know, the kind that wears the feather? His skin was dark, almost like a haji's but he didn't have no beard. His hair was black and kinda long. They called him 'Chief' at any rate. Anyhow, he comes running up to Sergeant Lowell and done asks him if he's all right. Course, Sergeant Lowell don't answer. So, then he sets to work on saving him. I'll be damned if he don't enlist my help too. I felt like some damned nurse assisting a doc with some big surgery. He locates the bleeds and stops 'em. Patches Sergeant Lowell up real quick."

"And what were the other men doing while this SF medic worked on Sergeant Lowell?"

"To be honest, I didn't have no time to really look, since I was help-ing with the life-saving bit. But, once the Indian had him stabilized or whatever, he said he don't need my services no more and asked me to pick up the trash pile he made."

"And did you?"

"Course I did! If a Green Beret asks you to do something, you do it. Anyhow, then I gets to looking around. Most of the soldiers was just sitting there all chill-like, keeping a lookout. Then, I noticed someone who wasn't no Special Forces. Hell, the damned terrorist we was sent to pick up from the village was sitting there in the truck, all bound up and this one soldier was standing over him with his M4 carbine fixed on him. One of the SF guys, I think he was the cap'n, must have noticed me looking cause he says to me, 'We caught him slinking away from the village on the north side.'

"Then, a few minutes later, the sun was coming up, and outta the sunrise, like some movie, was a black hawk. It lands and collects Sergeant Lowell and the HVT and flies away. Then, me the SF team went back into the village and we carried out each and every one of our guys and laid 'em down by the original convoy. A few hours later, a column of Humvees comes up from the south, to get me and my buddies."

Private Giles swallowed again and looked down at his food, looking ill.

"And then what?"

"And then, nothing ma'am. We come back here, and all this brass comes out and I spend the day sitting in some stuffy debriefing room. They only come to talk to me an hour or so ago and I told 'em all what I just told you."

"That's quite an ordeal to live through, Private."

"You're telling me, ma'am. It still hadn't quite sunk in. But, what can I say? It's just another day in the United States Army, ma'am."

"Thank you for your time, Private Giles." She stood to leave, tucking her pen into the top of her spiral pad.

"Ma'am?"

"Yes?"

"People back home, they don't care about us no more, do they?"

"No," she said. There was no point in sugarcoating it.

Private Giles nodded then bowed his head.

"That's why stories like this matter, Private. That's why I bothered to ask what happened out there."

They nodded to each other in mutual understanding. She attempted to give him a reassuring smile, but it fell flat. Instead, she turned with a sigh and headed back to the spot from which she had come, to wait for another story to materialize.

MARGARET MADIGAN

Hot Dish Heroes

THERE WERE only four of us left from the high school, as far as I knew; me, Colin, Lauren, and Tasha. We were the only ones who hadn't eaten the cafeteria hot dish for lunch. But it took us days to figure that out, and by that time it was too late to save the town.

"We never should have split up, Alex," Lauren said as we hunkered in the rocky ruins of the infamous *blah blah blah* Revolutionary fort in the state park. I couldn't care less about the history, and right now adrenaline was fucking with my memory. All I cared about was not being eaten by my zombified former friends and neighbors.

"It's a little late for should have, don't you think?" I snapped.

Colin and Tasha had run for the lighthouse, which I'd argued was a bad place to hide because we'd basically be trapped with our backs to the cliff and the ocean. They didn't care. They wanted the high ground, but I refused to be imprisoned at the top of the tower waiting for the zombies to shuffle-and-moan up the stairs and eat my brains.

"Maybe they won't find us?" Lauren whispered.

"No, we're pretty much screwed," I said. When she started crying—a completely useless response, in my opinion—I tried to reason with her. "Everybody's infected. For all we know, it'll go global."

"But it was just a rancid hot dish. How could that infect the whole world?"

"Didn't you see that shit? I mean, even on a good day it looks like someone's already eaten it, but it was especially soggy and gray on Monday. Mom's always ranting about that pink slime crap the stores add to hamburger now to make it go further. That's got to be what did it."

"Zombie hamburger?"

"What else could it be? Did you eat the hot dish?"

"No."

"Neither did I. And neither did Tasha or Colin. But if everybody in town was buying and eating hamburger with that junk in it, they'd get infected too."

At that moment I heard the sickening sound of hundreds of shoes scraping concrete. Lauren whimpered next to me.

"They found us," she whispered.

"What I wouldn't give right now for a shotgun."

"Why?"

I just stared at her and shook my head. How could one person be so uninformed about the fundamentals of the zombie apocalypse?

"The shotgun is the universal zombie-killing weapon," I said. "A headshot is all it takes to kill them."

She cocked her head and scrunched her eyebrows together like I'd just spoken in some alien language.

"What the hell are you talking about?" she asked. "You've been playing way too many video games, moron. These are *real* zombies, not Hollywood zombies. We have no idea what'll kill them. Besides, there are hundreds of them. Can you carry that many shotgun shells while also running away from them?"

That made a frightening amount of sense. I ran down a mental list of possible ways to kill a zombie: shotgun to the head, which Lauren had just shot down; a machete or sword of some kind could take their heads clean off, but I had no idea where to get a machete or sword. While yesterday we'd had a baseball bat, a crowbar, and a shovel, any one of which if swung with sufficient force (according to my physics teacher, who was now also part of the army of walking dead) could burst a zombie skull like a ripe melon, we'd had to vacate our hiding place so fast in the middle of the night to escape Mr. Carpenter the used-to-be janitor and a couple of guys from the swim team, we'd left all our weapons behind.

So I just shrugged. "I have no idea."

She glared at me as the moaning and shuffling grew louder. I think she'd finally reached the point where she was more pissed at me than she was scared of the zombies.

"Well, I do have an idea," she said.

She grabbed my hand and pulled me from the relative safety of the ruins until we were on the road and exposed to view. This zombie crowd, unlike in the movies when they're slow and easy to run away from, moved really fast when they smelled food. Once they sighted us, they snarled and growled and hightailed it right for us.

"What the fuck kind of idea is this?" I squealed when she took off running for the cliff behind us.

I sprinted after her at top speed, determined that all I had to do to save myself was outrun her, but when we were within yards of the fifty-foot drop to the sharp rocks and ocean below, she ran a play that the football team would have been proud of. She dodged to the right and I went left, and the zombies, with their numbed reflexes, went straight off the cliff like a herd of lemmings.

Lauren and I jogged back to the edge of the cliff in time to watch the last of them splash into the ocean.

"I can't believe that worked," I said, offering her a high five.

She slapped my hand and grinned. "Not bad for a lit geek, huh?"

"Nope, not bad at all. Let's go find Colin and Tasha."

We headed back to the lighthouse where another crowd of zombies was moaning and slobbering all around the base of the building.

"You think it'll work again?" I asked.

"It's worth a try, but we're going to have to get some weapons soon. We can't stay here forever, and there won't always be a handy cliff nearby every time we get cornered by zombies."

"True that."

She rolled her eyes at me, then turned and yelled at the zombies, waving her arms in the air to get their attention. "Hey, meat sacks," she said, then sprinted for the cliff again.

I wolf-whistled at them and followed her.

Predictably, the zombies ran after us. Apparently it was lunchtime, and we were on the menu.

We ran the same play, and it worked again. I lost count of the zombies diving over into the ocean, but they followed each other, one after another, out into the air and into the water. I didn't recognize most of them, but I saw the guy from the gas station, and our mailman. Just before I met up with Lauren, I watched the cafeteria lady waddle right off the edge of the cliff. I leaned over the top just in time to see her bounce off a rock and *sploosh* into a wave.

"Huh. Ironic."

Lauren joined me, and we watched Tasha and Colin leave the lighthouse and head our way. I never expected the world to end by high school hot dish, and even though the zombie apocalypse sucked, at least I'd never have to suffer through another cafeteria lunch again. I counted that as a win.

KELSEY KEATING

ALBATROSS

PART 7

I SUPPOSE we'll never know whether or not Captain understood what he'd created the day he named me Warrior. When he burst into my cabin, frothing with jealousy, everything happened so quickly, and yet time seemed to slow around me.

Braydon shoved me aside, taking Captain head on. With little effort and a quick slash of his blade, Captain cut Braydon across his chest and knocked him aside, his rage focused on me.

His fingers closed around my throat and he shoved me down onto my bed, his grip cutting off my breath as his other hand went for the button of my pants.

I struggled to find air, and suddenly my sad life played out before me: watching my father and mother die in the sky raids; Captain's crew stripping me of my clothes and discovering I was female; the crew member, pinning me to my bed in order to rape me, paying little attention as I pulled his dagger from the sheath at his side...and Braydon. Braydon, my only spot of sunshine in the hell of a hand life had dealt me.

Wrath—the wrath of a warrior—raged through me. With a guttural cry I kicked Captain in the groin. His groan of agony fueled me forward, but he caught me by the hair and yanked me around. I kicked out again, knocking his legs out from under him. We both went down, his fist colliding with my face. With another shriek, I rolled free and pounced on him, pinning his arms down with my knees as I sat on his chest. He struggled against me and I punched him full in the mouth, cutting my knuckles against his teeth.

"You don't own me." I reached down into my boot and pulled out the dagger I kept hidden there. "You will never own me." I placed it against his throat. "I am Warrior, and your life belongs to me. Beg me for mercy!"

"Please," Captain rasped. "Please spare me. I won't...I couldn't hurt you."

"Promise you'll let us leave."

"I promise," he said through gritted teeth.

"Liar." I spat in his face. "Pig!" I felt everything go calm as I made my decision, the air around me buzzing with energy. "I won't ever be free of you. Not so long as you draw breath."

"No!" Captain screamed and I raised my dagger. With all of the rage and power of the warrior he'd created, I drove the blade straight into his heart.

Shock flooded his face and his body lurched. I pulled the blade free and plunged it in anew, blood spurting up into my face. Again and again I drove my blade into him, sobbing as I did so.

"Sara! Sara stop!"

The sound of *my name* halted my madness. I looked up to see Braydon watching me in horror. "We have to go. We have to go now."

My door crashed open for a second time as Blade and Wrench rushed into my room. Mingled horror and surprise flickered through their expressions as they gazed upon me, topless, straddling Captain, covered in his blood.

"What the hell—" Wrench stopped short when Blade hit him hard from behind.

"Grab what you need and go." Blade's voice was low, dangerous. "This is mutiny, and I can't save you." When I didn't respond, he turned to Braydon. "Take her. Take her and go."

Nothing else is clear in my memory. I stumbled as Braydon lifted me, draping me in a jacket. He held my hand, but I can't remember getting on the airboat and pushing out into the clouds. I don't recall how long we sailed, or how long it took me to bandage Braydon's wound, which thankfully wasn't deep. I only remember his arms around me, the taste of his lips against mine as one phrase flashed over and over again in my mind.

Free. I am free.

KIRSTIN PULIOFF

WARRIOR'S PASSION

THE HARSH pull of the chains behind her brought her to her knees. Arianna swore as a warm drop of blood slid down her shin, clearing a path through her dust-covered legs. Her eyes narrowed and shot up, searching out the cause. Glistening under the silver armor, he was unmistakable. Thick ripples of muscles outlined his body as his hands tightened around her restraints. She watched the movement of white linen contrast against his olive skin as he walked closer. Her gaze moved upward. His chiseled jaw softened, brown eyes pooling with regret.

"It's time," he said. The deep timbre of his voice wrapped around her as he held up the metal collar.

Even as the pain pulsed in her legs, desire swept through her. She seized his outstretched hand and pulled herself up with a defiant curl of her lips. She tried to close her mind to him, to focus on the seriousness of her capture, but failed. Holding his hand, her mind raced with images of them together.

It hadn't been that long, but even a few days in the king's holding chambers mimicked years. As if somehow the thick walls had a way of blocking time along with the light. She doubted it had been more than four days, but the only warmth she felt blazed within her mind. Memories of her and Thiegan in the thick grass, his rough hands tickling her as they lay beneath the olive trees.

A sigh escaped. He must have felt the same; his hands found a way to her shoulders, their warmth prickling her delicate skin as he turned her around and secured the metal restraint around her neck. She shuddered at the resounding click as it locked in place.

"Thiegan," she breathed, closing her eyes, giving in to the passion rising inside. Memories swirled together. "I promise, we will be together again," she whispered. "Even the king cannot keep me from you."

"Don't underestimate the king," he warned.

"Don't underestimate me," she snapped, turning to face him, and then pursed her lips at his frown. "Sorry," she apologized reaching out for him. "The last few days…"

"Are a torture I never wished you to endure."

"And I won't for much longer," she insisted.

"I am counting on you being right." He clutched her hands. "We can still run. It's not too late."

"And have the entire army on us? No, he called for all the eligible women, and he'll know if anyone's missing." She twisted her forearm so the barely healed skin from the branding shone under the dim light. "We'll have to leave on our own, afterward."

His fingers rolled over the tender skin before lifting it to his lips. His eyes spoke the words he couldn't utter.

Arianna's heart beat wildly as he pulled her near. He gripped her with a fierceness that belied the tenderness in his eyes. The metal breastplate cooled her skin as he pulled her closer. He touched his lips to her hair. "If you're wrong…"

"I won't be. I can't be. It's you and me forever, like we planned. Like we vowed behind that olive tree."

"That tree," he laughed. "You know that was the first time I saw you. When I peeked…"

"You mean when I let you peek," she smirked and then sighed. "That seemed so long ago. There's never enough time."

"There never will be, my love. Eternity itself would not be long enough for me to cherish you."

"Thiegan," she said, turning with sadness she hadn't let herself feel since her capture. "I promise, just as we did before. My future belongs to you, no matter what the king or my parents say."

"I wish you didn't have to do this."

"I'm a warrior. It's the only way. It's always been this way. I will win my freedom, one way or another."

"I wish you didn't have to."

"Just promise me you won't give up on me, whatever happens. Believe in me. Fight for me."

"Forever Arianna."

Her hands slipped down to meet his, squeezing them once before letting go with a sigh.

Hearing rough steps crunch the dirt, and jingling of armor, she knew another guard approached. She didn't flinch when Thiegan stepped back, standing formally along the edge of the hallway. The chains pulled a taut tether between them.

She ignored their interaction until a loud click released the cold metal on her wrists. Risking one last look, she turned and caught Thiegan's gaze. Welling with regret, his eyes pleaded silently. She recognized the look. It was the same he'd given her before the king's men had taken her away.

Their silence grew into an awkward pit, swallowing the words they wanted to say. He pressed her forward, down the narrow torchlit hallway. Steel rings hung on the walls, larger versions of the shackles he'd just released her from. Focused on the gulf between herself and Thiegan, Arianna missed the chatter in the background. Sweet laughter and warm voices greeted her as they rounded the corner into a larger chamber.

Arianna's mouth dropped, and Thiegan bumped into her from behind as she stopped in the doorway. In contrast to the narrow hallway, the room before her was a vision of opulence. A red jeweled sash draped over the edge of a chair, cobalt blue hung from the steel rings in the walls, yellows as bright as the sun welcomed her into the room. Tension melted away as warm, familiar smiles greeted her.

Thiegan unclasped the metal collar and pressed her forward into the room.

Faces from her past greeted her. Women she grew up with, traded with at the market, and washed in the river now stood before her as equals. Each person vied for a way out, through the king or death. It didn't seem fair.

She didn't entertain their attempts at conversation, walking past their stunned expressions to the towering piles of fabric. No one expected to see her, especially at the hands of Thiegan. Even loving a royal guard didn't guarantee freedom. When the king made an order, everyone obeyed, even if it meant turning in your love. Her fingers trailed along the dresses, indulging in the smooth silks, rich velvets, and delicate sheers. Luxury overflowed from her hands. The air around her filled with an exotic smell as sweet plum wine mixed with the incense, numbing her mind.

A cough from the back of the room broke the magic of the moment, and Arianna took another look. Reality surfaced above the carefully arranged façade. Dust from the stone walls and ground left a soft layer of dirt on the silky fabrics. Smoke from the torches dropped soot to the ground, and the soft gleam of the guard's smile spoke of terror. And the silks, they were frayed and stained with blemishes. They were tarnished goods, just like all of them. Used and discarded at a whim. What condition would she be left in?

A sigh escaped as the silk dropped from between her fingers, and her eyes found Thiegan. She cursed herself for forgetting the reason she was there, even for a moment.

She walked around the room, noticing the way the guards' gaze followed them and hearing the rising cheers from the arena doorway. Along the far wall, a stone table held piles of similar silk gowns, studded jewelry, and a line of weapons. While the other luxuries put them at ease, this table suggested something more ominous. Weighted stares tightened the air around her as the women gathered, suddenly aware of the competition. Casting sideways glances at each other, they seized the silk in greedy fistfuls.

Without privacy or order, the women began throwing the fabric over themselves. Layers of sheer silk revealed their skin, leaving little to the imagination. Fabric swayed around her curves. Arianna tied the golden rope around her hips. The luxury soured as she looked at the other scantily clad women. Disgust at the infantile demands of the king and prince burned in her.

She grabbed the nearest spear. Her spirit hardened like the cold steel beneath her fingers.

The king didn't know what he was getting.

The calm demeanor in the room shifted as she took the first weapon. Metal rang behind her as the women grabbed, dropped, and argued over their options.

Soft silk fluttered against her skin as she moved past the other women, towards Thiegan. He stood at the doorway separating them from the arena. Light shone down on him, highlighting his strong body and serious face. The sun blinded her as she approached his side. She squinted up at him, and he looked back with tenderness, unspoken words connecting them in silence.

"Are you sure about this, Arianna? The king doesn't play kindly, and I don't want to lose you."

"It's the only way we can be together. If I lose you, then I lose myself. This is the only option," she whispered, brushing her arm against his. "We'll be together. I will win. At whatever cost."

"Some things aren't worth the price. Even if you win, the king doesn't bargain."

"The king won't get me," she countered, anger simmering with her words. "Why are you doing this?"

"Doing what?" he asked.

"Trying to talk me out of this."

"I just don't want to see you hurt, or worse," he admitted, looking hesitantly back to the other women and pulling her toward the edge of the room.

"There is no worse. I won't spend my life without you. That's final."

The commotion for their event had already begun. Cheers and jeers blasted as the arena overflowed with people. Colorful clothes, streamers, and banners fluttered in the crowd. She held her head high against the jeers and suggestive movements of the crowd. Her eyes settled on the man in charge.

Sitting in the upper compartments, the king stood with his arms open in welcome. His face glimmered in the sun as the light reflected off his golden chains and adornments. He moved with the grace of a young warrior, in spite of the silvered hair around his temple. Behind him, a row of beautiful young women clad in jewel-toned silk watched with distracted eyes. Beside him, she settled on the young prince. He lounged in his chair; the grace and presence his father possessed hadn't carried down the line.

Her gaze slipped away from the crazed crowd and settled on the playing field. Strategically placed around the stadium, ramps, stacked barrels, and hay bales formed an obstacle course. She itched with curiosity. In between the common obstacles, metal boxes flashed under the midday sun. She idly watched the boxes until something moved. Smooth, black velvet sauntered in and out of the box's shadows.

Then her stomach tightened against the smell of blood and fresh meat.

"You have no right to chain those animals up!" Anger flared in her eyes as rough hands grabbed her from behind.

Roars of laughter assaulted her as the eyes of the king appraised her. "You have a warrior's passion," he rumbled. "Let's hope that spirit can bring you to the end."

"I do not doubt it will, my liege," she spat.

The king elbowed his son. Arianna bit her tongue when Thiegan pulled her back. Her eyes burned with building anger.

"Now is not the time," he whispered. "Save it for the contest."

"Oh, I will," she breathed, her voice thick. "This adds fuel to my fire. I'll win this battle, and defeat him too."

She didn't have to wait long. With a quick gesture from the king, they were paraded into the center of the arena behind a lead guard. The crowd erupted as the sun shone through their gowns, erasing any remnants of their dignity.

Thiegan pulled her to the base of a ramp and squeezed her hand quickly, before anyone noticed. She looked around, feeling the heat from the midday sun beat down on her. Dust kicked up around the guards as they positioned the women throughout the arena. Once they retreated to the outer edge, she heard it. The pervading silence announced danger. In that brief moment, clarity shone. She saw it all, from the amusement in the king's eyes as he whispered back to one of his wives, the undisguised lust gleaming from his son, the fear drumming through her heart, to the rippling muscles of the panther as he leapt on his hind legs, reaching through the metal grates of his cage. One moment stretched until the bell rang, and then sped into a blur.

A loud click, a roar, and then the panthers were released. Beautiful cats, prized for their textured skins and the ivory masks around their faces.

Her grip tightened as she raised her spear, feeling it slip in her grasp. Her heart pounded, covering the roar of the crowd. As much as it turned her stomach to fight them, she had no choice.

Deepening her stance on top the ramp, she swiveled her head, on alert for attacks. Her heart dropped when she saw several women down, bodies littered beneath the hay and along the edges of the arena.

A cry cut the air. She saw a woman fall to the floor, a sword slicing her chest. The delicate gown fell, shredded and sodden in blood.

Gathering her breath and rage, she leapt off the ramp directly in the path of one of the panthers. Before it could move, she pierced his chest, impaling it on the shaft. She seized a dropped sword and moved to the next.

The air around her thickened, the roar of the crowd diminished beneath the beating of her heart. Sweat dripped from her temples, irritating her fresh wounds. Her mouth filled with the metallic taste of blood and the energy humming through her body. The rhythm of her movements blended with the swirling energy and cheers of the arena. Her body flew, twisted, and dove beyond the panther's reach. Taking advantage of the arranged course, Arianna moved fluidly, silencing the animals' roars with her quick strokes. The sword slipped between her hands. Fresh drops of blood spattered her as she pulled it from another body.

She glanced around, noticing the arena. The dusty ground stilled under pools of blood and sweat. Bodies of animals and women cascaded over the edges of obstacles, frozen in movement. Around her, the threat quieted. She spun around, on the lookout for any remaining dangers. No animals or women approached.

The hush of the crowd warned her. She spun, narrowly missing the tip of a blade. Her feet wobbled underneath her, and she fought to regain her stance and composure. Arianna saw a gleam of desperation as another woman approached. The flimsy green fabric stuck to her, the sheerness marred with blood and dirt. Their chests heaved in unison as they stared at each other. The woman's scream filled the air as she ran toward her, sword raised.

Arianna ran backward up the ramp. She leapt to the side, avoiding the fatal stab, and heard the *thump* of a hard landing. Lying at the bottom, curled into a ball, the woman whimpered. The anguish stung Arianna's heart. She looked at the woman and up to the quiet crowd.

The crowd sat poised at the edges of their seats, holding their breath. The king's face revealed no emotion, and the women behind him watched with horrified expressions. Only the prince seemed to be enjoying himself.

As she watched him, her stomach twisted with hate. Defiantly, she hurled the other sword away, smiling as it crashed into the edge of the ramp. Her hands wrapped around the fallen woman's and pulled her up, ignoring the lady's confusion. She turned to face the king.

"Your Highness," she began. She let the gown part, showing off her long legs. The crowd cheered appreciatively. "I would like to suggest an alternative. I see no reason that we both can't have a happily ever after. Surely a man of your prowess can satisfy two deserving women," she teased.

The other woman faltered, but struck an equally seductive stance. The crowd exploded in appreciation. The king's content smile twisted in mischief as he stood to address the crowd.

"A warrior woman with a passion to live, a passion to fight, and passion to share. If I were younger, I would take you for my own. Alas, if not for me, then for my son. Consider it done," he said.

The prince's attempt at a seductive wink failed as he rose from his seat. His awkward gait became more apparent as he climbed down the staircase to the arena floor and strutted toward them, seizing them both lustfully.

Looking over the prince's shoulder, her eyes sought Thiegan. For a brief moment, their eyes connected, and a shiver ran down her back. The tightness around his jaw softened, and a small smile touched his mouth. Her heart fluttered in response.

IMMEDIATELY FOLLOWING the event, a small group of women surrounded and ushered Arianna and the other woman, Merlia, to their chambers. The room, located on the top level of the palace, was much richer than the dungeon's scraps. Thick red velvet covered the windows. An oversized bed dominated the room, plumped with large pillows and dark colors. Fresh flowers lined the tables. Their sweet fragrance filled the air, relaxing her nerves.

Arianna smiled, watching Merlia lounge on the bed. She walked past the room to the bath. Already prepared for them, bubbles and scented oils overflowed the tubs. She hastily unhooked the golden rope. The stained fabric dropped to the floor, freeing her from the memory of the morning. Sighing deeply, she slipped beneath the silky suds, letting the warmth surround her. Her fingers traced the fresh wound on her thigh, remembering the gentle rubs of Thiegan's fingers on her skin. Teasing her desires with memories.

She dropped her head under the water, feeling the seduction of the bubbles and scents roll over her. Not all parts of winning were detestable. If she closed her eyes she could almost forget. Almost. The background chatter from the other room persisted. She languished in the bath until the water chilled.

As she emerged from the bath, her wet curls clung to her back as she rubbed oils over her body. The spicy flavor of mint and lilac stung as it slid over her legs. New bracelets and necklaces hung from her wrists, sticking to her wet skin. Unlike the bindings from earlier, she welcomed these adornments.

Sun flashed through the open window and danced on the back wall. A distinct pattern.

"Thiegan," she whispered, feeling her heart flutter. She looked out the window, searching out the flickering pattern of light. Her breath caught in her chest. The rough edges of the rocks bit into her fingers as she traced them over the stone wall. "I'm coming for you, my love. Just a little longer."

"Hmm?" From the shadows, Merlia appeared. Covered by a flimsy robe, the same sheer silk did little to cover her body.

Jumping away from the window, Arianna's blood ran cold with fear. "Nothing," she murmured.

Merlia's smile grew as she approached Arianna, looking over her toned stomach and shimmering skin with approval. The tips of Merlia's fingers trailed across her collarbone, drawing a line through the slick layer of oils. Arianna shuddered.

Arianna straightened and pressed her fingertips to Merlia's lips. She shook her head. "The prince would not approve," she said, grabbing and draping a blue robe around her.

"It is simply a way to prepare, to be ready for his conquest." Arianna saw the lust in Merlia's eyes. She slid her fingers beneath her orange robe, letting it drop to the ground.

With an overly dramatic sigh, Arianne picked up the dropped robe. "I assure you, I am ready for the conquest."

"Why did you save me then? Why save me to ridicule and mock me?" Merlia snatched the smooth fabric.

"My sweet Merlia," Arianna said, with a sad smile. "I did not save you to mock you. I saved you to save me."

They both jumped when the doors to their chamber opened and crashed against the far wall. Running to the doorway at the commotion, her stomach twisted, seeing the prince standing in the middle of the threshold. A crooked smirk rested on his lips, suggesting both an invitation and a threat. If the treatment of the door served as an indicator of his tenderness, she wanted nothing of it. She almost felt sorry for Merlia. As she looked at the other woman, any trace of guilt disappeared. In the time that it took the prince to enter the room, she had propped herself seductively against the overstuffed pillows.

"My lord." She nodded in deference.

Arianna glanced back to the prince, watching his jaw drop and his pants lift with enthusiasm. Maybe this would be easier than she imagined. She brushed the delicate spirals of her hair off her shoulder and walked forward. Lowering her lashes and letting the side of her robe drop over her shoulder, she pulled the golden rope from around her waist.

"Welcome home, my prince," she purred.

The prince's smile grew while he leered between the two women.

He kicked his boots off behind him and unbuckled his pants. Struggling to rip his leather vest off, he stumbled over his fallen trousers. Arianna walked over, feeling his greasy skin slide beneath her fingers as she helped pull him up. Standing there, bare-chested, her feelings about his over-compensation grew. The prince lacked more than the natural charm of his father.

Her fingers slid over his slick skin, nauseating her. It reminded her of a sickly child. She pressed him toward the bed. Glancing over his shoulders, she saw Merlia already at work, fingers stroking and pulling on the prince.

Showing little patience, he flung himself on the bed, twisting and opening his arms to welcome them. Before she could think of a way out, Merlia saved her. With a squeal Merlia plopped on top of him, twisting her fingers through the small mat of hair on his chest. Hiding her reluctance, Arianna tried to find a way to blend the prince with a memory of Thiegan. She failed miserably.

Arianna winced, listening to the light moans coming from the bed, wishing it could be different. The bed shifted under her weight as the prince pulled her on top. Her body rocked back and forth. A glint of envy flashed from Merlia's eyes as the attention shifted. Arianna reached beside her to grab Merlia's hair and brought her forward, inviting her in. Their lips connected, teasing each other. After a playful bite, Arianna shifted off the prince and pressed the more eager woman forward, encouraging her to please the prince. With one hand holding Merlia down, the other hand reached across the bed until she felt the cool, hard surface of the candlestick under her palm.

The vibration of the metal shook her as it connected with the prince, the force of the strike knocking him out cold. She thought she recognized fear before raising her arm to Merlia. The rod clanked as it rolled away.

Removing her trembling hands from covering her mouth, she appraised the damage. She moved a thick strand of hair out of Merlia's face, looking at the still beauty. Lowering her ear to her soft chest, she sobbed with relief at the faint thumps. She was alive, but knocked out.

Slipping out of bed, she raced across the cold stone floor. She looked out the window, looking for the one man who knew how to make her feel better.

Beyond the riverbank, hidden in the shadow of the olive trees, a flash blinded her, pulsing three times. Arianna let out her breath and twisted her own wrist into the light.

With no time to waste and no time to think, she grabbed the prince's leather vest and trousers, leaving without a backward glance.

"YOU'RE REALLY here," she said breathlessly, folding into his arms.

"I haven't left this spot since the event ended." He held her back and looked her over. "Did he hurt you?" he asked, searching her with concern.

"No, he didn't stand a chance," she said, squeezing his arms. "Nothing could keep me from you."

"From now until forever, Arianna, you are mine. I will not let anyone take you from me again, at any cost." His strong arms cradled her protectively as he lifted her chin up. His eyes devoured her. "I didn't realize the risk we faced. Not just to your life, but to mine. Without you, I am nothing."

He pulled her tight against him. Her breath caught in her throat. The light trail of his fingers tingled against her back as he claimed her body with his hands. Her lips parted in desire. Her back arched as a soft moan slipped out. His touch made her skin hum.

"Where will we go from here? We can't stay," she whispered, her eyes closing in delight as his lips traced the curve of her neck. The cool grass tickled her back as he pressed her to the ground.

"Wherever you want to go, my warrior princess. I plan to make your every wish and desire come true."

Her eyes sparkled mischievously. "I had the same idea," she said, pulling him on top.

KELSEY KEATING

Autumn's Last Stand

DEIDRE, COMMANDER of the Autumn Legion, let the grain fall from her hand, watching as the wind swept it from her long fingers and blew it south. She scanned the lush green valley below her, searching for any movement from their enemy. To her right, the thick forest jutted along harvested wheat fields and cast an eerie shadow in the setting sun. Brushing off her hands, she felt the internal fire flicker in her breast beneath her armor. A few paces back, her second in command, Audrelie, stood at attention.

Deidre clasped her hands behind her back, not an auburn hair out of place as she addressed the younger Nymph without looking at her. "They're coming. This will be Autumn's last stand."

"Commander?" Audrelie stepped forward, her brow furrowing.

"Summer won't allow us to survive. The Pixies are hell-bent on our destruction if we don't give them the key to our magic."

"But what of the Sprites? The Fairies?"

A humorless smile twisted Deirdre's lips as she turned to face Audrelie. "The Winter Fairies have already been pushed back behind the Stone Wall, their fairy dust cutoff. And the Sprites." She splayed her hands in front of her. "They were never ones for war. They've already receded or been absorbed by Summer. They won't have been killed; Summer values Spring water magic too much and Sprites won't mind trying to share to avoid conflict."

Audrelie remained silent as Deidre gazed out from their crested hill where the golden Autumn Fields met the low Summer Valleys. In the distance tents dotted the Pixie campsite—the inhabitants waiting for sunrise when they'd make their attack.

"I've made my decision. Every legionnaire with a family must return to the Leafdell and gather them up. Then, you are to lead them to safety."

"But Deidre—" Audrelie began, only to be silenced by a raised hand.

"Those who wish to stay and fight—and have no family—may do so. There's no reason to lose more Nymphs than necessary." Deidre turned to look back over her land. The setting sunlight was Autumn's best light, and the wheat bales gleamed majestically, surrounding her legionnaires as they polished their armor a good distance away.

"Where am I to take them?" Audrelie's voice trembled and Deidre watched her shakily brush back a stray strand of strawberry blonde hair.

"North."

Audrelie's large amber eyes widened. "North? To Winter?"

"Not exactly." Deidre squared her shoulders, preparing for the oncoming disagreement as understanding dawned on Audrelie's face.

"You want me to take them to the Ice Giants? Are you mad? They'll kill us!"

"Listen carefully to what I'm about to tell you," Deidre said, stretching to her full height of six inches. "Just east of the Winter Wood, on the very border between Autumn and Winter, there's a small colony of Druids. They're human, and different from the Ice Giants. Find Beatrice. She'll take everyone and keep them safe. You can begin again there, away from all of this."

"But what of you? What of Leafdell and the Fields?" Audrelie's hands gripped Deidre's own, clinging to her.

"Autumn will be lost, for now. I foresee a time when our descendants can return to this land and begin again."

"When? When do we return?"

"Not until Summer's power has waned. When Winter rises again and brings its full force—only then—will it be safe for Autumn and Spring to return." Deidre removed her hands from Audrelie's grasp. "It's time for you to go. If you leave now, you'll have just less than twelve hours before the sun rises again. The more time you waste, the more you ruin everyone's chances of getting out safely."

"And the rest of you?"

"We'll fight valiantly for our land. We'll be outnumbered, and we will lose. The purpose isn't to win—it's to give you time to escape." Deidre looked away, feeling pressure at the corners of her eyes. "Those who remain will be the ones who have already lost everything. Saving our kind will be our legacy." The image of her beloved Matthias swam through her vision and she pushed it away. She'd be with him soon enough. "Tell them this is a direct order from me. Now go."

Audrelie's face twisted with grief, her lips puckering as she failed to bite back a sob. She'd always been so emotional, Deidre often wondered if there might be Sprite in her blood. "Goodbye, Commander."

"Goodbye, my friend."

TWO HUNDRED Nymphs remained on the Autumn Fields, blades drawn at the ready, waiting for Summer to come up over the hill. At the front of the line, Deidre gripped her own weapon, glaring across the way. With fire rising inside of her, she faced her troops.

"Today," Deidre said, raising her voice so each Nymph legionnaire would hear her. "Today we fight for our right to freedom. We fight that we may be remembered as beings that would not stand down and let Summer take everything.

"We are here because we have lost much, but are willing to gain more. Our sacrifice will save the rest of our kind. Together we will end this war, for better or for worse."

As one, the legion let out a fierce battle cry. Deidre nodded, a wicked grin twisting her lips. Someone within the line gasped, pointing up into the sky. A flicker of hope flowered in Deidre's breast as she looked up and saw beings flying through the air.

Winter had come. All wasn't lost after all.

Someone shouted, and Deidre's hope died like a blossom falling from the tree. "The Pixies! They can fly!"

No. Her stomach clenched and a chill swept through her. They'd succeeded. They'd taken the Fairies' flight. Rage renewed, Deidre bared her teeth and turned once more to face her comrades.

"The Pixies have learned how to fly, but nothing they do will ever teach them our power!"

"What are we going to do?" a voice called over to her left.

Deidre's ruby eyes lit with the blaze of Autumn. "We give them what they want." Holding out her left hand, she conjured the fire of her people. It sparked in her palm, glowing hot and ferocious. Fires sparked in the hands of the legionnaires, until every Nymph held the Autumn blaze in one hand, a sword in the other.

"What are we going to do?" Deidre shouted at the top of her lungs.

Once again, the legion answered as one.

"*Burn them!*"

With another cry, Deidre raised her sword and ran out onto the battlefield.

ONE HUNDRED and eighty-two Nymphs were slaughtered, but four hundred and seventeen Pixies went with them. Several more were still being treated for severe burns, their condition uncertain.

Deidre, one of the eighteen taken, pushed all of her hate into the glower she fixated on Chief Gerralt, the head of Summer, and strained against the chains holding her. "You might as well kill me." She spat at his feet.

Gerralt chuckled. "How very feminine. I've always wondered how Autumn survived with females in charge. Apparently, it's because they behave like males." He grabbed her chin, squeezing hard. "Tell me what I want to know, and I'll let you die."

"There's no answer." She burned his fingers and forced him to release her.

"Liar!" Gerralt slapped her. "Fairies have wings, but without them we've learned how to fly. They have the dust they mine in their mountains. Sprites can grow fins and breathe under water, and they've shown us the plant to assist us in doing the same. What do you have? What allows Nymphs to create fire at will?"

"We are born this way. It can't be taught. There's no dust or vegetation that enhances it."

"We'll see if your answer changes once we've hunted the rest of your kind. When their lives hang in your hands, you'll sing a different tune."

Deidre laughed hollow and cold. "You'll never find them, not unless you want to face the Ice Giants."

Fear flashed through Gerralt's eyes and he sneered. "They wouldn't risk it."

"Why don't you go looking for them and find out? My answer won't change."

"Very well." Gerralt gestured for one of his soldiers to step forward. "If what you say is true and only Nymphs can create fire, we'll have to find another way. Did you wonder why we captured you and some of your females? One of our more intelligent members of the Pixie community believes we could breed the ability into our blood. I suppose there's only one way to find out."

Gerralt and most of the others left the room. Only the one soldier remained, advancing on Deidre.

AFTER DAYS of travel through the trees where Winter and Autumn collided, Audrelie gestured for the others to stop. To their left, large, dead trees creaked and crackled in the wind, covered in a layer of snow. In front of them, part of Autumn, a clearing opened through their orange and red trees. A dwelling larger than any she'd ever seen stood a large distance away from them. More could be seen beyond it. With little trouble, they found the druid human named Beatrice, who did as Deidre said she would.

As their community settled in their new, secret home, Audrelie silently thanked Dedire for her bravery. "I promise," she said to herself as the Nymph offspring played together in the trees. "They will know the stories. They will know what you did for them."

Enjoyed this story? Check out
A Stolen Kiss by Kelsey Keating free on Wattpad

J.S. BAILEY

THERE WE WILL BE

SOME PEOPLE stared straight ahead, unseeing. Some never glanced in his direction at all. And some flicked their gazes his way, became fraught with suspicion, and glanced around to see if anyone was with him before moving onward. They had much better things to do than wonder why a little boy in a torn shirt and corduroys sat by himself on a bench in the center of a busy shopping mall.

Brian was used to being ignored.

He hadn't learned his own name until he was three because Mommy and his daddies so seldom addressed him. Most of the time they smoked and drank smelly drinks that came in red and white cans, and after a whole huge box of the cans was empty and crumpled into the garbage, Mommy and whatever daddy lived with them at the time would start yelling at each other about grownup things like "trust" and "insecurity" and sometimes even a person named Pattie who was "some tramp."

They yelled about him a lot, too, even though he could never figure out what he'd done wrong.

That's when the darkness would edge in and Brian would cower in a corner, begging it to go away. Laughter lived in the darkness. Cruel, mocking laughter that spoke mean things that hurt him deep inside.

They hate you, Brian. The reason they fight is because of you. They wish you were dead.

And with tears running down his cheeks, he would whisper, "Please help me. Save me from the monsters."

Because what else could the voices be?

Brian's current daddy was a bald man named Craig. Sometimes when Mommy was out Craig would get mad and throw things. When Brian tried to explain to Mommy that the big bruise on his arm came from Craig's metal ashtray that had been hurtled across the room at him, Mommy slapped him hard across the face and told him to stop making up stories.

Another time Craig had thrown Brian down the back steps when he'd thought Brian had taken his cigarette lighter. Something had cracked in Brian's arm when he landed at the bottom, and when Craig rushed him to the hospital, he'd told the doctors Brian had tripped and fallen over a toy he'd left on the stairs.

Sometimes life was easier when you were ignored.

There hadn't been any food in the house that morning. The fight last night had been so scary that Brian almost ran away, and Mommy and Craig must have been worn out from all the yelling and screaming because neither of them responded to his knocks on their bedroom door when he wanted to ask about breakfast.

Brian's forehead had creased as he tried to think of what to do. He considered finding tools to get their door open and wake them up, but then the cruel voice returned: *They want you to starve to death, Brian. They want you to die!*

So Brian did the only thing he could think of: he left the house and ran.

After perhaps ten minutes of his chest hitching as he checked the roads for oncoming cars and raced across them when it was safe, Brian reached the Crosstown Mall. The mall had a food court with lots of restaurants and even a playground in the center of it. Sometimes his Aunt Sarah and cousin Blake took him to the mall when things at home got extra scary. Brian and Blake would play in the indoor ball pit and on the jungle gym and eat chicken nuggets and fries after that, and it would be so much fun Brian didn't want to go home.

As soon as he got to the mall that morning, Brian planted his rear on a bench in the food court, realizing too late that in order to get food, he would need to have money.

He couldn't remove his gaze from the nearest restaurant counter just a few yards away from him. The smells of cooking burgers and chicken nuggets made his mouth water, and hunger pangs stabbed his stomach like knives. Stealing was wrong—Mommy had said that to one of his old daddies before throwing him out of the house.

But if he didn't steal, he would die of hunger, and that was much worse.

He squinted at the counter where people ordered their food. In line stood a man, a boy in a ball cap, and a teenage girl talking on a phone. None of them paid any attention to him.

If he was fast, he might be able to slip around them and go behind the counter without being seen. Only a couple people were working back there, and Brian was short, so chances were good that nobody would notice if he snuck back there and took a burger for himself. And some fries. You couldn't eat a burger without fries and a Coke, too.

You're an evil little boy, Brian.

No, he said to himself. *I'm hungry. I'm not evil.*

He rose from the bench and ran toward the counter.

"Hold it right there, son."

Brian's limbs turned to ice. He looked up and saw a man towering over him wearing some kind of police uniform. His blue eyes were stern like Mommy's when she yelled at Craig.

Fear tightened Brian's throat so much he couldn't even say a word.

"Are you lost?" the policeman asked as he bent down eye to eye with him.

The lie came to Brian's lips without any thought. "I'm waiting for my mom."

The policeman's eyes narrowed ever so slightly. "You are? And where might she be?"

Brian pointed at the nearest store—one that had a bunch of almost-naked lady statues wearing underwear in the windows. "That one," he said, blushing. He didn't like looking at ladies' underwear. Things like that were supposed to be private.

The man gave a slow nod. "Okay, son," he said. "Just be careful out here because sometimes bad people like to run off with little kids like you. Where were you going, anyway?"

"Um…" Brian looked down at his feet to think.

This time he could actually see the darkness cloud the edges of his vision. *Good little boys tell the truth, so you're not good at all! Come with us, Brian. You belong with us.*

Brian shivered, and tears welled up in his eyes.

The policeman's expression changed to something Brian couldn't read. "You're not here with your mother at all, are you?"

"Please don't take me to jail!" Brian cried, the thought of being locked in a cage filling him with terror. "I'll be good! I promise!"

At first the man looked baffled. "Jail?"

"Y-you're a policeman. Policemen take people to jail. I've seen it on TV."

The man's expression softened. "I'm mall security, actually. My name is Harry." He held out a hand, and Brian shook it. "And who might you be?"

"I'm Brian. Are you sure you won't take me to jail?"

Harry smiled, but there was something sad in it too. "I'm sure, but I may have to call Child Protective Services if we don't find out where your parents are. So where are they?"

Brian swallowed a ball of fear that had lodged in his throat. Mommy might be angry if he told anyone that he often went places without her. Most of the time, he'd go down to the community playground and play with the other boys and girls on the blue monkey bars and bright orange swings while Mommy was away at work.

Come to think of it, the park was where he'd first met Aunt Sarah and Blake.

BRIAN REMEMBERED that day well. The sun had gleamed a dazzling yellow against a backdrop of cloudless blue, and the temperature was nice enough that Brian didn't have to dig through the closet to find a jacket. Mommy had gone out to see a doctor to have a "little problem taken care of," and Craig had been too busy dozing on the couch to notice Brian's departure.

The park lay two blocks down from their house. Dozens of children were there that day, some with parents, and some without. Brian recognized a few of them like Georgie and Garret, who lived with their grandparents across the street from him. There was Brayden, and Dawn, and another little boy who was either Martin or Marcus.

Today he saw two new faces in the crowd: a nicely dressed woman with red hair in a braid pushing her red-haired son on the swings. Brian sat down on the empty swing next to them and started pumping his legs to get higher and higher when the woman said, "Nice to see you here today, Brian."

Brian dug his feet into the pea gravel, grinding himself to a halt. He stared up at her, squinting, trying to determine if he was wrong about not knowing her.

"It's nice to see you, too," he said, blushing.

The woman smiled at him with such an expression of kindness in her eyes that Brian felt his own grow misty. "You don't know me, do you?" she asked, her eyes sparkling.

Brian shook his head. The red-haired boy stopped swinging to watch him.

"I'm Aunt Sarah," she said, "and this is my son, Blake."

"You're not my aunt," Brian said. Just who were these people?

"Sure I am," she said. "We just haven't met until now."

Brian scrunched his brow. Mommy never mentioned anyone named Sarah before. Mommy did have a sister named Monica, but this lady wasn't her.

"I can understand if you don't believe me," the woman said, "and that's okay."

That settled it in Brian's mind. "If you're my aunt, does that mean Blake is my cousin?"

"That's right!" Aunt Sarah beamed. "Now how would you like to go to the Crosstown Mall for lunch? I know you must be hungry."

Brian could scarcely believe his ears. The mall was just three streets over, and he had never been there before, though he had seen it plenty of times and heard Mommy talk about shopping there whenever she had enough money in her account.

He licked his lips at the thought of lunch. "But my mom…"

"Will never know you've been there if you don't tell her," Aunt Sarah finished. Some of the light left her eyes and she looked away for a moment. "Am I right?"

Brian nodded.

"Then let's go. You have nothing to fear. We'll keep you safe."

Blake hopped off the swing, and Brian followed suit. Aunt Sarah held out a hand for Brian to take. As soon as her hand made contact with his, he could feel himself filling with light that shoved away all of the darkness and scary things that had ever happened to him.

As the three of them walked to the mall, Brian felt lighter inside than an airborne leaf tumbling on the wind. At last someone was paying attention to him in a nice way. At last someone was showing they cared.

That first visit to the mall nearly overloaded Brian's senses. Since Mommy had never enrolled him in kindergarten (which, according to kids at the playground, was a place where you got to sit at a desk in a room full of other kids while listening to a person called Teacher who told you what to do), he had never seen so many people in one place. Aunt Sarah ordered lunch at a burger place in what she called the Food Court, and after they ate, Brian and Blake played in the ball pit until Brian wore himself out. Then they walked around and looked at shops, and Aunt Sarah drew to a halt outside a store displaying mannequins just Brian's size.

She looked him up and down, wrinkling her nose at his holey shirt and sweatpants. "How would you like to have a new outfit?"

He started to say he would love it, but what came out was, "But what will Mommy say?"

Aunt Sarah sighed and crouched down to be at his level. "Your mother is a confused and broken woman. I would take you away from there if I could, but unfortunately that is neither my job nor my place. I keep praying, though. You deserve so much better."

Brian nodded, not fully understanding what she meant.

"It's okay," Blake said. "I'll help you pick out something cool."

And he did. Brian left the store wearing new gym shoes, jeans so long they had to be rolled at the cuffs, and a bright red shirt.

All of his old clothes had gone in the trash.

After that, Aunt Sarah dropped Brian off at his door, gave him a hug, and said she'd be back another day.

"Where'd you get those clothes?" Mommy asked later that afternoon. Her eyes were red and puffy and a funny bruise was forming at her temple.

"A lady at the park gave them to me. She thought my old clothes had too many holes in them."

"Nice lady. Next time you should ask her for a million dollars, too." Mommy started laughing then and soon her laughter changed to sobs, and Brian slunk off to his room to be alone.

Aunt Sarah and Blake were at the park every time Brian went out after that, regardless of what time of day it was. One time he didn't even come to the park until after supper, and the pair had been there alone, waiting for him to come play.

Brian had been delighted. "You waited for me!" he exclaimed, grinning from ear to ear.

"We're always waiting for you, silly," Aunt Sarah said as she started to push Brian's swing. "We'll always be here for you. Whenever you need us, there we will be."

And they were right. Once when Brian ran away from a mean older kid who lived next door, he ran into an alley and hid behind some garbage cans, wishing with all his heart that Aunt Sarah would come save him. No sooner had he wished this Aunt Sarah and Blake appeared at the mouth of the alley calling his name.

Again, the light had come. Again, the darkness had been driven away.

DURING THOSE weeks, things got even scarier between Mommy and Craig. Glasses were thrown. Dishes were broken. Threats were shouted, and tears were shed.

One day when Craig went down to the store, Mommy stood at the sink washing dishes, her expression tight.

Brian glided over to watch her.

"What is it?" she asked without looking at him.

"You're sad."

Mommy set a glass upside down in the dish strainer and glanced down at him. "What makes you say that?"

"I just know, Mommy. Craig is a bad man and he makes you sad."

All because of you! the dark voices whispered.

Mommy's cheeks flushed and a shadow passed over her eyes. She made no reply and went back to her task.

THE NIGHT before Brian went to the mall alone had been the scariest of all. Mommy and Craig came home from a pizza place fighting. A dangerous look appeared in Craig's eyes as he looked from Mommy to Brian. "I don't know why you didn't have it done the first time," he said. "God knows you wish he'd never been born."

Brian's breath caught in his throat.

"Stop it!" Mommy shrieked. "You stop it right now!"

"It's true," Craig continued, staring right at Brian, his voice an eerie calm. "She wanted you dead. Told me so herself. She even went to the doctor that kills little worms like you, but your *father* made her change her mind at the last second. Too bad he was too much of a deadbeat to stick around for long after that."

Mommy was sobbing and clutching her stomach.

"Go ahead, Julia," Craig sneered. "I dare you to deny it."

Mommy just continued to cry.

Craig grinned. "See? I told you it was true. You ever wonder why she doesn't feed you half the time? It's so you'll die and give her a little peace of mind."

Brian ran into his room and wept for what felt like hours. Eventually the sounds of the fight subsided and their bedroom door slammed.

Brian found himself praying. *Aunt Sarah…Blake…please come be with me. I know you love me. I know you care.*

He waited and waited but they didn't come. At last he drifted into a light slumber and dreamed that Aunt Sarah was sitting at the edge of his bed, wiping the tears from his cheeks and assuring him that everything would be all right. Blake stood guard by the door, looking as stern as a six-year-old could.

"I love you, Aunt Sarah," Brian murmured, comfort washing over him like the warmth of a summertime breeze.

"And I love you too, child. I love you, too."

"WHERE ARE your parents, Brian?"

Brian jumped. His mind had been wandering, and he still hadn't answered the mall security man's question.

"At home," he said. "I'm here with my aunt."

Aunt Sarah, please get here fast, he prayed.

Harry gave him a dubious look. "Okay. So where is *she?*"

"I don't—"

"Brian!" exclaimed a red-haired woman who ran into the food court holding a giant blue shopping bag. "Where on earth have you *been?*"

"Aunt Sarah!" Brian ran into her arms and gave her a tight squeeze. "I'm so glad you found me!"

The patter of approaching footsteps told him that Blake had just caught up with his mother.

"Thank you so much for keeping an eye on my nephew," Aunt Sarah was saying to Harry. "He must have wandered off when I had my back turned."

"No problem, ma'am," Harry said, dipping his head. "I have a boy of my own so I completely understand. You have a good day now."

When Harry left them, Aunt Sarah frowned. "You shouldn't have come here alone. You could have been hurt."

"But I had to come here!" Brian said as tears filled his eyes anew. "I couldn't find anything to eat!"

Aunt Sarah nodded. "Let's go get you something, then."

THEY LEFT the mall a short time later, Brian's stomach splitting at the seams. "I should go home now," he said, though for some reason the thought of seeing his mother and Craig made him feel sick.

Aunt Sarah placed a hand on his shoulder. "Brian, honey, there's something we need to tell you."

Brian's chest felt tight. Something in her tone told him that something bad had happened—something worse than had ever happened before. "What?"

"Brian, you can't go home. We just found out this morning."

His mind spun. "You said you can't take me away!"

"Things have changed. I'm sorry."

Brian wanted to ask what had happened and realized he needed to see for himself. He broke into a run before Aunt Sarah could try to stop him.

Brakes squealed as he tore across the parking lot in front of moving vehicles. He stopped at the edge, watched for cars, dashed through a gap in traffic, and raced all the way home without looking back to see if Aunt Sarah and Blake were running after him.

He rounded the corner onto his own street and froze at the sight of flashing blue and red lights. Outside his house sat two police cars, an ambulance, and a big black van. His belly began to turn somersaults. Did this mean Craig was going to jail for being so mean to him and Mommy?

He continued slowly toward the house and halted a second time when he realized that Aunt Sarah and Blake were now standing on the sidewalk between him and his house. How had they gotten there so quickly without a car?

"I told you not to come," Aunt Sarah said. Her blue shopping bag was gone. "It isn't good for you to be here."

"Stay back," Blake pleaded. "Please?"

Brian shoved his way past them. He could go wherever he wanted. He didn't have to listen.

He halted two doors down from his house. Some men were loading a person-sized cocoon into the back of the black van, and he immediately pictured his mother still and lifeless like the bodies in the shows Craig watched on TV.

Oh, no…

See what you've done? the cruel voices hissed. *Dead, all because of you!*

Darkness closed in, but it vanished in a blast of light when a hand laid itself on Brian's shoulder. "Don't be afraid," he heard Aunt Sarah say behind him.

A messy-haired woman sitting in the back of a police car caught sight of Brian and started to shout through the glass.

It was Mommy.

"The creep can't ever hurt you again, Brian! I did it for you!" Tears ran down Mommy's cheeks. "I did it all for you!"

Brian could feel the darkness trying to creep back inside of him, but Aunt Sarah's light kept it away. Brian had thought he would go to jail for trying to take food that wasn't his, and now Mommy was going to jail instead.

"Where will I go now?" Brian asked, feeling a little scared even though Aunt Sarah told him not to be.

"I'm not exactly sure, but I do know you'll be sent to live with a new family who will take care of you and love you as their own."

That made Brian's heart skip a beat. Wide-eyed, he stared up at her. "A new family? But what about you? Why can't I live with you?"

The normally silent Blake was the one to answer that. "Because we're your guardians, silly. You can't live with us, but we can live with you."

Brian squinted at him, not fully understanding. "What do you mean?"

"We mean that even if you can't see us and can't hear us, we will still be there whenever you're in need. We were sent to keep you safe and send the darkness away."

"And," Aunt Sarah said, "we were sent to give you hope."

A woman in a police uniform was walking up the sidewalk toward them. "Brian?" she asked.

He felt himself nod.

The woman held out her hand. "Brian, I need you to come with me, okay? You can trust us. We're the good guys here."

Brian turned to ask Aunt Sarah if the police lady was right, but the sidewalk was empty. Aunt Sarah and Blake were gone.

But only to your eyes, he heard Aunt Sarah's voice say. *Remember, Brian. Whenever you need us, there we will be.*

And Brian believed it.

LADONNA COLE

THE FINAL ACT

HEART POUNDING in her chest, Liliana drew a deep breath and steadied her Glock. "I need an extraction, now!" she whispered into her com.

"Copy, Vixen. We are ten minutes out."

"I don't have ten minutes!" She pressed her back to the marble wall of the Library of Congress, the chill seeping through her thin cocktail dress. She slid to the corner where a slice of light dissected the shadows.

Ding.

The elevator door across the room opened and two men in camo uniforms exited, led by their Browning M2 HBs at the ready. Turning toward the north corridor, they stomped away from Liliana.

228 | READ, WRITE, MUSE

"Get to the third floor, Vixen." Her partner's voice crackled over the com. "We may have another…"

Liliana didn't hear the end of his sentence. She ran for the open elevator and skidded in just before it closed. She punched the three and checked her clip, chambered a bullet, and pressed her body against the wall beside the elevator doors.

They opened and Liliana peered around the corner. The third floor seemed abandoned. She slipped into the darkness, keeping her back to the perimeter wall.

"Vixen, did you get the documents?"

"Affirmative." Flipping the blonde wig over her shoulder, she scanned the shadowed room. Tall maple bookshelves eclipsed her view, and the odor of dusty books assailed her.

"Good," her partner sighed. "I'm gonna get you out safely, Lil."

"I know." Liliana's heart spiked at the tremor in his voice. She and Tim had been partners for seven years and lovers for three, inevitable from the beginning. The air sizzled when he was near.

The elevator dinged.

"They're here!" She escaped further into the back section of the shelves and wove between discarded desks and chairs.

"Lil, get to the last row of shelves on the north side."

"Why?"

"Just do it. I have schematics."

Keeping low, Liliana pressed toward the last row. She froze when a radio crackled on the next aisle.

"No sign of the intruder." A deep voice faded away.

She inched back. Her foot struck something on the floor, and she staggered. A hand grabbed her ankle.

She clenched her teeth to keep from screaming and whirled around. Bright white FBI letters cut through the dark.

"Help me," a man rasped and clung to her calf.

"Shh." She squatted down beside him and placed her finger on his lips, then checked behind her to see if the guard had heard. He was still moving toward the elevator.

"Agent Keller, FBI," he breathed, barely a whisper. "National security risk...must get..." He gurgled out the end of his sentence.

A rusty smell rose from the floor and warm fluid seeped into her shoes. This agent was gone.

"Did you hear something?" the guard asked his partner.

"Back there." They jogged toward Liliana.

"Vixen, are you there?" Tim asked.

"Yes."

"Top shelf to your right, seventh book down, *Photogenics A-Z*."

"I don't have time!"

"Pull the book! Now!"

Liliana yanked at the tech manual. The bookcase slid back like a patio door, revealing a staircase winding down into darkness.

"Down here! I heard something!" the guard bellowed at the end of her row and spat a volley of bullets.

Liliana dove into the stairwell and the bookcase door slammed closed. Bullets pelted the steel door.

"Tim. Tim!" Liliana tapped her com but it was silent.

She placed a stiletto pump on the next step and carefully descended, spiraling into the dark unknown. Gun supported between both hands, Liliana delved into pitch black.

With her eyes useless, she honed in on her other senses. A waft of stale air fingered through the strands of her wig and she could hear the fading sounds of the guards above trying to blast through the door.

As she crept deeper, sounds above yielded to other noises. The click of her heels on the stone steps, a scramble of tiny claws and squeaks fled before her. Her pounding pulse and ragged breathing clamored. She spiraled deeper.

The wall fell away and the steps ended. Sliding her foot forward she felt a cobbled stone floor and sensed open space ahead.

Another sound pierced the darkness. Someone else was in the room with her. She could hear them breathing. A masculine scent filtered past her, familiar and intoxicating: Grey Flannel, Tim's favorite cologne.

A light flared and Liliana flinched as the pain stabbed her eyes. She blinked and peered through her lashes.

"Tim!" Relief washed over her and she stepped toward a safe embrace. "How did you…"

She stopped. Tim aimed his gun directly at her heart.

"Give me the documents, Lil."

She peeled back the slit in her gown and withdrew the folder of documents. "What's going on, Tim?"

"This is my last job, Lil. I'm done. I'm out. When I deliver these documents to my employer, I will be filthy rich." His eyes flashed with wild ambition.

"Your employer." Liliana slowly lifted her Glock. "I assume you don't mean the CIA."

Tim snorted. "No."

"You're a double agent?"

"I prefer to think of myself as freelance."

"Traitor," Liliana growled.

"Now, Lil, no need to get hostile." His eyes scanned her lean form. "Come with me. We can get that beach house in the Caymans."

"You killed the FBI agent up there, didn't you?"

"He shouldn't have interfered."

"You are never going to touch these." She waved the documents at him.

"You don't know the combination to get out of here. If I die, you are stuck here, forever."

"You said we would be together, forever. That was the only time you told the truth!"

Liliana and Tim glared, eye-to-eye, gun-to-gun, and fired. Documents scattered into the air and both agents slammed back against the walls and emptied their clips into each other.

Tim convulsed then stilled. Liliana slid down the wall, leaving a bloody smear as US government seals and Top Secret stamps fluttered to the ground and soaked up her final act of patriotism.

MEET THE AUTHORS

J.S. BAILEY

As a child, J.S. Bailey escaped to fantastic worlds through the magic of books and began to write as soon as she could pick up a pen. She dabbled in writing science fiction until she discovered supernatural suspense novels and decided to write her own. Today her stories focus on unassuming characters who are thrown into terrifying situations which may or may not involve ghosts, demons, and evil old men. She believes that good should always triumph in the end.

Bailey is the author of *Servant*, *Solitude*, *Rage's Echo*, *The Land Beyond the Portal*, *Weary Traveler*, and *Vapors*. "Rochelle's Pizza Run," a short story sequel to *The Land Beyond the Portal*, is available in the Read Write Muse anthology *Through the Portal*. She lives with her husband in Cincinnati, Ohio.

Learn more about Bailey's stories at
www.jsbaileywrites.com

E.D.E. BELL

E.D.E. Bell was born in Cleveland, Ohio in 1976. She grew up in Southeastern Michigan, and graduated from the University of Michigan with a Master of Science in Engineering (MSE) in Electrical Engineering. She worked in engineering and data analysis in Northern Virginia for several years, and now works in Southeastern Ohio as an advisor in the technical intelligence field. She married husband G.C. Bell in 2002, and they have three children together. Bell is the author of the novel *Spireseeker*, and is currently working on the *Shkode Trilogy, Book 1: The Banished Craft*.

AMBER E. BOX

Amber E. Box is an editor and freelance writer of fiction and poetry. She is currently working on her first novel as well as a young children's series. Amber resides in Texas with her husband and three small children. Her work has recently been featured in *The Penmen Review* and *The Literary Yard*. She is currently pursuing a degree in English from Southern New Hampshire University. She credits her Scribes family with challenging her to become a better writer every day.

You can follow her experiences on her blog at
www.amberebox.com

E.P. BROWN

In this bustling world virtually brimming with Eric Browns, this particular one is a freelance writer and punk rock "musician" and songwriter. Eric writes weird fiction and scripts comic books. His short stories have appeared in various anthologies. Eric has material published as both Eric Brown and E.P. Brown. He lives in Pittsburgh, Pennsylvania.

HOLLY & JARED BROWN

Holly Brown has been creating and writing stories since she was five years old, growing up in a small farming community in rural Idaho. Wife to Jared and mother of three young sons, she spends her time and talents attempting to create a nurturing and safe environment for her family.

Absolute Despotism is her first novel. The second book in the Supremacy Rising series, *A More Perfect Union*, was released in November 2014. The third installment will be published in early 2016.

ISABEL BROWN

Isabel Brown is the author of *Son of the Tides* and is a Netflix aficionado. She adores chocolate-covered strawberries, anything by Edgar Rice Burroughs, and anywhere she could sink her toes in the sand. When she isn't writing, Isabel is thinking about writing or dreaming about writing. She believes every moment of her life can become a scene in her next novel so watch out—you might be the next person who inspires her. Isabel lives with her husband, her lovable dog, and her sweet kitty in Columbus, Ohio.

Visit her at
www.isabelbrownbooks.com

LaDonna Cole

LaDonna Cole thrives in the Smoky Mountains of Tennessee with her children. She sings, writes, and travels as much as possible. A psychiatric nurse and incurable optimist, she draws on her zest for adventure, passion for family, and journey through faith to release the soul of each new story.

Visit her at
www.ladonnacolern.wix.com/ladonna-cole

S.R. KARFELT

  S.R. Karfelt is thrilled to be a part of this Warrior Anthology. Most of her own battles are with her muse, and she has the best job on earth doing what she's been made to do: share stories. Action adventure fantasy is her main genre, and her books focus heavily on relationships and internal struggle.

  Karfelt's contributions to this anthology are previously-unpublished scenes from her novel *Heartless: A Shieldmaiden's Voice*, and she's pleased that they've found a home and that readers will have a chance to meet Carole Blank as a young girl. *Heartless* is a Covenant Keeper novel and ties into other books in the series, including *Kahtar: Warrior of the Ages*.

  Karfelt would love to hear back from readers and can be reached through social media or her website: *www.srkarfelt.com*

KELSEY KEATING

Author, blogger, and developmental editor Kelsey Keating doesn't know the meaning of the word "bored." Living by day as an executive assistant, she moonlights in the writing world, helping other authors achieve their dreams through her knowledge with *Literary Lies* and *Tales from the Blade*.

When she's not writing, this shieldmaiden can often be found soaking in all that God's beautiful earth has to offer…even if she's not so fond of actual "earth" (ewww. Outdoors!). A student of media, Kelsey considers acting a hobby, critiquing movies a calling, and riding unicorns through rainbows a daily expectation.

Driven by her love of fantasy, Kelsey's novels reflect the wonderment she's always felt of what the imagination can dream up. For more on Kelsey, check out her blogs or see her other works in *Through the Portal* and *Monstrosity*, coming in 2016.

Visit her at
www.lifeunpublished.blogspot.com

D.M. KILGORE

D.M. Kilgore is a freelance writer, novelist, and literary hitwoman. She loves being a writing gypsy and dipping her toes into the sparkling stream of whatever genre she happens to be dancing by when inspiration strikes.

After midnight, D.M. can be found dancing through the moonlit waters of multiple genres with a bloody pen in one hand and a magic wand in the other.

She's currently prancing through poetic puddles, making a splash in the blood-tinged waters of suspense-filled thrillers, and twirling her toes in the glittery streams of young adult paranormal fantasy.

She insists she's found her niche, if not her groove.

If you can hear the music, dance along at
www.dmkilgore.com

MARGARET MADIGAN

Margaret Madigan lives in the vast northern plains where it's quiet, mostly empty, and conducive to letting her imagination run wild. She writes romance and sci-fi and dabbles in other genres just for the fun of it. Her post-apocalyptic fairy tale retelling *Hero for Hire* released through *Lyrical Press* in 2013, and her historical romance *Gambling on the Outlaw* is scheduled for release through *Entangled* in June 2015.

When she's not writing, you'll find her in a college classroom teaching English, or working as a literary agent for an amazing agency…and of course, enjoying time with her family.

RYAN T. NUHFER

Ryan T. Nuhfer is an author and freelance writer who has dabbled in short stories for over a decade. He is currently working on his first novel, *Gh05t Proxy*, a cyberpunk thriller. Ryan lives in Warren, Pennsylvania with his wife Crystal, his son Logan, and two hyperactive black labs.

Catherine Jones Payne

When she isn't dreaming poetry or writing fiction, Catherine Jones Payne serves as the managing editor at Quill Pen Editorial Services. She holds a degree in English literature from Wheaton College and has been influenced by Virginia Woolf, Flannery O'Connor, Toni Morrison, and Denise Levertov. She lives in Waco, Texas with her husband Brendan, plays a mean game of racquetball, and can't stop reading Julian of Norwich.

Kirstin Pulioff

Kirstin Pulioff is a storyteller at heart. Born and raised in Southern California, she moved to the Pacific Northwest to follow her dreams and graduated from Oregon State University with a degree in forest management. Happily married and a mother of two, she lives in the foothills of Colorado. When she's not writing an adventure, she is busy living one.

Learn more about Pulioff and her stories at
www.facebook.com/KirstinPulioffAuthor

ELLE K. WHITE

A textbook introvert who likes to burn the textbook every once in a while, Elle K. White discovered a love of storytelling at a young age. When well-meaning but unimaginative adults told her there wasn't a living in writing books, she grudgingly got a day job, but writing is still her full time passion. She dabbles in all sorts of sci-fi and fantasy subgenres, with a particular fondness for cyberpunk, steampunk, and clever retellings of classic fairy tales.

LEXY WOLFE

Wife, mother, semi-professional cat-herder, and lover of shiny things, Lexy Wolfe is the author of the highly acclaimed epic fantasy novels of The Sundered Lands Saga. After her time in the Army as a Russian linguist was cut short due to injuries, she has continued a tradition of serving as a translator, now between technical and business folks.

Lexy enjoys learning as much as she can about everything, with a special love of all fields of science. Unfortunately, she never could decide on a single field of study to focus on. Having to set aside a childhood dream, inspired by Carl Sagan, of becoming an astronaut and traveling to other worlds, she now weaves vivid worlds and vibrant characters into intricate stories.